"Shh. Don't move. . . ."

A snowy egret was lifting above them, spreading its wings in graceful majesty. As she gazed skyward, Eden felt an uncontrollable rush of emotion. "It's wonderful," she murmured, "like a blessing to end our day."

"I *am* blessed, my darling Eden, to have found paradise with you." His hands framed her face. "I see the beauty of your heart shining in your eyes—and I am humbled by your sweetness."

His touch, his controlled power, was starting a firestorm in her deepest recesses. "Derek, my love," she whispered, "you have the look of a Viking warrior, but the soul of an Irish poet. I do truly adore you." His fingers moved along her cheeks, caressed her chin and her throat as if he sculpted her from living clay.

"You've given me back my life," he murmured. "I want to teach you all the joys of love."

She closed her eyes to receive his kiss. His lips were tender as he brushed one eyelid, then the other. When she sighed, his mouth covered hers, demanding, searching. His tongue penetrated, claiming her with sweet invasion. The boulder where they reclined was still warm from the sun when he eased her down. . . .

CRITICS AND BOOKSELLERS ADORE KRISTA JANSSEN'S

CREOLE CAVALIER

Books by Krista Janssen

Ride the Wind
Wind Rose
Creole Cavalier
Indigo Fire

Indigo Fire

Krista Janssen

POCKET BOOKS

New York   London   Toronto   Sydney   Tokyo   Singapore

An *Original* Publication of POCKET BOOKS

POCKET BOOKS, a division of Simon & Schuster Inc.
1230 Avenue of the Americas, New York, NY 10020

Copyright © 1995 by Rhoda Poole

ISBN: 0-671-51907-7

First Pocket Books printing September 1995

10 9 8 7 6 5 4 3 2 1

POCKET and colophon are registered trademarks of
Simon & Schuster Inc.

Cover art by Franco Accornero

Printed in the U.S.A.

With love to
Brent and Angela

Special thanks to my editor, Caroline Tolley, for her enthusiasm, encouragement, and expertise.

And kudos to my agent and friend, Nancy Yost, for making business a pleasure.

1

Barbados—June 1731

"Ye bargain like a shark, Miss Palmer—despite yer dimples and curls. The indigo is worth twice that—and well ye know it." The aging buccaneer grinned at her, his eyes becoming slits in his round, bewhiskered face.

Eden clasped her hands beneath the table and gave him her most audacious look. Dimples and curls! Really! Why, he made her sound like a bit of fluff with no sense at all. She supposed her youth went against her in these negotiations—and her ruffled taffeta dress was not at all appropriate for her visit to the pirate's rustic shack—but she was determined to prevail. She gave him a pointed look and leaned forward. "I'm not a child, Mr. Hawkins, nor am I a helpless violet. I'm a farmer—as experienced as any in the Carolinas. And I didn't come all this way just to sail home empty-handed."

In the silence that followed, Eden felt moisture gather along the back of her neck and bead along her temples. Everything—her home, her land, her entire future—was hanging in the balance at this very moment, dependent on the whim of this old rascal facing her across the table.

"A farmer, eh? A rich slave owner from Carolina, I'll warrant. With milksops for menfolk, 'tis plain. Why would a man send a chit to do his trading?"

"I'm unmarried, sir, though that's no concern of yours. My stepfather did indeed build the plantation with the help of slaves, but from his deathbed he freed them all." She gave him her most officious look. "I, Mr. Hawkins, now own—

1

and manage, I'm proud to say—Palmer Oaks Plantation. And I assure you I've been well-trained for the job."

"Har." He smirked at the idea. "I admire your spunk, lady, but I wouldn't bet a barnacle on your chances of succeeding. You say ye're converting the rice fields to indigo?"

"I am. I've studied the possibilities and believe indigo to be a far superior enterprise. With less than a hundred acres in cultivation and a dozen free laborers, I expect to make a handsome profit."

Bull Hawkins looked dubious.

Stiffening her spine, Eden met his look with cool determination while a fervent prayer whistled through her mind. *Please Lord, let him take the offer.* There on the table between them sat her last pouch of gold; it was all she had been able to scrape together since the poor rice crop last spring.

Brushing a trickle of perspiration from her cheek with the tip of a gloved finger, she met his doubting scrutiny. She would try a new tack. "I was told in Charles Town that you're an expert with indigo and would sell your prize seedlings." She reached for the pouch and began to tighten the drawstrings. "But if you're unwilling to accept my price, I'm sure I can find someone else on Barbados who'll be happy to take my offer."

He stayed her hand with his own. "Nay, ye've come to the right man."

She pursed her lips to hide a smile and silently complimented herself for recognizing his greed. She moved the pouch several inches in her direction.

He leered across the table at her, his thick lips parting to reveal several blank spaces between yellow teeth. "But the cap'n of the ship in the harbor has made me a better offer for the same seedlings." His expression was neither cruel nor friendly, but rather curious and suspicious, like a dog being offered a bone that had a peculiar odor.

Eden could see his lurid past written in his face. She had heard that as a buccaneer he had plundered the Caribbean alongside Kidd and Blackbeard. But he was clever enough to stash his loot and give up the trade before he was hoisted to a pirate's gibbet or opened up by a Spaniard's cutlass. She figured he was also clever enough to lie about having a better offer for the plants.

Well, she wouldn't allow either the old sea dog's menacing looks or the oppressive heat in his tiny hut to defeat her. She would keep a clear head and, above all, wouldn't let Bull Hawkins know how desperate she was.

She must take a chance, she thought, mustering her courage. Since the money on the table was insufficient, she would have to take the gamble of her life. She rattled the coins in the pouch just a bit. "I have a proposition, Mr. Hawkins. I think you'll find it quite interesting."

He lifted his brows and encouraged her with a smile. "Let's hear it then, lady."

"You sell me the seedlings, and make certain I have full knowledge of the plant's preparation for market. This purse of gold is yours to keep—and you'll have the right to purchase Palmer Oaks if I fail to bring in the crop."

His eyes widened. "What's this?"

"I owe the English Crown one last payment to own the plantation in fee simple, free and clear. It was an arrangement made by my stepfather, Charles Palmer, when he took the land grant seventeen years ago. If I don't make the payment by November, I lose the property. I can assign you the legal right to make that payment and secure the property for yourself before anyone else can buy it. It's not terribly important to me," she lied. "I have wealthy relatives—the Wentworths, in Bedfordshire, England—who have been pleading with me to reside with them ever since my stepfather's death. But I like living in America, and I prefer to stay at Palmer Oaks." Leaning back in the rickety chair, she opened her fan and waved it gracefully near her cheek.

3

"Hm." He scratched his beard and thought a moment. "I've always 'ad an itch to be a gentleman," he said at last. "That means owning land." He stared at her hand on the pile of coins. Outside the shanty, a parrot's shrill call cut through the sultry stillness.

Eden's throat was dry, her palms wet with sweat. Could he hear the throbbing of her heart? She clenched her teeth to keep from saying one word more.

"Aye. I'll take your offer, Miss Palmer."

Her spirits leaped, but she merely closed her fan and smiled. "Good. Then it's settled. I'd like to sail as soon as possible. Time is critical, as you know."

"Ye're in luck. That frigate in the harbor docked yesterday and 'tis headed for Charles Town. I'll make arrangements to have your indigo plants delivered this very afternoon. I'll even include some prime seed which ye can store or plant as ye like."

"I would appreciate that. After luncheon today, I'll go to the ship and introduce myself to the captain. I need to arrange passage for myself and my servant. I assume he'll be agreeable."

"He's a haughty sort. One of them Huns, I reckon. Has hair the color of a Spanish doubloon. Speaks English plain enough, but with an accent like all them Dutchies. If he gives ye any trouble, ye let old Bull know. I run things in Barbados—if ye get me meaning."

"I understand," she said rising.

"Oh—ye'll have to keep the plants watered as ye go."

"Of course. I'll be sure there's an ample supply before we sail."

"Ye must 'ave a talent for growing things, lady. Ye've bitten off a mighty hefty chunk, in my view."

"Farming is what I love most," Eden said with complete honesty.

Bull pulled up his considerable bulk and walked around

4

the table. "Don't ye worry. The young plants will flourish if ye follow my instructions."

"And when we meet in November, I will match this pouch of coins with an equal amount."

"Agreed. I'll write down the details of our arrangement so we can sign it."

"Naturally. Good day, Mr. Hawkins. I'll see you later at the dock."

Eden walked on trembling legs from the ramshackle hut. She had hoped to buy the indigo for less, but at least a bargain had been struck and she would soon be on her way home. There, she would work day and night, do whatever was necessary, to bring in the crop and pay off the Crown. Nothing meant more to her than owning Palmer Oaks, the home she loved more than anything on earth.

Baron Derek von Walden arrived at the Government House of Barbados at precisely one o'clock. At his side strode Dr. Hans Messenbaugh, his botanist, on whom he depended for guidance in his new occupation of commercial farming. Derek had been born and raised to rule the ancient barony of Neuchâtel, but he'd learned that in the New World, survival skills were far more valuable than any royal European title.

Derek was eager to meet with Governor Barclay and to get a first look at the survey map of his land grant in South Carolina. He was certain Lord and Lady Barclay's luncheon would be a dull affair in the hottest part of the day, offering polite tête-à-tête in the garden along with weak tea, tiny sandwiches, and minuscule cakes. Of all the things he admired about the English, their insipid social gatherings were not among them. Hopefully he would be able to pay his respects to the lady, corner the governor just long enough to obtain the map, then return to the Bridgetown wharf to settle this new problem with Bull Hawkins.

"I hope to God we can take care of business quickly," Derek growled to Hans. "I want to obtain the official copy of the survey and get back to the ship."

Hans followed Derek up the sweeping path leading to a broad veranda. "Everything's ready," he observed. "The cane and farm equipment are all on board. What does Hawkins want with us now?"

"Something about a woman and some damned indigo plants. She wants to go to Charles Town and take several hundred seedlings in our hold."

"Hell, we're crowded as it is, Derek. If she expects the plants to survive, she'll have to have extra water. *Nein*, I would just refuse."

"I intend to—though Hawkins has tried everything from bribery to thinly veiled threats. He's insisting we take her aboard. My guess is the woman has paid him plenty, and part of the deal includes my hauling the plants to Carolina. He'll be at the wharf when we get back, and we'll settle the matter once and for all."

Derek and Hans were welcomed at the door by a liveried butler and escorted at once to the manicured garden where luncheon was being served al fresco to approximately two dozen well-dressed guests. They were greeted by the governor and his wife, then introduced all around.

Stationed under a spreading cherry tree, Derek balanced his cup and forced himself to give polite attention to Lady Barclay, who insisted on engaging him in conversation.

The lady fanned her rouged, plump cheeks and addressed him in tinkling tones. "We are delighted to meet a member of such an old and noble house, Baron von Walden. Tales of your courage and sacrifice have spread as far as our English enclave here in Barbados. Please tell us more about your exploits."

He shifted uncomfortably and looked to Messenbaugh for help, but at this moment the brilliant botanist was standing tight-lipped with an inane look on his face.

Derek cleared his throat. "We had to leave our native homeland of Neuchâtel, my lady. King Louis of France sent his papists to ravage our valley."

"Yes, Baron," she simpered, "we've heard how you fought the French forces, how you heroically rescued hundreds of your people from slavery and brought them to England. How you gained the attention of Their Majesties and won a land grant in America for your Swiss settlers. Do give us the details."

He answered with as much courtesy as he could muster, "The story is lengthy and boring, I'm afraid. I'm sure there are better subjects for such a fine afternoon."

"But we rarely have such a noble guest in Barbados. Surely you will share stories of your adventures."

Derek waited, hoping Messenbaugh or Governor Barclay would make some comment, change the subject, do something to rescue him from this embarrassing conversation. No one spoke.

Finally he said, "You've already described it succinctly, madam, though some points are exaggerated. As a matter of fact, I consider myself more of a failure than a hero. I lost the battle for my homeland, lost my family and many friends; I lost my fortune entirely. Only through the generosity of the English king have I found sanctuary and a new life for my people."

She fanned vigorously. "Why, you're much too modest, sir. Don't you agree, Mr. Barclay?" she added without glancing at her husband.

"Why, yes indeed," the governor replied in a lackluster tone.

The lady continued, "You speak excellent English, Baron."

"Danke schön," he answered in German, wondering if this would turn her flattery elsewhere.

"Oh my," she tittered. "You see, I almost forgot you're—"

"Swiss. From the Swiss Confederation. Would you care to comment, Hans?" he said to the doctor, hoping to prod him into speaking.

"Nein," said the doctor flatly.

"Does he not speak English?" she asked Derek.

He glared at Messenbaugh, who continued to sip his tea as if uncomprehending.

The awkward silence was broken by a servant delivering trays of the dreadful tiny sandwiches which could be held between two fingers and constituted half a bite in a hungry mouth. It wasn't worth the effort, Derek decided, and declined the offer. Looking across the gathering, he saw all eyes turned his way. At his bold stare, however, the guests quickly resumed their conversations, and the drone of laughter blended with the hum and buzz of tropical insects in the surrounding shrubbery.

At last Derek was able to hand his cup to a passing servant and speak hurriedly to Governor Barclay. "Pardon, sir, but I would like to conduct our brief meeting right away, if possible. Though your party is a delight, I have many duties awaiting me at my ship. I hope to sail tomorrow with the tide."

"By all means, Baron. Come into my study. I have the document waiting for you."

With Messenbaugh in his wake, Derek followed the governor to his office. There, unrolled on the mahogany desk, was a survey map inscribed: *Walden Survey—1730— by order of His Majesty King George I.*

Eagerly, Derek studied the survey while Messenbaugh observed at his side.

It was official at last. Thirty thousand acres of prime land with a mile of the Ashley River running through it.

"You're a lucky man, Baron," said the governor. "You must have made quite an impression on our sovereign."

Surprised by Barclay's brittle tone, Derek peered down at him. The puffy-faced official with his coiffed and powdered hair seemed suddenly in a testy mood. "I made my request through the usual channels," Derek stated. "The king wanted hardworking Protestants on the land. He concluded my Swiss immigrants were perfect for the task."

"No doubt. But I could just as easily have settled the land with *English* subjects. I'll speak plainly, Baron. I see no need to bring in foreigners for such a project."

So here was his first brush with prejudice. He and his people would have to learn to deal with it without malice. "Then you're right, my lord. I *am* in luck to have the king making these decisions rather than you," he said with only a hint of vexation. "Now if you'll answer a question or two concerning the survey, I'll be on my way."

Derek turned back to the paper and traced one finger around the perimeter of the survey line. "Who owns the adjoining property? In time, I may want to enlarge our holdings."

"To the northeast—Henri Poinsett, a French Huguenot. He settled ten years ago and has a flourishing plantation."

"And here? I understand some English commoner recently died, leaving a house by the river. It looks like the property is part of my grant."

"That I wouldn't know. I haven't traveled beyond Charles Town myself."

"Never mind. I'll soon see it with my own eyes." Derek swiftly rolled up the document and turned to Messenbaugh. "We should leave, Hans—and allow Governor Barclay to return to his party."

Barclay motioned toward the garden. "If you please, Baron, just a few moments more. Several important guests have just arrived who are eager to meet a Swiss nobleman with such an impressive reputation."

Derek caught the note of sarcasm in Barclay's tone, but he chose to ignore it. Disgruntled, he cocked an eyebrow at Hans and dutifully followed his host back into the garden.

* * *

Eden was late for the governor's luncheon, very late. But the mid-morning meeting with Bull Hawkins had been terribly draining. She had been limp as a steamed noodle when she finally escaped his dockside shanty and arrived at her rooms at the inn on the hill above Bridgetown. Part of her weakness was caused by sheer relief at having accomplished her objective—obtaining her plants and arranging for their passage to Carolina. A few months ago she had given up hope of keeping Palmer Oaks, but then she had heard the intriguing rumor about Bull Hawkins and his prime indigo—and of the secret process he used to produce the rare product that was valued everywhere in the world for its exquisite blue color.

It was a stroke of luck that a ship was available to transport her right away to Charles Town. Time was crucial if she was to make a profitable crop by November—and pay off both the Crown and Hawkins. Today she would make certain her precious plants were put safely on board.

With her maid Laykee's help, she had bathed and changed into a silk dress and straw bonnet. She was still breathless when she presented herself at Government House and stopped to inspect her gloves and adjust the fan dangling from her wrist. Resigning herself to the ordeal of sipping tea and making foolish conversation for the next half hour, she entered the garden and placed a smile on her face. She would escape as soon as she had paid her respects to the governor of Barbados.

Very soon she was surrounded by curious guests, most of them men in elegant formal dress and powdered wigs. Lady Barclay hurried to greet her and guide her among the visitors, who fulfilled Eden's worst expectations by talking incessantly about subjects that were deadly boring.

She accepted the obligatory cup of tea and took up a position in the shade. While smiling at two talkative matrons, her eyes wandered past the verdant flowering shrubs to the back portico of the house. Emerging from the interior was a tall, extraordinarily attractive man in an odd military uniform which seemed incongruous with the fashionable dress of the rest of the gentleman present. What he lacked in fashion, he made up for with broad shoulders, a rugged profile and startling golden hair bound at his nape. Shifting her attention back to the ladies, she tried to concentrate on their dull chitchat. It was all she could do to appear to listen. How much longer was she obligated to stay here? At last she extricated herself from the women and opened her fan to hide a yawn. She was inching toward the door when a hand touched her shoulder.

"Don't move," came a low masculine voice.

She froze. Something in the voice carried a tense warning.

"My lady, do you have courage?" asked the man who was out of view behind her.

"I would hope so," she answered coolly.

"Then I must ask you not to turn around, or scream or faint."

Eden rolled her eyes, but kept her head perfectly still. All she could see was a man's hand resting on her sleeve and sense a large figure at her back. "What on earth is wrong?" she asked with the beginnings of alarm.

He coughed and moved near her ear. "Do you know what a tarantula is, young lady?"

She reflected on his odd question. "Why yes, an enormous black spider. Not too uncommon, they say." Her throat knotted. "Why do you ask, sir?"

"Please don't be frightened, but I must warn you that one of these spiders is sitting just below your curls on the back of your gown."

❧ 2 ❧

Eden's mouth went dry, but she held her position without flinching. "Can you do something—knock the spider off?"

"Yes, but it might leap onto someone else."

"What can I do?" she asked in a tight whisper.

"Do exactly what I tell you. Walk very carefully through the door and go to the front porch. I'll guide you and keep a close eye on the ugly creature."

"You're sure it won't bite when I move?"

"Not if you're careful not to frighten it. There is a layer of fabric between you and its mouth."

"Mouth," she mumbled and started to move ever so slowly toward the door. She felt the man close behind, his hand firmly on her arm. "Is it moving?" she whispered, not daring to breathe.

"No. Just continue walking and we'll soon be outside."

At last she was on the veranda. Halting, she stood as still as a stone and waited for him to sweep away the spider. After a second she whispered, "Do something." When nothing happened, she pleaded again, "Please get rid of it—quickly."

Strong hands turned her around. Startled, she looked up into the face of the handsome man she had noticed in the

12

garden—the man with the golden hair. A smile teased the edge of his lips.

"But—where is the spider?" she asked.

"Gone."

"Oh?" She twisted to take a look, then took a deep breath and returned his smile. "I'm sure I should thank you—" she began.

"No need," he said. "The spider didn't exist. I just needed an excuse to bolt from that godawful assemblage. I borrowed you because you appeared as bored as I was."

"You *borrowed* me?"

"Don't deny you were yawning behind your fan."

"Why, how dare you! That's the most high-handed, rude—"

"You've described me exactly, *fraulein.*"

"I demand an apology. You frightened me half to death."

"For that I apologize." He didn't look the least bit sorry.

"How will I explain to the governor?"

"I suggest you escape while you have the chance. No doubt your many admirers will swarm out here looking for you any second."

"What you did was unforgivable—cruel. Outrageous to say the least. I might have truly fainted. What would you have done then?"

"Exactly what I intend to do now. Leave you here on the porch—since you seem determined to risk being trapped again."

"Well, I declare—"

"You appear to be a woman who can take care of herself. *Auf Wiedersehen,* madam," he said briskly, and hurried down the steps to enter a waiting carriage.

Aghast, Eden stared after him. He deserved a severe tongue lashing, but she'd had no chance to give him one. They hadn't even been introduced, and he'd manhandled her and scared her beyond words. Then he had marched off without even a by-your-leave. She couldn't imagine why the royal governor would have such a crude person at his soiree. Why, the clumsiest oaf in Charles Town wouldn't leave a woman alone on a porch without making certain she was not in distress.

"Pardon me," came another voice with the same peculiar accent as the stranger's.

She turned to see a plump, balding gentleman with hat in hand.

"Have you seen a man—a tall man in a uniform—pass by?"

"He's in that carriage," Eden snapped. "And I'm going to mine."

Her nerves were tingling when she climbed in beside Laykee.

"Did you meet a gentleman?" asked Laykee. "I saw you come to the veranda."

"Not a gentleman—quite the opposite. Why, you won't believe what that wretched man did. If I ever lay eyes on him again, I'll give him a piece of my mind. Umph. Driver, take us back to the inn." She would forget this unpleasantness, change into a more comfortable dress and go directly to the docks.

The open carriage clattered up the hill. Eden settled in her seat and secured the ribbons of her hat. To her surprise, she found a smile slipping across her lips. Regardless of the man's unforgivable behavior, he had done her a favor by saving her from another ghastly minute at the party. And despite her resolve, she couldn't forget the warm strength of his hands as he guided her from the garden—or the enigmatic smile he'd given her before he rushed away.

In less than an hour she and Laykee were traveling through Bridgetown's streets. The linen stays beneath her sheer bodice felt like bands of heated iron. Pulling the wide brim of her straw hat down to protect her face from the sun's intensity, Eden gazed out at the colorful kaleidoscope of humanity surrounding her. Native Barbadians with chocolate faces beneath bright bandannas crowded the streets, bustling, flamboyant, laughing, arguing and hawking their wares under a sky like tempered brass.

Laykee leaned near and spoke above the noise. "It's worse than Charles Town in August—like an ant colony in a forest fire."

"This time tomorrow we'll be at sea. Mr. Hawkins promised to have our plants loaded before sundown."

"I saw the ship at the wharf when I was buying fruit for breakfast," Laykee said. "Looked like plenty going on around it."

"I just hope it's a stout vessel whose captain knows the shortest route to Charles Town—and the fastest."

"Your papa wouldn't have approved of any of this, Miss Eden. You should have done what he told you on his deathbed—marry and let your husband worry about plants and such."

With a tug of sadness, Eden recalled how her stepfather had been tossed from his stallion that terrible day last spring—of how desperate she had been to say or do anything that would ease his suffering. "I did what he asked," she said. "I agreed to marry Landon. But Papa Charles wouldn't have expected me to marry so soon after his death. It wouldn't be proper, and besides, I hardly know my cousin—and he's never paid court like a gentleman should." It was hard to think of Landon Palmer as a relative, even if he did carry the Palmer name. He had been raised and educated in England, the only son of her stepfather's brother. A year ago he had arrived in Charles Town and taken a house, then proceeded to establish himself in society while enjoying his large inheritance.

"I saw Mr. Landon eyeing you like a hungry hawk when he came to the funeral," observed Laykee.

"I was much too upset to notice," Eden said wistfully.

"But I do wish Papa hadn't put both Landon and me in such an awkward circumstance."

"I don't think Mr. Landon minds a bit, from what I've seen when he comes calling."

"Oh, he's just being polite with all those flowery compliments. Though I do think he intends to keep his pledge to Papa."

Laykee shook her head. "Your papa was right to tell you to marry, but you don't have to marry Landon Palmer."

"Maybe not," Eden sighed. "But it's an old tradition to marry family. Like marries like. It keeps things on an even keel—and property isn't lost to strangers."

"Property. That's for sure a poor reason to marry. The Cherokees don't possess any land, and we get along just fine."

The carriage came to a jolting halt, blocked by several donkeys loaded with cane stalks.

"Oh bother, we're going to fry like bacon before we get to the dock. Uh," Eden grunted as she was thrown back against the seat when the horse suddenly started forward. Progress was jarring and tedious. She fanned vigorously in the heat. "I'm just not in a hurry, Laykee, to become the wife of some arrogant male and do his bidding. Papa taught me all about running a plantation, and I intend to manage Palmer Oaks on my own before I take a husband."

"He did leave the plantation to you in his will. I heard him say so."

"But he knew that my husband will become its sole owner when I marry. Men think that's the best way to protect their womenfolk, but I know more about what's needed at Palmer Oaks than anyone else in the world—especially my cousin Landon. Why, he's only seen the property a few times."

Laykee shook her head. "Too bad. My people have a different law—and women have more say-so."

"I like that idea."

"You're an English lady. That's a different matter from being a Cherokee. You don't belong to a tribe, so you *have* to be some man's wife."

"And his possession," Eden added. "Well-tended chattel bought with pretty words and fancy dresses and the need for protection—and children. Oh, don't look so shocked. I suppose I might marry Landon Palmer. Maybe love will grow between us. And I do want children someday. Only, I won't think of marriage until I bring in the indigo crop and pay off the note to the Crown. On that day, I'll be a free woman, free and a landowner, and happy as a meadowlark. Then if I marry Landon, he will always know his wife was once a woman of property and didn't marry him from necessity. He'll have much more respect for me, I'm sure."

Laykee flashed a grin. "He'd better, Miss Eden. You're mighty headstrong for such a young lady."

"And you're my best friend, Laykee. Working together, we shall conquer all." She laughed. "Whether it be an old pirate like Hawkins or a new husband like Landon."

The carriage slowed again. The mulatto driver twisted in his seat. "I am sorry, ladies. It's a busy market today."

"How far are we from the ship?" Eden called over the clamor.

"Not far. It's at the end of this street. Look there, you can see the mast."

Leaning forward, she glimpsed the tip of the main mast with its rigging tightly furled. "Stay with our trunks," she said to Laykee. "I'm going to walk down and see if the plants are aboard yet. And I'll arrange for our accommodations if Mr. Hawkins hasn't done so already." She flung open the door and stepped down.

"Oh, Miss Eden, be careful."

Raising her parasol, Eden made her way through the crowd until she reached the wharf. There, stacked in neat rows of pots, were her green indigo seedlings. She was about

17

to do a quick inspection when she heard shouting from near the gangplank. She turned to see Bull Hawkins waving his meaty fist in the air.

"Ye don't have a choice, ye bloody Hun. I've made the deal and ye've got to make space for the cargo."

Eden shaded her eyes and took a better look at Bull's adversary. The man was apparently the ship's captain and in a fine fit of anger.

"Nein! No, by heaven, I will not unload my supplies!"

She moved toward Hawkins. This could be a serious problem.

The man on the ship's deck continued shouting. "Everything we need is in place, Hawkins. I'm telling you, there's no more room, and I sail tomorrow."

Moving closer, she took a good look at the captain. Her heart skipped a beat when she recognized him. It was the very same man who had played such a ridiculous trick on her at the governor's party. He looked different now— shirtless, with his flaxen hair unkempt around his shoulders —but it was definitely the same scoundrel. And he had the power to destroy her plans to transport her indigo to Charles Town.

Bull called up to him. "I've struck the deal, Cap'n. I helped ye round up yer supplies, now ye must take the indigo plants."

"Dammit, Hawkins, you told me last night you wouldn't interfere. We're loaded and ready. I took you for a man of honor."

Bull grunted. "Honor . . . aye. Stuff that comes and goes with the tide in most places. Me honor is as good as any man's once gold has crossed me palm. I've sold the indigo, and the purchaser is in a mighty big hurry to transport it to Charles Town." His voice lowered. "Here now, Cap'n, ye can make room somewhere, can ye not? I'll pay ye well for your trouble."

"I don't have a trading ship, Hawkins. I'm transporting a

colony of settlers to America. I came here for cane and farm supplies and now I'm leaving."

Eden propped the umbrella handle on her shoulder. So Bull Hawkins had lied about the captain bidding for the indigo, and tricked her into paying too much. Well, it was too late now. What really mattered was getting that horrid captain to agree to take the plants to Charles Town. If he refused, she was facing certain disaster.

The men were still arguing hotly when she hoisted her umbrella, gathered up her skirts, and started up the gangplank.

"Hold it right there, madam," ordered the blond giant. "Who gave you permission to come aboard?"

Eden stopped in her tracks and used her umbrella to steady herself on the plank swaying gently above the water.

"I'd like a word with you, sir."

"I'm busy."

"I beg your pardon, but that is *my* indigo waiting to be loaded. I've paid for it, and my price includes delivery to Charles Town."

The man hesitated. "In that case, I'm sorry. But you've been misled by Hawkins. I've a full load already."

"But I *must* take my indigo to America." Her heart was in her throat. "At least allow me to speak to you. I insist—" Eden started to move upward when a gust of wind caught her parasol and pulled her sideways. She screamed as she leaned precariously over the water.

The captain leaped onto the boards and rushed to catch her. He caught her wrist just as she was about to fall backward into the sea. Her parasol sailed over her head, and she grabbed for him with her free hand. Gasping, she looked up at him. Suspended at the full length of his muscular arm, she would not fall, but she was helpless to pull herself upward. Surely he must recognize her, she thought while looking into the most astonishing eyes she'd ever seen. They were the very color of the indigo dye she hoped to produce,

19

and framed by golden lashes. She hadn't noticed them before, but now they absorbed her in blue fire. From arrogant prankster to ship's captain. The man had changed his appearance, but not his manners.

He could have lifted her to the plank—but he didn't. She was confident he wouldn't allow her to fall, but he refused to pull her to safety.

"Haven't we met?" he asked as one eyebrow lifted.

"Not formally. Now please help me up."

"You're quite safe. I told you not to board my ship, and now see what has happened."

"Nothing has happened," she said, her cheeks burning under his bold appraisal. "The wind merely caught my umbrella, that's all." She clamped her lips. Oh, he was the most impossible man. But she must measure her words or her hopes of loading her indigo would be dashed.

His brow knitted. "I do recall our meeting. You rescued us from the governor's tea party."

"I thought *you* were the hero of that occasion."

"It was nothing. I often perform heroics on the spur of the moment."

"Especially involving nonexistent spiders."

"I apologize for that."

"I might be more civil if you weren't dangling me over the water."

He made no move to help her up, but swept her with his eyes. "So you're the woman who has bought Hawkins's indigo."

"Yes. Now, please—" She gripped his forearm. His flesh was hot beneath her fingers, his muscles rippling and powerful as he easily supported her weight.

His earlier annoyance had changed to amusement. Now she saw decision in his expression.

He cocked his head toward Hawkins. "Our friend, Mr. Hawkins, has offered to pay me well for shipping your produce to the coast."

"It's extremely important to me. I pray you will allow it," she said, swallowing her pride.

"Hawkins!" he called, without looking away. "You've already been paid by the lady?"

"Aye, but only 'alf," shouted Bull from his spot near the gangplank. "Don't drop the wench. If she drowns, I'll lose my chance at her riches."

"Excuse me," Eden said coolly, "I'd like to be in a safe spot while we continue this discussion."

"I won't drop you," he said nonchalantly. "And I have another question or two."

"But this is ridiculous." A quick turn of her head showed filthy water lapping between the ship and the dock several feet below her.

He frowned. "I hope I'm not hurting you."

My, he loved to play absurd games. She wasn't about to let him get the best of her. She relaxed and let go of his forearm. If he opened his hand, she would certainly fall into the water. It was worth the risk if she could call his bluff. "No. But I've heard you Dutch have a streak of cruelty. I guess this is proof enough."

"I'm neither Dutch nor cruel."

"Then you have an odd sense of humor."

"I've been told I'm lacking that as well."

"Then why won't you raise me up?"

"The reason would flatter you too much, I'm afraid. And your surge of confidence would work against me when we negotiate."

"Negotiate?"

"The price of your passage. I assume you will be accompanying your plants to Charles Town?"

"I'll pay a fair price for me and for my maid. I'll insist Mr. Hawkins have his men do the unloading and loading for the price he's already received. And I'll care for my own plants during the voyage. They're not large and won't take up much room."

"You'll share quarters with your maid and ask no special favors. I do have forty men aboard, some perhaps with the cruel streak you mentioned—though I doubt it. Mostly they're gentle farmers with wives and children waiting in Charles Town."

"Agreed."

Nodding, he allowed his gaze to roam slowly from her hair, which had come loose from under her hat and was drifting about her face and shoulders, along her rounded bodice, down her billowing skirts to the tips of her shoes, balanced on the edge of the plank. A suggestion of a smile played around his lips as he carefully drew her toward him. Then swiftly he cupped his hands around her waist and lifted her to the center of the gangplank.

She swallowed hard as she tried to keep from staring at his magnificent chest. Her hands were resting feather-light on his shoulders. After one heartbeat she yanked them away as if his skin was fire to her touch. "Thank you, Mister . . ."

"Baron Derek von Walden. From the Swiss Confederacy."

"Baron?"

"A worthless title now. Which is fine with me."

"Royalty?"

"It's a noble heraldry. But I'm setting it aside the minute I claim my land in America. I understand a man must *earn* his titles there—by toil and sweat and brains—and a bit of luck." He released her and stepped back. Standing above her on the sloping plank, his legs encased in fitted thigh boots, he appeared eight feet tall.

Eden smoothed her blouse and straightened her tilted hat. Controlling her voice, she said, "I'm sure you'll do well— and it's lucky for me you saved me from a dunking in that dirty water."

"If I added to your discomfort, I apologize. As I recall, you like apologies." He reached down and drew her hand to his lips.

"Only when they're earned," she said sharply, to conceal the effect his unexpected kiss was having on her senses.

Bull interrupted. "'Tis bloody hot for a teatime chat. And if I understand rightly from your recent conversation, I'm to be loading this ship with indigo before the tide goes out. If we're agreed, I'll be about the business."

"We are agreed," said the baron. "Come aboard and I'll show you what goods will be moved." He turned and strode to the deck of his ship.

Bull marched up the plank and eased his way by Eden, giving her an approving wink as he passed.

She had started to return to the dock to look for Laykee when the baron's voice stopped her.

"Pardon, my lady, I didn't get your name."

With an effort to restore her damaged dignity, she glanced over her shoulder and gave him a haughty look. "Miss Eden Wentworth Palmer—of the Carolina Palmers."

If she had hoped for a smile or friendly comment, she was doomed to disappointment. The captain gave her a curt nod and disappeared below decks. As she continued down the gangplank, she reassured herself that everything was going as she had planned. She would sail to Charles Town with her indigo. But her knees were shaking and she had the odd feeling that she had just encountered a force that could be beyond her control.

3

Derek watched as Hawkins's hired hands loaded endless numbers of small brown pots into the hold, each one containing a minuscule green sprout of indigo.

Propping one foot on a barrel, he asked himself why he had agreed so readily to take Miss Palmer and her plants to Charles Town. He'd had no obligation to do so and it was certainly an inconvenience. He'd moved out of the captain's cabin and in with Hans so the lady and her maid could have comfort and privacy. The old doctor had grumbled mightily over being forced to move his prize rose cuttings off the spare bunk and to the storeroom belowdecks, but he'd been given no choice. All this shifting around because of the wishes of a very determined lady. Derek pondered the reason for his decision. Surely not for the few extra shillings she'd agreed to pay him.

He recalled how she'd caught his eye at the governor's party, how he'd figured she was one of the little bits of fluff that he so often encountered at such gatherings—pretty, mindless, and extremely dull. He'd seen her yawn, and instantly thought up the tarantula trick to extricate them both from the boring occasion. He had been unprepared for her youthful beauty when he spun her around, and for the way her lovely eyes flashed when she discovered his deception. But he could have put her entirely from his mind if she hadn't suddenly arrived on his gangplank, confronted him boldly with her demands, then nearly plunged into the waters of Bridgetown harbor before he could rush to her rescue.

Derek smiled as he recalled Miss Palmer's cry, her parasol wafting over her head, her ruffled skirt caught in the wind, leaving delicate ankles and tiny feet exposed to view. If she really had been frightened, he would have lifted her at once to the gangplank and had an end to it. But with his hand firmly gripping her delicate wrist, she had looked at him with more curiosity than fear. Remembering her scornful speech on the governor's porch, he hadn't been able to resist testing her temper once again.

When he looked into her eyes, he'd felt something pass between them, something unexplainable but powerful. It wasn't that she was a heart-stopping beauty—though her hair was indeed glorious as it swirled thick and radiant from the confines of her hat. Her eyes, too, were exceptional: green like an alpine meadow, but with flecks of umber and gold, and dark, feathered lashes surrounding them. And her figure, as he'd held her at arm's length, was perfectly positioned for him to see its perfection: her waist petite, her captured breasts straining under her bodice, her neck graceful, the veins throbbing beneath the delicate alabaster of her skin, so typical of English ladies of quality. A slightly sunburned nose only added to her charm. He had seen more beautiful women—but there was something extraordinary about Miss Eden Palmer.

She had recovered her composure at once, despite her near disaster and her awkward predicament. She had registered more surprise than fear, and then indignation. When he'd held her momentarily suspended, her surprise had turned to annoyance. He deserved her anger, but then—and most fascinating of all—was the way her manner had become one of arrogant nonchalance, as if her precarious position meant nothing, and she herself was in command of the situation. It was an open challenge, and he had answered it with light teasing. She responded with increased indifference to her plight and merely negotiated her passage and the space for her damnable plants.

Well, she'd had her way, the little fox. He'd always been prone to making quick decisions, and sometimes he made mistakes. This could be one of those times, but it was too late now to change his mind; the lady's plants would soon be aboard. At least she had promised to stay out of the way, and with so much to keep him occupied, he was sure he could forget she existed. The challenge of his life lay ahead of him, and he had no time nor interest in a dalliance with a pretty woman. As for any serious attachment, he'd given up such dreams long ago. For the coming week, until the ship dropped anchor at Charles Town harbor, Miss Wentworth Palmer of the Carolina Palmers would travel under his protection along with the others. Once he knew she was settled and comfortable in his cabin, he would put her completely out of his thoughts.

Eden spent the first two days at sea confined in the tiny cabin, nursing a seasick Laykee and doing her best to control her own queasiness as the ship struggled through deep swells and heavy rain squalls.

On the third afternoon, however, a benign sun shone from a turquoise sky, and a pleasant trade wind blew steadily, filling the canvas and hurrying the frigate on its way.

She assisted her maid to a chair before an open window and stretched out on her cot with Bull Hawkins's notes laid out in front of her. In nearly illegible scrawl, he had written down the terms of their agreement and also the specific requirements for processing the indigo.

For a time the project had Eden's full concentration. She hoped Joseph, her overseer, was hard at work as promised, draining the rice fields and getting them ready for the indigo seedlings. In her mind's eye she could see the vats completed, the storage sheds ready, the men busy preparing the dye stuff for market.

Eden hadn't realized how homesick she'd become for Palmer Oaks, for her vegetable garden, her early morning rides in the meadow, and for the views from her upstairs window of the Ashley making its gentle turn toward the sea. The plantation meant everything to her. She had no recollection of her first two years in England, and had come to love every nook and cranny of the house lovingly built by Papa Charles. Her earliest memories were of digging with a small spade in the rich black soil above the river, of exploring the woods with the workers' children throughout long steamy summers, of sitting on a high stool in the kitchen watching her mother fry up fresh-caught catfish, cornpone, and peach fritters for the family's supper. Later a tutor had come out from Charles Town several times a week to augment her mother's efforts at teaching. Eden wondered what sacrifices had been required in those days to provide her with a decent education.

Her mother remained a vivid picture, though she'd been gone almost nine years: a sturdy woman with dark red hair worn beneath a variety of caps and bonnets to shield her fairness from the unforgiving sun. A woman who laughed often but who wept over the loss of a rosebush or the necessary felling of a tree as if they were her darling children. A woman who worked from dawn till dusk without complaint—and who died years before her time.

After her mother's death, Eden became Charles's constant companion, dogging his steps in the fields and hovering over his shoulder when he struggled with his accounts in the library. There wasn't one aspect of the plantation that she didn't know how to manage as well as he. He wanted it that way—and she took to life at the plantation as if she'd sprouted from the soil itself.

She heard Laykee groan. "I'm sorry you're seasick," she offered. "Could I bring you some tea to settle your stomach?"

"No, thank you, ma'am. I'll live or I'll die. Don't much care, either way."

Poor dear. Eden remembered the day twelve years ago when the young Indian girl had been bought from Yamassee traders at the Charles Town market to be her playmate, her companion, and eventually her personal maid.

"You musn't die, Laykee. I couldn't do without you."

A sudden shout from outside drew Eden's attention. Feeling the press of cabin fever, she decided to venture out. Besides, she must see to her plants today. They would need frequent watering if they were to survive the voyage in good condition.

After a reassuring word to Laykee, Eden picked up a pail and made her way to the steps leading to the hold. She tried to be as unobtrusive as possible, remembering her promise to Baron von Walden to stay out of the way. So far, that had been easy enough. The only member of the crew she'd seen was the young lad who brought their food from the galley and who spoke almost no English.

When Eden reached the storeroom with its bank of open windows, she was enormously relieved to find the plants looking green and content with new signs of growth. The pots had been placed side by side in long rows, some on the floor and others on raised benches and shelves stacked nearly as high as her head. Walking along the rows, she hummed a tune and occasionally complimented a particularly handsome seedling.

"That's a good girl," she crooned over a leafy stalk. "Or maybe you're a *boy* plant. My, I should have asked Mr. Hawkins about that." She shook her head and smiled. "No, I couldn't have asked such an intimate question. But I must find out before next season to be sure you're properly germinated." She continued on her way, humming again.

Abruptly she stopped and leaned to inspect a plant that was brown and bent double. "Why, I declare, you look just awful. You're certainly a sickly one. Or are you just depressed?" She tapped her cheek. "Let me see, I'll sing something lively. Maybe that will help." She began a song: "Merry go the bells, and merry do they ring, merry was myself, and merry did I sing; with a merry ding-dong, ding-a-ling, dee, and a merry singsong, merry let us be!" Lifting her voice, she moved along the aisle toward the water barrel. "Merry have we met, and merry have we been, merry let us part, and merry meet again; With a merry singsong, ding-a-ling, dee, And a merry ding-dong, merry let us be!"

"Your plants are fortunate to have such a talented mistress," came a low voice from the door.

Heat flooded Eden's cheeks as she whirled to face the speaker. Observing her with a hint of a smile was the baron. She'd done her best to forget the overbearing man—and been annoyed at her lack of success. But at least she hadn't seen him since the day they sailed, nor been forced to speak to him—until this minute. What was worse, she again looked the fool while chirping in her untrained voice to a roomful of indigo plants.

She'd have to brazen it out. "I do what I can, sir," she said crisply. "But what they need this morning is a good watering."

Pretending she didn't feel his eyes following her, she moved to the nearest cask and held her bucket beneath the spigot. A firm twist failed to turn the handle. "Lordy mercy," she muttered. A glance toward the baron showed he wore an amused smile.

"Too bad," he commented dryly. "Neither a song nor a prayer seem to help. Perhaps I can be of assistance."

"No, I can do it," Eden snapped, wondering why the baron's simplest words held a note of challenge. As he approached, she put all her strength against the handle.

He stood watching her, his thumbs hooked in his belt. He was as imposing a figure as she remembered, and intimidating at this close proximity. She tried to ignore him despite her accelerating pulse. Concentrating on the handle, she twisted it with all her might, but to no avail. If only he weren't standing so near, his eyes cool and amused.

Annoyed at her failure, unnerved by his close observation, she stepped back, but kept her pail under the faucet. "You may try, if you like, but I fear it's jammed. I really must water my plants."

He gripped the handle, then strained to force it open. With a loud crack the fixture broke off in his hand, taking with it a sizable piece of wood.

Dark golden liquid with the rich aroma of newly made rum squirted in all directions.

"What the devil!" Walden swore. "Rum!"

Dropping her bucket, Eden jumped backward, but not before she was sprayed with the rum from her hair to the hem of her skirts.

The baron looked around for something to stem the flow, then with a curse pulled his shirt over his head and stuffed it into the hole. In seconds the cloth was soaked and was pushed outward, where it fell to the floor in a sodden heap.

Wiping her skirts, Eden felt a laugh starting deep inside. The captain was finally in a predicament, and he was a comical sight as he gaped helplessly at the raging rum. The tables were turned, and she couldn't help feeling a bit of perverse pleasure in Baron von Walden's difficulty. Touching her lips, she tasted the rich flavor of the liquid on her fingers. She giggled, then gave up and let laughter erupt while she attempted to wipe the sticky drops from her cheeks and chin.

Scowling, he ordered, "Place your pail under the flow. We might as well save some of the stuff."

Controlling her merriment, Eden retrieved the bucket and

held it beneath the spewing rum. "My pail won't hold a fraction of the liquid in that huge barrel."

He grumbled, "It's enough to send twenty lads into their cups. We'll need a larger container if we're to keep the floor from swamping." Having said this, he merely stood looking from the mess to her with his forehead knitted in consternation.

Eden ignored his frown and ran her tongue around her lips. This was her first taste of rum. It had a delightful flavor, she decided, though a bit tart. Her bucket overflowed and she pulled it away. "What can we do, sir?" She felt her lips twitching, but contained her amusement in response to his glower. My, the man didn't have the slightest sense of humor. Or maybe the situation was more serious than she knew. A terrible thought struck her. "Oh dear, you don't suppose *all* the casks contain rum?" she asked suddenly concerned. "My plants will die!"

"No," he said wiping his hands on his breeches. "I'm sure some of these have water. We've drawn from them several times."

She hurried to one of the other casks and easily turned the spigot. Fresh water flowed out. "Good," she said, and with studied nonchalance poured the rum from her bucket to the floor, purposely adding to the accumulation, and placed the container under the faucet. As the pail filled, she watched him slyly. Where he had been so self-assured, so domineering, a few minutes ago, he now looked like a small boy who couldn't figure how to mend a broken toy. She liked him better this way, but she was certain the impression was fleeting. "You do have quite a mess here, Captain. I'd like to help, but . . ." Her voice lacked conviction.

"Never mind," he said sharply. "The keg has nearly quit flowing." It was no surprise when he reverted to his former officious manner.

Ignoring the sticky liquid spreading across the floor,

Walden approached her. "Please be conservative, Mistress Palmer. Since we're short a barrel of water, we may need to ration bathing and drinking before we reach Charles Town." Shirtless, reeking of rum, he studied her with an imperious look. The incongruity between his appearance and his royal bearing was so amusing, she was hard-pressed to keep from laughing again.

"Ration? Are you suggesting that bathing is more important than the lives of my indigo seedlings?" she quipped. "Why, if the voyage lasted six months, I'd still use the water for my plants—and hold my nose if necessary when I encountered my fellow travelers."

"Or you could soak the plants with rum," he suggested without the trace of a smile. "Or bathe in rum as we've just done. The results might be quite interesting." One eyebrow cocked as he awaited her response.

The sudden vision of the two of them bathing together in a tub of spirits caused her heart to flip-flop under her ribs. The man did have a sense of humor, after all—and it was daringly suggestive. To conceal her agitation, she said, "You could be right, at that. I should have asked the indigo which they preferred—water or spirits?" She put one hand on her hip and watched his reaction.

He appeared to make a special effort not to smile. But at least he didn't look nearly so grim. "You'll need some help, especially with the high shelves. Otherwise it will take you hours to water all these pots. Frankly, I think you're wasting your time."

She faced him squarely. "Why do you say that? Indigo is a wonderful new crop—once one knows how to raise and process it."

"I discussed the matter with my botanist. He doesn't believe the wilderness land of Carolina is suited to growing indigo. He tells me the growing season is too short, the climate too cool, pests are a threat, and the process of obtaining the blue product both complicated and delicate."

"He's quite mistaken—" Eden began, then caught herself and looked down at the plants while collecting her thoughts. She knew she could dispute every point, but why should she? Apparently the baron was taking a sizable group of people to settle in Carolina. With so many workers, he could do quite well growing rice and sugar. But if he planted indigo on hundreds of acres and learned to process it successfully, he could put her out of business within a year or two—either that or send the price into a downward spiral. She gnawed her lip while giving him a sidelong glance. Should she mention that indigo grew wild in South Carolina? Was she being selfish not to offer this man and his settlers the benefit of her knowledge?

"I'll be happy to introduce you to Dr. Messenbaugh, my botanist," Walden said. "He's an expert, I assure you. He could save you a year of fruitless labor, endless hours of backbreaking work. The captain leaned his weight on a post. "Don't you have a man—a father or brother—to make such decisions for you?"

His insulting implication countered his physical allure and erased any twinge of guilt she'd felt over withholding information from his settlers. She smoothed back her hair, aware of spreading the sticky rum in the process. "If you're suggesting I'm inept because of my gender, I hasten to correct you. I helped manage my father's plantation for years before his death. Now I'm completely in charge."

"My apologies. I'm sure you're more than competent," he said, looking at her with eyes laced with doubt.

Eden decided it was best to ignore his unsettling gaze. Turning to the next pot, she said, "But I'd be happy to meet your botanist. Maybe *I* can instruct *him* in some of the finer points of farming in the New World."

"I have no doubt you could," he replied.

She had no choice but to move toward him as she pretended to pour water into the pots. Controlling her annoyance, she decided the baron was as self-centered as he was unfeeling. In Carolina, a woman was spoken to with respect, showered with compliments, placed on a pedestal. Although she'd always suspected this display of courtliness was a veneer of sugar over a hard core of male egotism, she expected such courtesy from a gentleman of class. And wasn't Baron von Walden a gentleman? He did carry a royal title, though she had no idea how royalty conducted itself in that cold distant land of his birth.

She was very near him now and would have to brush past him if she was to gain the door. Would he let her pass? He looked almost threatening as he relaxed there, studying her with a solemn expression. With eyes lowered, she inched forward. A strange fantasy sent shivers along her spine. Here she was in the bowels of this man's ship, alone and with no one to come to her aid if he—well, misbehaved. He had been silent for so long, just watching her in quiet scrutiny. What if he decided to toss her overboard and keep her plants for himself and his clan? Who would know? Besides Laykee, of course, and he could toss her overboard just as easily.

He won't harm you, she chided herself. On the other hand, what did she know about the baron? He might be one of those uncivilized barbarians with flowing hair, vile tempers, and bearlike hands who pillaged and raped helpless women.

Nonsense, she told herself. But she stole a look at his hands. No, they had no resemblance to a bear's, but they were large and strong, quite capable of doing extreme damage if that was his will.

What was his will?

From the corner of her eye Eden scanned his powerful physique. The light was failing now. She had the urge to drop the pail and dash past him up the stairs to her cabin. In the silence, the ship creaked; the rum cask dripped blobs onto the floor; from some distance came the sound of a bell and a seaman shouting to his mate.

34

Yes, she must leave, but the baron blocked her way. Why didn't he speak? She started to take a step, but her foot was glued to the planks. The other foot, too. Oh, this was becoming a nightmare. She tried again and her foot came loose so suddenly she nearly toppled. The rum. Her slippers were soaked and sticking to the floor.

She wasn't aware she had dropped her pail until he strode to her side and retrieved it.

"Allow me, Mistress Palmer." His voice was throaty, seductive.

Eden snatched the bucket from his hands and tried to walk past him. First one foot, then the other, popped right out of its slipper. Syrupy rum seeped through her hose, causing the delicate fabric to shred.

He was inches away. She dared to look up at him and caught a glint of pleasure behind his narrowed eyes. Her urge to escape was replaced by the most astounding desire to wrap her arms around his bare shoulders, to lift her face to his, to feel those half-parted lips crush against her own.

Ridiculous. Ignoring her sticky bare feet, she walked swiftly with her eyes fixed on the open door. "I don't need your help, sir," she said more shrilly than she intended. "I'll finish watering tomorrow." It was all she could do to keep from running, and her feet were making a strange sucking sound with each step, which detracted a great deal from her dignified exit.

Collecting her skirts, she climbed up the companionway. Blue sky at last. Fresh air. Mustering her self-control, she walked with head high to the safety of her cabin.

By the following morning Eden was angry with herself for allowing the baron to wreak havoc with her usual good sense. Maybe the strong vapor from the spirits had gone to her head. He had only tried to help her, and she had treated him with extreme rudeness. As she slipped into her calico dress, she chided herself for being such a silly twit. The baron must think her either a dreadful snob or ready for the madhouse.

She stepped out onto the deck and blinked in the sudden brilliance. Closing the door softly behind her so she wouldn't disturb Laykee's first sleep in days, she gazed across the bow of the ship. The day was diamond-bright, tinged with sapphire blue at its edges. There was no wind at all, and the canvas sails hung limp along the mast.

The sound of laughter from near the prow caught her attention as her eyes adjusted to the glare. A group of men were squatting in a patch of shade, apparently engaged in some sort of game. One thing was plain: the frigate was making no progress toward Charles Town.

Eden shaded her eyes and saw with surprise that there were women aboard the ship. She had assumed from the captain's earlier comments that only a skeleton crew of men were on board. But several women, similarly dressed in ankle-length skirts and embroidered blouses of white muslin, were hanging wash to dry on a makeshift line stretched between posts on the deck below her. They chattered in their foreign tongue, though she occasionally caught a few words of English. They were brave souls, she thought with a rush of admiration, braver even than her own mother who had traveled to a new land, but at least a land ruled by England, where her language and customs were basically unchanged.

One of the women noticed her and spoke to the others. Their conversation stopped and the six ladies stared up at her.

Eden smiled and lifted a hand in greeting.

A stout gray-haired matron wearing a straw bonnet waved back. "Hello," she said. "Come join us, mistress."

Eden was happy to oblige and made her way down the wooden steps and joined the ladies.

"Good day," said the matron, greeting her with a warm smile. "My name is Henny Mueller. This is my daughter,

Katya." She indicated a rosy-cheeked girl whose eyes were as azure as the sky. Her thick blond hair was braided and bound into two large buns, one above each ear.

Katya curtsied and said, "Hello."

Eden offered her hand to Mrs. Mueller and to Katya, then to each of the other ladies. It appeared the remaining four were either too shy to speak or didn't know the language at all.

Henny Mueller explained, "Katya and I spent several years in London. For us, the English comes easily. The others will learn, though, as soon as we're settled in America."

"It's a pleasure to meet all of you," Eden responded. "I thought my servant and I were the only women on board."

"Most of the women and all the children did go to Charles Town on two other ships. But a few of us wanted to go to Barbados to help select supplies for our new homes and gardens." She smiled once more. "And to keep our husbands out of mischief."

"Then you're all married?" Eden inquired.

"All except Katya. But she has her cap set for a gentleman—and likes to stay as near to him as possible." She looked fondly at her daughter.

Katya blushed and shook her head. "Mama—*bitte!*"

Henny laughed. "Now Katya, it's no secret. Only the gentleman in question is unaware of your designs. I expect you'll have him in front of the reverend soon after we're settled in our new home."

Katya smiled broadly. "Maybe. We'll see. Oh, here he comes now."

Eden turned to see Baron von Walden approaching. He was plainly the man Katya intended to wed. She felt an odd sense of disappointment stir under her ribs. No wonder Katya was smitten with the man. His good looks in the clear morning light would melt a block of granite.

∾ 4 ∾

Watching Walden's approach, Eden felt more foolish than ever for acting like a frightened goose yesterday when she'd confronted the baron in the ship's storeroom. Was there any hope he had put the incident from his mind?

His first greeting was a bow to Henny Mueller. Next, a word in German to the others. At last he turned her way. The knowing look in his eyes revealed he had not forgotten at all. One side of his mouth crooked upward. "Good morning, Mistress Palmer. I took the liberty earlier of having your plants thoroughly watered. *Water*, that is, not rum. Oh, and your slippers have been cleaned and set to dry in the sun."

She was surprised and touched, but hid her feelings with a crisp response. "Why, thank you, Baron. But I promise you, I'll assume the responsibility myself from now on."

"As you wish. But today my men are idle—due to the lack of wind for sailing."

"Do you think we'll be becalmed for long?"

"Hard to say. I'm unfamiliar with these waters."

"At least my maid is feeling better since the swaying has stopped," Eden said in an attempt to keep the conversation light.

"I'm glad to hear it—though a servant's unsettled stomach would be a small price to pay for a quick journey."

"Well, of course—" she began, but he had turned his attention to Katya. So much for small pleasantries.

"And Miss Mueller, how is the bruised elbow today?"

The girl's eyes were wide and adoring as she pulled up her sleeve to show him her injury. She started to speak in German, but the captain shook his finger near her lips.

"English, my dear, English. We must all practice, you know."

Katya nodded vigorously, and Eden could see that she would do anything the baron suggested—even walk on hot coals if he asked. A sympathetic smile broke across his lips as he inspected Katya's elbow. To her annoyance, Eden felt her heart jump at the sight. My goodness, such a charming smile, and so rarely given. She almost envied Katya— no, to be honest, she did envy Katya. She would have enjoyed very much receiving such a look from Baron von Walden.

But the smile was gone when he turned back to her. Still, his expression was not unfriendly. "On a day such as this, we enjoy a rest and a game or two. Perhaps practice our marksmanship with the crossbow."

"Oh yes, let's do that," Katya interjected, pulling his attention back to herself. "Of course, Derek, you always win. Another William Tell, you are." Her voice dripped with honey.

"Hardly as daring as Tell, I'm afraid," Walden said.

"May I ask who is William Tell?" Eden ventured.

"A Swiss hero. One of our great legends—though some say his story is true. The man was ordered by the bailiff to shoot an apple off his son's head with an arrow. Having done that, he then shot the bailiff."

"Impressive feat, I agree," Eden said, attempting to appear merely friendly when his gaze was catapulting her heartbeat.

"Come watch," he suggested. "We'll set up a target—no

39

one's son, of course—and stage a contest." He winked at Katya, causing her hand to flutter to her throat. "The prize could be a kiss from Mistress Mueller—if she's willing."

Henny Mueller pretended shocked annoyance. "Now, Baron, none of that. My daughter's lips are sacred until her wedding day."

He tapped Katya's pink cheek. "I kissed these innocent lips the day you brought her into the world, Henny."

"But you were a lad of twelve then, sir. It's a different matter now."

"Let Katya decide. After all, it is a gamble. I might not win."

Katya laughed and tossed her head. "You? Lose an archery contest? Impossible. Certainly you may claim a kiss as your prize."

"Fine. We'll get started." He walked away, leaving the girl tittering behind him.

So he *could* tease, Eden thought. He must have been teasing her when he held her over the water. It was a type of reckless humor she had never encountered.

She spoke to Mrs. Mueller. "The captain, Baron von Walden, seems very nice."

"Nice?" The lady's eyebrows popped upward. "Nice? Why, the man's a saint. Oh, maybe not a saint, but a great hero. Certainly as great as old William Tell. He fought the French for years, risked his life time and again, sacrificed everything. And now he leads us like Moses to the promised land. My daughter is terribly attracted to him. She would like to help him overcome his heartache over his lost love."

"Lost love?" Eden couldn't resist the query.

"A girl from Neuchâtel whom he planned to marry. It happened years ago, but he's never courted another. She was murdered by the French invaders."

"Oh, how sad." So he was no stranger to deep feelings, after all—nor to pain, Eden mused. She had misjudged him.

Maybe that explained the haunted look behind his occasional smile.

"We all idolize him," Henny continued. "He arranged everything—met with King George and the queen. Sold his family's jewelry to buy the ships, obtain the grant, the thirty thousand acres of prime land for our township. Why, we'd all be starving in Switzerland by now. Starving or slaving for French masters." She placed her palms together before her face. "Praise the Lord for such a man. Even if he is full of mischief at times," she added with a sly smile.

Eden was impressed. A Swiss Moses. Why, that would impress anyone. It was true his commanding presence was fascinating. No doubt he could inspire his people to acts of courage and sacrifice. And the winsome Katya intended to make this heroic figure her husband. Maybe the girl would succeed, she thought. Again, this idea disturbed Eden more than she cared to admit.

"Mistress Palmer?" came a voice from above.

Eden looked up to see Laykee outside at last. "Come down," she called. "We're going to see a shooting contest. The fresh air will do you good."

Joining the onlookers, Eden took a seat on a barrel, with Laykee beside her.

Each man took a turn firing an arrow, until only the baron was left to compete. The target was a small white rag nailed to the mast some distance away. Derek took up a position farther than anyone else, brought the bow to his shoulder, took aim and let the arrow fly. It pierced the rag dead center.

Applause and shouts of congratulation exploded from the audience.

"He wins again!"

"Derek can't be beaten!"

"What's the prize this time? The baron always collects."

Other comments were in German, but the meaning was the same.

Laykee leaned near Eden. "A good shot—a fine-looking man."

"I claim my reward," called Derek. "Katya, come here please." He was not only smiling—he was grinning, on the verge of laughter.

Eden watched enthralled. She felt the blood pounding in her temples—and there were stirrings elsewhere in her body.

A delighted Katya had to be prodded forward. She stood before him, her hands behind her, her face lifted toward his.

He cupped her chin and kissed her firmly on her lips as the crowd cheered and shouted encouragement.

Eden released her breath, only now aware she'd been holding it. Oh yes, Katya Mueller was a very lucky girl, she conceded. Eden would have been happy to trade places with her and receive the baron's kiss.

Katya had no sooner rejoined the tittering ladies when Derek called over the din, "Mistress Palmer, we're honored you and your maid have joined us. Come here and I'll demonstrate the crossbow for you."

For a split second Eden was too startled to respond. Then she left her seat and walked toward him. If this was some new test of her spirit, she was determined to appear fearless. She was the only one who knew how her heart was hammering in crazy rhythm.

"I told you about William Tell," he said. "One never knows when such a skill could be of great benefit. Are you willing to learn to shoot?"

"Of course," she said lightly, keeping up a show of confidence. "As long as I don't have to shoot an apple from anyone's head. As a matter of fact, I'm not completely ignorant of weaponry—even of bow and arrow."

He cocked an eyebrow. "You're an archer?"

She knew everyone was watching closely, but it was the baron's scrutiny that unnerved her and scattered her concentration. Her courage faltered. "No, not exactly. I have shot the native weapons used by the Indians of my country, however."

"Ah, the American Indians. I've heard of their prowess." He looked around. "Does anyone have a longbow?"

"I do, Derek. Shall I fetch it?" offered one of the men.

"Please. We must give the lady a fair chance to win the contest."

"Oh, I'm not in the contest. I mean, I don't really know how to shoot *that* well. Besides, you've already won." She was positive he was bent on upsetting her, making her feel foolish once again. Why? He must be annoyed that she'd outmanipulated him in Barbados, she thought, and that she'd laughed at him when he stood splattered with rum. No doubt this great hero, this Moses, this legendary leader of his people, wasn't used to such belittling treatment, she concluded wryly. She wished she could suddenly become invisible. But she merely threw Laykee a helpless look and waited for whatever might happen next.

The longbow was produced, and she had no choice but to go along with the baron's game. The bow was certainly the largest she'd ever held. Her first attempt to insert the arrow and draw the string was awkward, but then she pulled with all her strength and let the arrow fly. It arched past the target and disappeared into the sea.

"An excellent first attempt," said Derek. "I doubt if I could have done better myself."

Now Eden was certain he was toying with her. Of course he could have done better. She felt her color heighten under his condescending smile.

"Next the crossbow," he suggested, reaching for the weapon.

"I've never shot one," she hastened. "I have no idea how it's done." She started to turn away, but he stopped her with his hand on her arm.

"Wait. I'll help you," he said with an invitation in a low voice that left no room for refusal. Placing the crossbow in her hands, he positioned the missile. He spoke for her alone. "The arrow is called a quarrel. Draw it toward you, secure it there—and release the trigger."

When she tugged the bowstring backward, the quarrel slipped from her fingers and clattered to the deck.

Embarrassed, she flashed him a pained look. His lips were twitching as he picked up the arrow at her feet.

She could see he was thoroughly enjoying himself.

"Remember how *expert* I was when opening the jammed faucet of the rum barrel?" he noted. "Too much strength—and not enough intelligence, I fear."

She glanced up at him. Was his admission a sort of apology for his former lack of friendliness? Was he actually joking about his awkwardness of yesterday? His sudden pleasant manner was more disturbing than his coolness. What if he turned out to be *likable,* as well as the most devastatingly attractive man she'd ever set eyes on? Certainly he was physically powerful, and she could tell he was remarkably intelligent. Combine that with humor and charm and he could be downright irresistible.

Eden made a new attempt to insert the arrow into the crossbow. Abruptly, his arm went around her shoulders, his hand covered hers and clasped the string. She shifted to look back at him. His eyes captured her with their intensity, their unexpected warmth, their sensual challenge. Her senses reeling, she stared again at the target. How could she concentrate with his body so close, his arms encircling her, his lips brushing her hair? She felt his muscles contract along her arm and across her back, his legs press against hers through the layers of her skirts. His mouth was so near her cheek she could feel his breath on her skin. Slowly he drew back the quarrel, taking her hand inside his. She was part of his body, encased in his embrace, his strength hers, his concentration absorbing her as if he, and she, and the weapon were one. Her left arm was extended. His left arm was beside it, lending his power until he took the entire pressure onto himself. At that instant a sense of elation raced through her like a shooting star in a predawn sky.

"Now," he whispered. As one, they fired the missile. It sped away and struck the rag in the same hole as his previous shot.

Eden was barely aware of the cheers as he released her as quickly as the quarrel. Her ears were ringing, her breathing uneven. Her fingers and arms tingled from the effort of drawing the string as he took the bow and gave her a look of satisfaction. She read volumes in that look: condescension, admiration, masculine pride, desire, challenge—it was more than she could understand.

"Thank you," was her inane remark as she turned and made her way back to her seat. Everyone was clapping, smiling, offering pleasant comments in two languages. Everyone except her two newest friends, Henny and Katya Mueller. She could only guess they were none too pleased at the baron's sudden interest in her shooting skills. She avoided their eyes as she sat beside Laykee.

A sudden gust of wind caught at her skirts and ruffled her hair. It spelled the end of leisure for the day. The men leaped into action as she and Laykee headed for their cabin. Sails were adjusted and the frigate shifted into the wind.

Eden's emotions were a wildly whirling vortex. She relived the feel of the baron's body next to hers, the latent power of his arms around her, the intimate look in his eyes. She knew she would never forget the feel of Derek von Walden's embrace—not if she lived to be a hundred.

⤞ 5 ⤝

Derek took the wheel and watched the sails billow and strain in the brisk winds. Overhead, the flag of England snapped in the breeze, a bright banner against a crystal sky. In seconds the sea had shifted from serene silk to surging swells with snowy peaks. The well-trained amateur crew of Swiss farmers and craftsmen lashed the rigging and prepared to make the most of the renewed wind.

For those few minutes, Derek almost put from his mind the feel of Eden Palmer's slender young body pressed next to his, the fragrance of her hair drifting near his cheek, the sight of her small hand forcefully gripping the bow beneath his larger one. He had thought he was too experienced, too smart, to let a woman get under his skin and awaken emotions he buried years ago.

In another lifetime he had allowed such feelings to wrap him in their web of fantasy. Heidi had been the enchanting daughter of a prosperous farmer in the next valley. With a heart bursting with love, he had ridden across meadows of wildflowers, past gurgling steams of melted ice, blind to the magnificent mountains soaring on either side of his path. He had met her often that summer of his youth, loved her beyond endurance, and in the fall watched as her ravaged body was laid to rest in the village churchyard. He himself

46

had discovered her pillaged farmhouse; all that was left was a blackened shell. Inside were the bodies of her parents. He'd found Heidi's corpse in the barn, where she'd been raped and her throat cut from ear to ear. That day, his youth ended. He didn't know the identity of the perpetrators, but he knew Louis of France had inspired them. He had spent the next ten years fighting with absolute determination. In the end he had lost his own land, and only by moving heaven and earth had he been able to extract his people from the bondage of the old world and bring them to the freedom of the new.

He thought his heart had died with Heidi. There had been other women, of course, some rare beauties, too, though none had touched him deeply. But Eden Palmer had stirred him beyond explanation. His gaze drifted to the deck outside her cabin. There, she stood in the wind, her skirts swirling, her hair turning to fiery gold as it caught the midday sun. She was staring out to sea, but he would have sworn she looked away the instant he'd turned toward her.

"Sail ho!" came a shout. "Off the starboard bow!"

Jerked from his musings, Derek shaded his eyes. A ship approached—and was closing fast upon them.

"What flag?" he shouted.

"None, sir," came the reply.

"Are you certain?" he called. No ship plied the waves without its country's flag—except for pirates and privateers.

"No flag, Baron. None at all."

He turned the wheel to try to avoid the mystery ship's course. Maybe the vessel would pass them by with a friendly salute. If it pursued them, however, he must be prepared for trouble. He knew pirates operated in these waters—both English buccaneers and Spanish cutthroats. His frigate was in good condition and had ample speed, and it had eight cannon and a large store of ammunition. But it would be no match for a converted man-of-war.

"There it is!" cried the lookout. "The skull and cross-bones! It's a pirate ship, sir, sure as hell."

"Clear the decks!" shouted Derek. "Prepare for battle! Women inside. Karl, get your men to the cannon. Remember our drill. If we can't outrun the bastards, we'll have to fight it out."

It was soon apparent that escape was impossible. The large ship bore down on the frigate like a white-winged hawk attacking a helpless pigeon.

Derek leaped to the deck and tore open a box of muskets. "Fire!" he ordered.

The starboard cannon exploded simultaneously, rocking the ship and filling the air with black smoke and the smell of gunpowder.

A handful of men hurried to take muskets, pistols, and swords and line up behind the gunwales.

Undamaged by the cannon's volley, the pirate ship hove to alongside the frigate. Grappling hooks flew through the air, snaring the smaller ship in talons of iron.

Derek jammed two pistols into his belt and brandished a cutlass. There was no time to think, to plan, to maneuver. The modern eighteenth century pirate was a highly skilled professional, more rare than the earlier breed, but equipped with the knowledge of his predecessors' tricks of the trade.

Derek knew his farmers were badly outnumbered, but he also knew they were fearless and would fight viciously to the last man.

Armed men were pouring aboard the frigate in an endless wave. From the corner of his eye Derek saw his cannoneers rushing up from below to meet the attacking hoard with small arms and knives. Dear Lord, it would be a bloodbath. The tragedy of it was that his ship carried nothing of real value—no gold, no jewels, no great store of weapons—only grain and seedlings and tools for farming. That thought gave him an idea, not particularly heroic, but a plan that might save all their lives.

Dashing in front of his men, he fired both his pistols in the air. "Hold your fire," he shouted. "It's no use. We'll negotiate."

"Hell, Baron, kill the vermin!" cried one of his men.

Several others cursed in German and tried to argue while they aimed their pistols at the advancing hoard.

"No. Stop," yelled Derek. "Don't kill anyone and we may yet survive. We have nothing they want—nothing!"

As the smoke cleared and vision became possible, Derek whirled to face the attackers. With dramatic flair he threw his pistols at the feet of the man leading the attack, then offered his sword, hilt forward.

"Take him," ordered the bare-chested buccaneer. "He's the leader. He's surrendering. An easy catch, I swear."

Chafing at the insult, Derek forced himself to hold his temper and let himself be captured. In seconds he was grabbed by rough hands and bound with ropes. His men were herded into a group and their weapons seized. He saw amazement in some of their eyes, disgust in others. It went against their nature to be overcome without a fight; their pride was trampled and their spirit tortured—but they lived, he told himself. From what he'd heard, most pirates were in the business for financial gain, not blood lust. The settlers' best hope lay in the measly value of their cargo—and the pirates' humanity, if such a thing existed.

A tall red-bearded man swung across the ship's side and landed near where Derek stood in helpless bondage. The pirate gave him a sweeping inspection with eyes as black as nuggets of coal. "Who ye be?" he demanded.

"Derek Walden. This is a merchant ship bound for Charles Town with a cargo of plants and supplies. I'm afraid you've wasted time and effort, Sir Pirate."

"God's blood—search the ship, men."

Derek, who was a head taller than his captor, looked down solemnly at the pirate while several of the motley gang scattered to inspect their prize.

"If ye're telling the truth, Mr. Walden, we'll amuse ourselves by filling you full of holes and sending your worthless ship to the bottom of the sea."

"What would that gain you, Red Beard, other than a hangman's noose?"

"Ha ha," spouted the pirate. "I've earned that long afore now, I'll warrant."

Derek kept his expression calm though his hopes swiftly sank. It appeared he'd lost his gamble. Some of the men might be taken as crew for the pirate ship and could survive. But what of the elderly such as Messenbaugh, and the eight women? Hell, maybe he should have allowed the fight to continue. At least they would have all died with honor and taken a few villains with them.

His jaw clenched as he saw the women herded forward by several armed cutthroats.

"Look here, Cap'n Hardy. They're not all young, but one or two look pretty saucy."

Another pirate emerged from the hold. "He's telling the truth, Cap'n. Nothing down there but a store full of damned pot plants."

The red-bearded captain cursed under his breath and turned toward the women.

Derek wished to heaven Eden Palmer didn't look like a swan among geese. His Swiss ladies were garbed in black skirts and modest peasant shirts. Miss Palmer's canary-yellow dress with scooped neckline and puffed sleeves drew the men's eyes like wasps to sugar. She was supporting the Indian girl as if she herself were the servant instead of the reverse. He thought he knew now, when it was probably too late, why he'd been drawn to Miss Palmer. Her beauty was most pleasurable, but her courage and spirit tempered with gentle caring was a rare combination. Even now she appeared unafraid and mostly concerned for her ailing maid.

"Hmm." The pirate leader gazed at the crop of females. "A poor kettle of fish," he observed, "except for the two young ones. You're right about one thing, Walden, there's nothing aboard this vessel worth the powder to sink it. No wonder ye gave up the fight so easily. Bloody saints, I wish we'd passed ye by."

"I disagree."

Derek twisted toward the sound of a husky female voice coming from the pirate ship. To his amazement, a stocky woman wearing breeches and a brace of pistols in her broad leather belt, and a Spanish-style wide-brim hat sporting a bright pink feather, jumped down from the gunwales and sauntered up to him.

By no stretch of the imagination could she be described as pretty, but her thick auburn hair fell to her waist and her dark eyes flashed fire and unrestrained excitement.

"Now, Jen," the pirate said, "this time we'll hang the wretch. I remember what happened the last time ye got that look in your eye."

"Leave me be, Jack," the girl said hotly. "This one's different."

"God's eyes, ye say that every time, sister." The pirate known as Jack shook his head in annoyance.

Derek stared at the two. Yes, he saw a strong resemblance between them. Brother and sister, no doubt. What unfortunate mother had spawned two pirate offspring from the same womb? He'd heard of female pirates, but this was the first one he'd seen. The wench was certainly giving him a close eye.

With no hint of ladylike coyness, she stood before him, then ran her hand along his chest where his shirt lay open. Her touch was rough as a scouring cloth, but he felt the tide suddenly turn in his favor.

"Balls of fire, he's built like a castle keep. Just as big too." Her hand moved up to his shoulder, then trailed across his shoulder bone and gripped the side of his neck. "Hard as Dover rock," she said.

Derek could have sworn he heard a gasp from one of the

ladies, but he didn't dare look their way. Though he was mildly embarrassed at being probed like a ham at market, his hopes to save his ship were soaring. Maybe he did have a negotiating tool, after all.

He laid his most seductive smile on the girl and asked as if he cared, "Is Jen a nickname for the lovely name Virginia?"

She was plainly distracted by his smile and friendly tone, but covered her confusion by stepping away and swinging her hips. "It is," she said haughtily. Then she grinned. "But I gave up the virgin name at the same time I gave up my maidenhead." She laughed heartily while awaiting his reaction.

He was sure now that more than one lady behind him gasped. It was a wonder they didn't all swoon, he thought, good women that they were. As for him, he had encountered crude wenches before. "I'm sorry I wasn't the one to win that treasure," he said lifting one eyebrow.

"I'm sorrier than you, Captain," she purred, moving to thrust herself against him, pressing her well-rounded breasts against his chest. With one thumb hooked in her belt, she reached an arm up to encircle his neck. "But it's better late than never, so they say. We can have a fine romp, if ye like."

She'd taken the bait. "Perhaps we can discuss some sort of trade."

She stiffened, then backed away to gape at him. "What? Well sir, ye don't have much choice now, do ye?"

"I don't have to give myself up without a fight—one that would probably cost me my life one way or the other."

She scowled at him. "A waste, I do agree."

Jack grabbed her arm. "Dammit, Jenny, let the cocky villain swing. We'll scuttle the ship and be on our way."

She was piercing Derek with a look like a heated dagger. "No. If there's anything I detest, it's an arrogant male who's too stupid to know when he's trapped." She moved close to him and ran her hand along his forearm, then down to his hands tied behind his back. Almost in a whisper, she said, "I could force you aboard my ship—take what I want. You couldn't stop me."

Smiling slightly, Derek put his lips near her ear and murmured, "Rape? Is that what you had in mind, *fraulein?*"

She encircled his nape and dragged his lips down to meet hers. Her fingers tangled in his hair as her lips parted and she urged his tongue between her teeth and into her waiting mouth. Her other arm went around his shoulders as she forced the kiss to continue until they were both gasping for breath.

"There," she said shakily. "I've given ye better than ye've ever had before."

He cocked an eyebrow as he looked down at her. "I'll hang before I give in to you, *Virginia,* but—"

Her lips were moist, trembling with frustration and desire. "But *what?*"

"I mentioned a trade."

She looked about to explode. "A trade!" she fairly cried. "So that's it. You want your freedom, no doubt—and maybe coin, as well. Hah! Hah hah." Her laughter held no humor. "I'll call your bluff, Captain . . ."

"Walden," answered Jack at her side.

"Hang him, Jack. I'll pay for no man's favors."

A girl screamed.

A pirate produced a rope and flung one end over a yardarm, then wrapped the free end around Derek's neck.

"No! No, Derek," the girl screamed again.

Jen motioned toward the ladies. "Shut her up. She must have a hankering for this stubborn worthless—what is he? A farmer?"

"He's not," cried the girl. He's—"

Derek turned in the noose. "No, Katya, don't—"

"He's a baron," Katya cried. "He's royalty. He is Swiss, but he sails under King George's protection. The king himself will have you drawn and quartered if you kill this man."

Jen again studied Derek. "Royalty? Swiss? So you're one of them Dutchies. I've heard they're grand in bed—kinda mean and heavy-handed. I think I'd like that. Besides, I've never been tumbled by royalty."

Inwardly he groaned. "You'll never know if you hang me, now will you, Virginia?" Derek held his breath in the long silence that followed. It was easy enough since the rope was tight around his throat.

She was angry; she was annoyed; but the look in her eyes told him he had won.

"So what is this trade?" she hissed between her teeth.

"My ship," he said. "My ship and all aboard will sail safely to Charles Town."

"Hell, that's no great loss to me," she said sharply. "If I agree—what do I get from you?" She put her hands on her hips and fixed him with her gaze.

"You get exactly that—me."

She moved near. Every eye on the ship, whether pirate, settler, or stunned lady, was glued to the scene. The ship rocked in the heavy sea, the wind whistled through the rigging, as the moment hung between life and death.

Her voice was hoarse as she asked, "In bed—willingly—with vigor?"

He hesitated. "No promises—only that you'll have me—and my ship goes free. That's the deal—take it or leave it."

"Done." She whirled to her brother. "Cut him down, Jack. Get him aboard and let these fools go on their way."

As Derek's bonds were being cut away, Katya broke from the group and flung herself against his chest. She was sobbing hysterically.

"Katya, Katya," he whispered. "For God's sake, be strong."

"They'll kill you. I'll never see you again. I want to die!"

She was beside herself. His hands were free now. He lifted her away and gripped her chin, forcing her to look up at him.

"Katherine Mueller, where's your courage, *mein helden?*" he asked sharply.

"Get rid of the bitch," spat Jen.

Jack kept a pistol aimed at Derek.

"Karl, come get her," Derek called.

"No," snapped Jack, "none of the men are to move. Not a step. Not until we're off the ship. And if a shot is fired, we'll blow this tub to kingdom come."

Derek looked at Eden. She was staring open-mouthed, pale, but her back was straight and her eyes dry. Katya continued to cling to him.

"Mistress Palmer, would you give Katya some assistance? She's overwrought, I fear."

Slowly, trancelike, Eden walked over and looked up at Derek. She was biting her lip; he saw a trace of blood.

"I admire your strength, mistress," he said, feeling a little of his own courage slipping. "Miss Palmer—would you take Katya's hand. Take her to her mother, please."

"No!" Katya gave an anguished cry and tried to hold onto him.

Eden Palmer wrapped her arms around the girl and eased her away, step by step. All the while, she held his look, and he saw her lovely eyes pool with tears. At the sight, he nodded and gave her a smile of encouragement. He was touched that she cared enough to shed tears for him. For the first time in years—since Heidi—his heart felt a stirring of life.

"Are you coming," Jen demanded, "or will my brother have to shoot you?"

"Wait just a damn minute!" snorted Jack. "If you take *him,* I'll claim a prize, too."

"Well, hurry and take your pick," Jen said, keeping her eyes on Derek.

"The wench in the yellow dress will do."

"No!" Derek protested. Before he could take a step, four

pirates surrounded him. One hammered the butt of a pistol into his head. Derek was dizzy when he was shoved onto the pirate ship, but he was able to see Jack carrying Miss Palmer on board. If she fought or screamed, he couldn't tell.

Eden was dazed, completely in shock. Everything had happened so fast, she hadn't had time to think or react. That rough, stinking pirate had scooped her up, carried her to the captain's cabin aboard his ship, and bound her to a post. While Jack went on deck to get the pirate ship under way, she was going to be forced to watch that terrible woman torment Derek Walden. A filthy handkerchief was tied around her mouth; her wrists were chafed and bleeding. She could struggle or she could faint, but she wouldn't be able to scream.

A bank of diamond-paned windows stood open to the sea and sky, showering the room with silvery opaque light. At the foot of the four-poster bed, Jen Hardy stood facing the baron, whose hands were bound to the bedpost behind him.

His head was leaning against the post; blood seeped from a wound along his hairline; his vest was gone and his shirt torn from his belt and hanging open down the front.

Jen was bare to her waist, her breasts fully exposed. A curved dagger was tucked into her wide leather belt. Below her waist she wore a filmy petticoat. Beneath that she wore nothing at all. Her hair hung in wild disarray down her back and swayed with the motion of the ship.

Eden's heart was racing out of control. If only she could do something. But she was helpless, and Baron von Walden was at the mercy of the pirate.

The woman's eyes were narrow, heated by desire, her lips slightly parted. Walden's look was stoic, impassive except for the hard glitter of his eyes.

Slowly, snakelike, Jen raised her arms and slipped her hands inside the collar of his shirt and pressed her naked breasts against his chest. One knee came up to rub his thigh. She raised one bare foot to stroke his calf and began to trail kisses along his throat and down the center of his chest.

His eyes closed and his teeth clenched, as if the woman's touch was more pain than pleasure. His voice was husky. "Nay, Virginia. You cheated me. Our deal is off."

"What do ye mean—off?"

"Just that. The girl wasn't part of our bargain. Let her go, keep her safe until you make port. Then we'll bargain again."

"Hell, she's Jack's prize. I have nothing to do with it, and he wouldn't give her up if I asked him to."

"Then you'll get nothing from me."

She nuzzled her lips into his chest, then peered into his eyes. "How's that, my noble captain? I'll let ye possess me. Your girl there can watch."

"Forget it."

She stood on tiptoe to press her lips to his. Wrapping her arms around his neck, she leaned back so the tips of her swollen breasts brushed his flesh. "You can't fool me, Baron. Your man's lust can't be hidden."

"Revelation is one thing, lovemaking another. My life is yours to take. My love is mine alone to give."

"Your *love!*" Stepping back, she slapped him hard across

the mouth. "Love be damned. It's your body I crave. What kind of man are you anyway?"

"A man who won't be forced, my lady. Nor would I risk creating a child with—with a she-pirate."

"You bloody bastard!" she shouted. "Ye think because ye're royalty ye can treat me like scum."

Quietly he said, "Let's just say—you're not a woman I care to bed."

She whipped the dagger from her belt. "I warned ye, didn't I? Ye'd best cooperate or—"

"Or what? You'll kill me?"

She put the blade to his throat and moved her other hand along his crotch. "I could slice your gullet right now," she said between her teeth, "or have ye stripped and turned into a eunuch. Which is it to be, my high and mighty lord? Choose."

Eden felt bile rise in her throat. She struggled in her trap like a moth caught in a spider's web.

"Do what you please, woman," Walden said flatly. "I can't stop you. But think about what you'll miss if you destroy my manhood."

Jen dropped her knife and flung herself against his body. She ran her hands along his shoulders and moved over him, half sobbing, half pleading in an agony of frustration. Forcing his mouth to hers, she molded herself against his large frame.

Hypnotized, Eden was drawn into the scene. It was *her* lips he kissed, *her* body pressed against his, *her* fingers entwined in his length of golden hair. As if in a dream, she heard his whispered words, "I love you, Eden Palmer, and I would die to save your life." She closed her eyes in a desperate effort to shut out the vision.

The pirate clenched her fists; her eyes narrowed with repressed fury. "I gave you a chance," she growled. "You could have lived, sailed with me. We'd be rich and free as the wind. This is your last chance, Baron. Deny me and ye'll feed the sharks."

His scornful eyes flashed back at her. "What better use of worthless human flesh?"

"Ahhh," she screamed. "So be it then, ye stinking rat from the foulest sewer." She grabbed a shirt off a chair and pulled it on over her head. "Jack," she shouted, throwing open the door. "Come get this blighter and toss him out. I'm bored with the miserable fop."

Eden was frantic with fear, her skin on fire, her body damp with sweat. She pulled, she moaned, she fought against the ropes until her wrists were raw and burning.

Jack appeared, and with an ugly leer dragged her from the room and marched her to the ship's upper deck, where she would be a witness to the execution of Baron von Walden.

When the baron was brought out, the pirate crew gathered and called insults amid crude jokes and guffawing. One man stepped forward and laid a cat-o'-nine-tails hard across his back. His shirt was torn to shreds and streaks of blood smeared his flesh.

Derek flinched and stumbled, but quickly straightened as he was forced to the gunwale by four stout buccaneers.

Eden's throat was closing. She felt like she was strangling as her pulse pounded in her ears.

"I want his boots," someone yelled.

"Get the ankle irons!" shouted Jack.

With his back to the rail, Derek gave Eden a lingering look. He smiled, but his smile was heavy with regret. "Have courage, Eden Palmer," he said gently. "God forgive me, I'm sorry this had to happen."

All she could do was nod, and pray he knew she didn't blame him. She wanted to die with him. Later, perhaps, she would die. But for now she could only gaze at him with a breaking heart.

The pirates returned with the chains and pushed him

backward, holding him across the railing. He made no resistance, but took a deep breath and looked skyward as his boots were pulled off and irons locked around his ankles.

Jen bent over him. "What's it to be, Baron von Walden— the sharks are waiting."

"Send me to them, madam," he calmly replied.

"Eeeee!" she screeched, and raised her dagger above his heart.

"Sail ho!" came a shout. "Port bow!"

Jen swirled to look. "Bloody hell," she cried. "Get these two into the hold until we see what flag it flies."

Eden was half carried, half dragged down steep steps. Behind her Derek was hauled by two of the crew.

Derek looked down at Eden Palmer. Her face was lost in shadow, but he knew she was crying. When she drew away the gag from her mouth, he saw the damage done to her small wrists by the ropes. "The bastards," he muttered.

She appeared near fainting, and he reached out to draw her into his arms. It was as natural a gesture as taking his next breath.

"Let's sit," he suggested. He guided her to a place on the floor where they could lean against the curved ribs of the timbered wall. The only light was a few patches of sun filtered from a broken board in the ceiling. The air was dank and thick; somewhere in the dark, a rat scurried away from the intruders.

She looked so forlorn, so exhausted, Derek forgot his own pain and took her hand in his. "Take heart, Miss Palmer, we seem to have a reprieve."

She gazed up at him, her eyes red rimmed, her lips slightly swollen, her cheeks smudged and damp with tears. Damn Jack Hardy, he thought. What kind of monster would mistreat a sweet, innocent young woman like this? A long-buried vision of Heidi's tortured body flashed through his mind. Yes, there were insane beasts loose in the world. It had been too late to help Heidi, but he might be able to offer some comfort to Eden Palmer.

She was shivering despite the stuffiness of their prison. He figured it was nerves and shock rather than cold, but he pulled her gently against his chest. Her shoulders were smooth as ivory above the buttercup-yellow ruffles of her sleeves. The low-cut bodice revealed the rise of her young breasts. Mistress Palmer held far more allure for him than the bawdy, half-naked Virginia Hardy. If only fate had treated him and this gentle lady differently, he might have paid court to her—become her close friend, and maybe more. If he were still a wealthy and powerful lord instead of a penniless immigrant, and they were not about to die—he would have relished a courtship with Eden Palmer. But at this point he figured what remained of their future would be spent here in this cramped, smelly hold—and it would be brief.

Her hands were clutched in her lap. He covered them with one of his and noticed they were icy. Her fingers tightened around his hand as if seeking warmth and reassurance.

"I'm so frightened," she whispered.

"You showed great courage earlier today, equal to any of my men. If you're frightened now, it's only a reaction to all that's happened this past hour. And you're not alone in your fear," he added gently.

"I was sure they were going to drown you. That horrible woman." Tears pooled in her eyes, caught in her lashes.

Derek noticed the delicate sparkle in the light filtered from over their heads. Smiling encouragingly, he said, "I thought so, too, but I suppose hell will have to wait awhile to collect my wayward soul."

The ship lurched and shuddered as it made a sudden tack to starboard. The girl was pressed tightly against his chest. He found he was increasingly aroused by the softness of her, the fragrance of her hair, the feel of her small hand in his.

She withdrew her hand to dab at a tear escaping along her

cheek. His heart tugged when he saw she only managed to smear the dirt on her pale flesh near the curve of her lip.

"Do you think we're going to die?" she asked barely above a whisper.

He had to do something to help her through this. He guessed one of three things was most likely to happen. The ship that approached would avoid the pirates, and eventually Jen and Jack would carry out his execution. Or there would be a battle. If the pirates won, his fate would be the same, and Miss Palmer faced worse than death. If the pirates lost, the ship could be blown apart. He and Eden Palmer would probably drown—or burn to death in this stinking hold. Drowning didn't bother him so much, but God, he hated the idea of burning. He admitted it was the one thing he feared most. He had seen his home go up in flames, his parent's burned bodies, the charred animals, the stench. Damn him for a coward, but it made his skin crawl to think of it.

"Death is a possibility, I must honestly admit," he said.

A distant roar of cannon fire punctuated his words. From above came the sound of a loud cracking, like wood being torn asunder. The ship tacked sharply and they were thrown heavily to the plank floor.

Pain shot across his ankles as the irons cut into his already raw flesh. A groan broke from his lips as he lay with his chest on the floor.

She knelt over him. "Oh, your poor back. It's deeply cut from the whip." Her fingers brushed his shoulders. "And those cruel irons. Captain—I'm so desperately sorry—what can I do?"

He pushed upright and fought against his pain. Sitting opposite her, he enclosed her hands. "Your presence is all the comfort I need, *fraulein*. Although, God knows, I'd give anything if I were alone and you were on your way to Charles Town."

She was looking at him with such compassion and misery,

he hated himself for his weak outcry a minute ago. Smiling, he settled once more against the wall and draped an arm over her shoulders when she rested beside him. She was warm now and her trembling had stopped. He would engage her in conversation and hopefully distract her from their likely fate.

"There's hope, Miss Palmer," he offered in a positive tone. "We're alive and the ship could come to our rescue."

"I hadn't thought of that," she said, her face brightening. "We can pray, I guess. Do you pray, Baron von Walden?"

Stretching out his legs, the ankle chains rattling as he did so, he held her close.

She cuddled against him as if she had done it a million times before, and rested her head on his shoulder.

He said, "Under the circumstances, why not use our Christian names? I'd be pleased if you called me Derek."

"Yes, and I'm Eden, as you know."

"A lovely name. Reminds me of paradise." Or temptation, he thought to himself. Eden Palmer's abundant physical charms coupled with the spirited challenge in her amber-green eyes could lead a man into sin in the space of a heartbeat.

The cannon's boom grew closer. She moved against him and encircled his chest with one arm.

"Tell me about your home," he said in as casual a tone as he could muster.

"We have lovely gardens. My mother's favorite pastime was gardening. I love it, too, though I'm not as skilled as she was. She learned her skill in English gardens, you see, when she was living there with my real father."

"Your real father?"

"A colonel in the British army. My mother was a Wentworth, and when my father left for battle, she stayed with her family. He died when his ship—when his ship sank off the French coast."

Derek saw the similarities of her father's death and her

present circumstances register in her face. Would she follow her father to the bottom of the sea? She tilted her head bravely and continued. "My mother married Charles Palmer when I was two years old, and came with him to America to take a land grant and build a home west of Charles Town. That was seventeen years ago. She died when I was ten."

"Tell me more about your home, Eden."

"It's beautiful. It was a wilderness once. My stepfather, Charles, and my mother built the house on the Ashley River. I've worked beside Papa Charles, but it's been difficult to make ends meet without slave labor. We used to have a few slaves, but Papa freed them when he died, and I'm glad he did. I never thought it was right to own human beings. Of course, nearly all the planters do." She gave him a tentative smile. "But with the indigo, I'll be successful, I'm sure. Only a few hands are needed to bring in the crop."

"Is it so important to you—keeping the plantation, even though you're alone?"

"It's the most important thing in my life. The plantation is all I have now. Mother and father, sister, brother— family. Everything. I love every rock and tree and flower and bird. Palmer Oaks is my very soul."

"Then I hope with all my heart you succeed." What an amazing woman, he mused. She had the face and figure of an angel and the same indomitable spirit of his Swiss pioneers. What a tragedy they would probably be dead within the hour.

"Tell me, Derek, about your home."

The ship tacked again. Somewhere beyond their vision boxes shifted and rats scampered along the floor.

Eden pulled up her knees and tucked her skirts tightly around her legs. But she made no verbal complaint.

He considered how most women would be in a swoon by now, and his admiration for her continued to grow.

Looking up at him, she studied his face. He saw a lack of guile, no attempt at a flirtation. But he saw his interest in her matched by hers in him. She was proud, she was intelligent, and she honestly cared about his thoughts and feelings. Instead of rattling on and on about herself, she was waiting quietly for him to speak about his experiences. He rarely did so, but considering their present circumstances, he was tempted to share some of his tragic past with her.

He began hesitatingly. "My family, the von Waldens, have ruled the mountains and valleys of Neuchâtel in Switzerland for generations. My father was the eighth baron. After his death, I held the title, but nothing was left of our property and possessions after the French invasion. I learned years ago that possessions are meaningless if the people you love are dead."

She nodded, absorbing his every word.

He went on. "My parents—died when my home was burned."

Her hand squeezed his. "Yes, Mrs. Mueller told me about your loss. Also about the girl you planned to marry. Does it pain you to speak of her? It's not that I'm curious, but my Cherokee maid said it's very healing to speak of deep hurts. Don't, of course, if you'd rather not."

"No, your maid is right. My fiancée's name was Heidi." Absently, he stroked Eden's hair and gazed into the darkness of the hold. "Heidi was as lovely as a rose in early bloom. Hair the color of flax, delicate skin like fresh cream, and a laugh as innocent and guileless as a child's. I loved her as only a youth can love for the first time. And she returned my love completely. There were stolen kisses in a landscape locked with ice and snow, promises, plans, a future full of endless joy that we believed in with all our hearts. The end came so suddenly, so viciously—" He stopped speaking; he clamped his jaw to contain his feelings.

"Derek—don't go on. I'm sorry. Later, perhaps."

He looked at her, saw the shared pain in her eyes. "It's all right. Your maid gives good advice. It's a purging that needs to be done." His hand roved along her arm. He had never spoken so freely with anyone, but Eden's sympathy and understanding reached into his heart. "Heidi was killed by several men. I found her body. I believe—at least, I pray— she died quickly, or was unconscious when they did their worst. The sight sent me to my knees. Later I scoured the countryside in a rage so blind, so furious, I would have hacked to pieces the perpetrators if I had found them. But they had disappeared into their mountain fortress, maybe back over the French border. Eventually I turned my anger and frustration into the battle against the invaders—but lost that, too. One day I rode back to my castle in Neuchâtel, to find it in flames. I tried to get inside, but—"

"Oh, Derek—"

"It was too late. I couldn't get to them. Later, I found their bodies, my parents, my sisters, all dead in the smoking debris."

"Dear Lord—don't say any more. Enough is enough."

"Now I work for my people. I've done all I can to see that they're settled safely in America. Thank God they're on their way. They will make it now without me, if they must."

"You're a very brave man, Derek Walden. I admire you greatly." Her compliment was spoken shyly and touched him deeply.

"I have fears like any man. But I've seen hell here on earth, so the real place holds no terror for me."

She shook her head. "You've had so much pain—and now this."

The acrid odor of gunpowder mingled with the smell of stagnant seawater. "I'd like to ask a favor, if I might," she said.

"My ability to grant favors is limited, I'm afraid. But please ask and I'll do my best."

"I'm assuming we might die. I mean, it's possible, you know. Would you kiss me good-bye?" Hastily she added, "If we don't die, of course, we'll pretend it never happened."

"I'd be honored, mistress. Nothing would give me greater

pleasure." He put an arm behind her back and lifted her chin with one hand. He touched her lips, feather light, but to his surprise she slipped her hands behind his neck and pressed her mouth firmly to his. The kiss ended all too soon as she drew away.

"Thank you," she murmured. "I've never kissed a man before and I didn't want to die—"

"My darling Eden, if that is true, we must try another." He pulled her into his arms and covered her lips, parting them with the tip of his tongue, enjoying the pleasure of her willing response, the feel of her petite waist in the curl of his arm, the fragrance of her hair, the rise and fall of her breasts against his bare chest. This time he kissed her long and expertly.

Afterward she remained cradled in his embrace, her moist lips just touching the flesh along his collarbone.

Gunfire sounded above them. Smoke was pouring under the door.

As if startled from sleep, she got to her knees and stared wide-eyed in renewed alarm. "Oh dear heaven! You don't think we'll *burn* to death, do you?"

His mouth dry, he forced a bantering air. "Of course not, my dear. We will drown long before that."

Footsteps were pounding down the steps outside the storeroom.

Derek stood, despite the listing floor. "We'll soon know our fate, Eden." He tried to shield her as he faced the door. He had no weapon but his fists. He would give as good account of himself as possible.

"Derek Walden," Eden murmured, her arms clamped about his waist. "I'm proud to die at your side."

Damn, what a woman, he thought as axes crashed against the door.

The wood splintered. A harsh voice called, "Nothin' in here—wait—some captives. You blokes get goin'. This ship's headed for the bottom."

~ 7 ~

From the rolling deck of the East India merchantman, Eden and Derek watched the death throes of the pirate ship as it burned and sank beneath the blue-green sea. The infamous Hardys, along with their surviving crew members, had been hustled belowdecks and locked away, where they would travel with the British to stand trial in Kingston.

Eden was numb with relief—and embarrassed over her lack of courage during the past hour. She also felt extremely uncomfortable under the curious stares of the English sailors. What on earth were they thinking? That she and Captain Walden, who was practically a stranger to her, had coupled in that filthy hold while awaiting probable death? Of course, they didn't *know* she and the captain were strangers. Nor did they know anything about the backgrounds of the man and woman they had just rescued. She certainly looked anything but proper with her dress torn and smudged, and Captain Walden was half naked and in his stocking feet, though at last his ankle chains had been removed.

Closing her eyes, Eden breathed deeply of the invigorating ocean breeze and chided herself for worrying over appearances when she and the baron had just come within a hair's breadth of dying. And after all, *she* knew—and Baron

68

von Walden knew—that nothing really awful had taken place while they were captives in the pirate's storeroom.

On the other hand, she had behaved scandalously, pleaded for his kiss, lain against his body as if she had every intention of seducing him. Her cheeks flamed at the thought.

She glanced up at him. To her instant horror, she saw he was smiling down at her, that all-knowing half smile that hinted he was reading her thoughts, that he acknowledged the intimacies that had taken place—and suggested more were yet to come.

She averted her eyes and said sharply, "I do hope we will have accommodations provided right away." She smoothed back her hair. "I am completely exhausted. Such an ordeal." Her speech did nothing to erase his smile. "Captain, if you please, I would like to speak plainly."

"Indeed, Mistress Palmer. Say what's on your mind."

She took note of his formal address. "When facing certain death, I behaved badly, I'm afraid."

His smile widened as he leaned on the rail and looked at her from beneath half-lowered eyelids. "As you can see, *fraulein,* nothing is certain—not even death. At least not advance knowledge of the time it will occur."

Eden was too tired, too flustered, to think clearly. "But you know what I'm saying, sir. I expected to die . . . well, I was quite frightened, I admit. At any rate, I would never have—"

"Don't worry," he interrupted. His look was annoyingly patronizing. "What happened in the pirate's hold will be our secret. I am a gentleman, after all. And frankly, the experience was the high point of my visit to the Hardys' charming vessel."

"Thank you. But I do hope you will forget it entirely," she said archly.

"I can't promise that. But I will try."

Heavens, he looked so incredibly appealing, standing there shirtless, his moist disheveled hair curling around his forehead, the flat plane of his stomach in plain view above the belted waist of his skintight breeches. And he had the air of a man who had just sauntered in from a game of tennis at the king's pavilion.

An officer approached them. "Excuse me, madam—sir, may I conduct you to quarters we've prepared? The cabins are small, but two of my officers have vacated to allow you privacy."

"Separate quarters, naturally," Eden said, cocking her chin.

"Naturally, madam. I was told you're not a married couple."

She threw Walden a grateful look. "No, we were merely seized from the captain's ship at the same time." She held out her hand to the British commander. "Again, my deepest thanks, sir. My family is prominent in Charles Town, and I'll see that you receive proper accolades."

"My pleasure, I assure you. We'll deliver those rascals to the authorities as soon as we reach Kingston. With luck, however, we may yet overtake your vessel bound for Charles Town. Captain Walden will help us in that effort. It will save you quite a long journey out of your way."

"Oh, that would be wonderful. I do have urgent business in Charles Town. Extremely urgent."

Was Walden smiling at her again? She felt he was, but she didn't dare look. Her business *was* urgent. Just because she was a woman didn't mean she had nothing to do but sip tea and sew. Derek knew about her indigo and how important it was to her. Of course, he didn't know she must sell the crop to pay for Palmer Oaks. No one knew that, no one except Laykee and Bull Hawkins.

She freshened up in the tiny cubicle provided for her and rested for a brief time. Then a polite seaman arrived to announce the captain's ship had been hailed and they would soon be transferred. At last she could resume her homeward journey.

The reunion was tumultuous. Eden heard the cheering before they reached the side of the vessel in their longboat, and it increased as they climbed up a ladder and were hauled aboard by a dozen wildly exuberant Swiss.

Naturally, the baron was greeted with more unbridled joy than she, but the settlers gave her a round of applause. Katya Mueller was beside herself and clung to Walden hysterically, as if he were her private possession.

Eden was embraced by a joyful, weeping Laykee, who assisted her to their cabin. She noticed a few cool looks aimed her way, especially from the women. Only now did it occur to her that they, more than anyone, would wonder what had taken place aboard the pirate ship. Did they think she'd been raped by Jack Hardy? Used by his men? Or even seduced by Derek Walden? She supposed her reputation was at extreme risk. Well, she would have time to reassure them during the remainder of the voyage to Charles Town. That is, if they believed she was telling the truth.

That evening, after a bath and a hot meal served in her room, the first note appeared under her door. Written in childlike scrawl, it read, *Leave Derek alone. He's mine.* She was sure it was from Katya.

For two days Eden remained in seclusion. Not because of the note, but because the kidnapping had left her more fatigued than she realized. Also, she wasn't sure what kind of reception she could expect from the straitlaced immigrants. Besides, she had no need to go out since Laykee was reliably tending the indigo plants and reported they were flourishing.

But by the third day she was sick of being caged in the small cabin with nothing to occupy the long hours as the ship plowed northwest toward its destination. In a day or two they would arrive in Charles Town—and then she would have to face Landon. How would her fiancé react to her experience with the pirates? And how would she explain her friendly relationship with the captain? Would Derek Walden still want to visit Palmer Oaks to see her flowers? Or had those been empty words to comfort her in a time of crisis? It was true, he had been uppermost in her mind ever since the extraordinary adventure they had shared. How could she ever forget his willingness to sacrifice his life for his people—his breathtaking courage when he expected to be tossed to the sharks, and the way he held her, comforted her, kissed her when she had been half crazy with fear?

She strolled outside her cabin and for a while observed the crew at work. The winds were favorable and they were making excellent time as they scudded through the white-tipped waves. She spotted Katya and Henny Mueller alone on the deck below and decided to take the opportunity to face the two and allow them to air their opinions.

"Good afternoon, Mrs. Mueller—Katya," she said in her friendliest tone, putting out of her mind the note she'd received. "We'll soon be in Charles Town, thank goodness."

Mrs. Mueller nodded, but her slight smile was blatantly false. "Yes, what a blessing," she said without warmth.

"Katya, I'm sure you're going to love it in Carolina. So many young ladies to meet. So many nice things to do—the theater, dances, picnics." She was sure she sounded completely sincere.

For her effort, she received a frigid blue stare verging on hateful and condescending. "I'll have work to do at our new town," Katya said. "I'll be busy helping Derek with the chores."

"Oh, of course," Eden said hastily. "But surely there'll be some time for fun. For getting acquainted."

Katya's look held daggers. "I don't need new friends. And I expect to marry before long."

"My, I didn't know. You mean . . ." Her voice trailed as the meaning of Katya's words registered. "You are engaged?"

"Yes. At least, we have an understanding."

Mrs. Mueller looked at her daughter. "Katya. You shouldn't mislead Fraulein Palmer."

Katya pouted. "Everyone knows I'll marry Derek. It's been understood for years."

Eden was stunned at how her heart plunged at Katya's words. She herself had no claim to the baron. Why, they had only just met, and he had been close to the Muellers all his life. His kiss, the way he'd looked at her, the warmth she felt when they had their conversation in the storeroom, none of that was truly significant. She and Baron Walden had only been doing their best to pass a tense hour together in most difficult circumstances. She must forget him—and she must remember *she* had a fiancé waiting in Charles Town.

"I believe I'll return to my cabin," she said, feeling her mood turn bleak despite the sunshine. "I haven't quite regained my strength."

"I'm sure it was a terrible experience," said Mrs. Mueller, with more condemnation in her voice than sympathy.

Eden left them before her temper could betray her feelings. Katya thought she was trying to steal Derek; Mrs. Mueller suspected she had been ruined by the pirates. It wasn't fair, Eden thought. She hadn't asked to be kidnapped and frightened half to death. She straightened her spine. But no one had guaranteed that life would be fair. And she would not let the prejudices of the settlers make her feel guilty for crimes she hadn't committed. She didn't go out again, and that night another note appeared under her door. Footsteps hurried away before she could fling the door open and catch the culprit. This note said, *Derek thinks you're a loose woman.* She crushed the paper and tossed it aside. But the note had done its work. This time, she agonized, the message might be true.

Eden stayed inside the following day. It was cool and rainy and she was fighting a headache. After a quiet dinner with Laykee served on the small table of their cabin, she felt better and decided to take a look at the indigo. Tomorrow they would be arriving in Charles Town, and the plants must be moved very soon for planting at their new home.

She had reached the first deck when she heard her name being called.

"Mistress Palmer, where have you been keeping yourself?"

Holding her shawl around her shoulders, she turned to look at the captain, who was walking toward her with a pleasant smile on his face. Splashed with the last colors of a dying sun, his hair tied neatly at his nape, he was every bit as handsome as she'd envisioned him in her dreams. And now his effect on her was even more devastating since she had been held in his arms, kissed by those inviting, sensuous lips, shared danger and faced death at his side.

She forced herself to remember Katya. "I've been busy in my cabin," she fibbed. "I have much to think about since we dock tomorrow." Hopefully, her voice held no hint of the tumult of her emotions.

He moved close, too close. "I was concerned that our capture had made you ill."

"No, no, I'm quite recovered. In fact, I haven't given it a second thought. My mind is completely fixed on my plans for the future. I'm sure you have much to think about as well—a new settlement and all." There. Just the right amount of nonchalance and flippancy in her voice.

His brow knitted as he gazed down at her. She tried not to stare at his eyes, his lips, his broad shoulders.

"Yes. I have a great challenge ahead of me. But it's my dream, as you know."

"Yes, I know. Leading your people to the promised land." She wanted to bite her tongue for sounding so sarcastic. She saw a suggestion of surprise flit across his eyes.

Then he laughed and said, "You make me sound like a Biblical saint, Miss Palmer. And we both know that isn't the case."

"Actually, I couldn't say, sir. I barely know you, after all." She was amazed at how harsh her words sounded when her heart felt like it was shredding into a million pieces. Better to be strong now, she told herself, than risk heartbreak and humiliation once they reached Charles Town.

After a pause while he continued to give her a half smile, more heartrending because it held an element of disappointment that she knew she had caused, he lifted her hand and brushed her fingertips with his lips. *"Auf Weidersehen,* mistress. With luck, we'll have a chance to become better acquainted in Carolina." He spun away and headed toward the prow of the ship.

Eden hated the lump in her throat as she continued on her way to look at her plants. She began to wonder if she could see anything in the lower hold now that the sun was gone and clouds had gathered to obscure the moon. Was the floor still sticky from the spilled rum of a few days ago? It had been so short a time since that unsettling experience. It seemed a century had passed since she'd boarded Derek von Walden's ship. She changed her mind at the last minute and started back to her cabin. As much as she cared about the indigo, she was no longer in the mood to inspect it. She wondered how long it would take her to recover her senses and end this ridiculous longing for a man who would never be hers.

∞ 8 ∞

With enormous relief and a prayer of thanksgiving, Eden saw the familiar shores of home, Charles Town harbor with its dozens of ships anchored at the wharf and the charming houses facing the water along East Bay Street.

On this steamy July day the dock was crowded with several hundred Swiss colonists who had been watching the sea for days, waiting with increasing concern for the baron's overdue frigate from Barbados.

Skirting the throng of immigrants, Eden avoided looking at Derek Walden. He was surrounded by hundreds of admirers and would have no time for her, even if she tried to say good-bye.

A pale Laykee walked beside her as they gained the street and searched for a carriage to take them to the town house leased by Charles for overnight stays in the city.

"Eden—Eden, my dear cousin. I came as soon as I heard the ship was sighted." A dapper Landon Palmer bowed over her hand, then reached to take her elbow. "Are you hungry? We can lunch at the Oyster House—or would you rather freshen up first? You do look a bit peaked, dear."

Eden was unprepared to deal with Landon. She had hardly given him a thought during the trip, and his presence only muddled her thinking. She was tired and wanted to see to her plants before she did anything else. Some had died during the voyage, but thanks to her diligence, most had survived in good health.

"Hello, Landon," she said with an effort to be polite. "Thank you for coming, but I must make sure my plants are safely stored until the barges can take them upriver."

"Oh yes—the indigo. You made the purchase?"

"I did. And I must get them into the ground as soon as possible if we're to have a harvest in November. It's very important," she added, noticing the bored look on his face at the mention of farmwork.

"Yes, of course," he muttered.

"I shouldn't be too long," she said. "I arranged for overnight storage in the warehouse. All I need to do is make sure they're carefully unloaded, then Laykee will take a message to Joseph to alert him the plants are on their way. Tomorrow I'll go home and get right to work."

Landon shook his head. "My dear girl, I wish you'd give up this unladylike business and sell that place in the country. As soon as we're wed, you'll be living in town and have no need to bother with such nonsense. If you insist on keeping the plantation, we'll hire a proper overseer and put Joseph to work in the fields where he belongs. I'll find someone who is experienced in husbandry and who will turn a profit for a change."

Eden kept her temper in check. No use arguing with Landon before she'd had a chance to catch her breath. "Joseph has been faithful to my family for years. And I've pointed out many times, I intend to keep Palmer Oaks, Landon—always."

"We'll see, we'll see," he replied with an indulgent smile.

"Excuse me, Mistress Palmer."

Eden turned to see the Swiss botanist, Dr. Messenbaugh, approaching.

He bowed before her. Before she could introduce him to

Landon, he said, "Pardon, mistress, I'll see to it that your indigo is moved to the warehouse."

"That's kind of you, Doctor. Thank you very much."

"The baron asked that I do this for you."

"How very thoughtful."

"You and I disagree, you know. I don't believe your indigo will make a successful crop."

"The baron told me that was your opinion."

"I don't think the plants will survive for long in this country. And the process to make the dye is too difficult. Derek said you are determined to make the attempt and ordered me to help you."

"I'm deeply grateful, sir—though I hope to prove you wrong."

The doctor started to turn away.

"One moment, Dr. Messenbaugh. Where is the exact location of your settlement?"

"It lies on the banks of the Ashley and is quite beautiful, I've been told. Our town will be named Waldenburg in the baron's honor—though he modestly suggested other names. The land is fertile—virgin soil with stands of huge trees ideal for building our first homes."

"Why, it must be near my farm. Perhaps we'll be neighbors."

Without returning her smile, he gave her a curt nod. "Good day, mistress. I must go. I have much to do." He turned on his heels and marched back toward the ship.

"Rather a dreary fellow," observed Landon at her elbow. "Though I must agree with him about the indigo."

"The settlers have had a hard journey. I'll explain over luncheon, if you like." Eden turned to Laykee. "Do you feel like walking to the house? It's only a block away."

"Yes, Miss Eden. The feel of solid ground beneath my feet will be most welcome."

"Go along then, and air out the rooms. As soon as you feel strong enough, I'd like you to take a boat to the farm and alert Joseph that the plants will be arriving tomorrow. And so will I." She took Landon's arm. "Poor Laykee," she said as the girl hurried away. "She's been seasick for most of the voyage."

Landon guided her to his waiting carriage. Giving him a sidelong glance, she was aware that he wasn't bad-looking, but he paled in comparison to Baron von Walden. She wondered how she could ever have thought of marrying Landon Palmer. Even if she never saw Derek Walden again, he had changed her view forever of what a man should be. She might not have a chance to marry Mr. Walden, but he would always be the standard by which she judged other men. And Landon would never come close to measuring up.

Landon settled beside her. "Eden, I must remind you not to pamper your servants. Why, you treat that Indian woman almost as an equal. If you must have free blacks and Indians working for you, you should insist they keep their place."

Eden leaned her head against the cushion and closed her eyes. "Please don't admonish me, Landon. Not today. Besides, I told you Laykee has been ill. And I do consider her my friend."

"Humph. That's what happens when ladies are raised in the country with little chance to mingle in polite society."

"I love the country," she said quietly, wondering why he didn't understand how much her home meant to her.

"That's only because your education, your opportunities, have been so limited."

What an insufferable snob, she thought, clamping her lips to hold back a scalding retort. There wasn't a thing wrong with her education. And he gave her no credit for taking the reins of Palmer Oaks after Charles's death.

"Landon, I don't believe I'll have lunch after all. Take me to my house and I'll see if Laykee needs help."

"*You* help your *maid*? I do say." He snorted with raised eyebrows. "One doesn't count a maid as a real person—that is, no one but you," he added with a derisive tone. "That girl

79

should look after herself, and you should have a full staff of slaves to do your bidding."

Eden's temper was near the breaking point. "As you know, cousin, my father freed our slaves before he died. I pay my workers—and right now money is in short supply."

He took her hand, his face laden with sympathy. "Ah, my dear, that will all soon be behind you. I repeat that we must sell that place as soon as our holy bonds are sealed. It's worth a great deal, you know. But without slaves to work it properly, it will be an albatross around our necks."

She pulled her hand away. "You presume, sir. It's too soon after Papa's death for our engagement to be official. As a matter of fact, we must have a serious talk about our betrothal."

"Whatever you say, Eden. But when your father was dying, you did agree to be my wife. Naturally, I think of you as my responsibility. You're just tired from your voyage. Understandable, I'm sure."

She knotted her hands in her lap to keep from exploding. "You're right—about my being tired. I haven't told you, but our ship was attacked by pirates."

"Pirates! My God! What happened?"

"Our captain, Baron von Walden, offered himself in exchange for the lives of everyone else."

"What a brave sacrifice. Was he killed?"

"No. He was rescued. I was captured, too, taken aboard the pirate ship. But as you can see—I'm quite unharmed." She faced him and waited for his response. It was exactly as she'd expected.

"You—were captured? Dear Jesus, you weren't— weren't—"

"No. I wasn't." She could see he was appalled, disgusted.

"But—what will people say? How will they *know* nothing happened? Everyone will be wondering."

"I'm telling you nothing happened," she snapped. "I

won't discuss it again, and you can tell *everyone* anything you please."

"I warned you about traipsing off to Barbados—taking on the responsibilities of a man. I did my best to hide your escapade from our friends here in Charles Town, but naturally everyone is talking about it. And now this. Next time, you'll listen to my advice, I dare say."

Being scolded was more than Eden could stand. As they pulled up to her house, she said, "I'm going in and I don't wish to be disturbed the rest of the day."

Landon started to assist her from the carriage, but she pulled her arm from his grasp. "No thank you, Landon. I can manage. I'll be busy at Palmer Oaks for several weeks. I don't know when I'll see you again." He actually looked relieved.

Eden entered her town house and sank into a comfortable chair. Laykee was busy in the bedroom, and Eden was glad to rest and collect her thoughts. She would break her engagement to Landon Palmer at the earliest opportunity. She had never really thought of herself as his fiancée, and she was sure he didn't love her. The few times they had spent together, he'd lavished her with compliments, then found her dull after ten minutes. She realized now how little she cared for him and wondered when such negative thoughts had first begun. Before her trip to Barbados she had thought Landon might be a suitable match when she finally decided to marry. But then she met the baron. The image of Derek Walden filled her mind and sent butterflies into her stomach. That was it, of course. Derek had awakened something within her that she had never known existed. He'd sent her emotions soaring beyond anything she'd experienced. But he would marry Katya Mueller. Could she settle for second best, go happily into the arms of someone who could never give her in a lifetime what she had felt in those few minutes in Derek's arms? Never. It was just

81

her luck to have every other man in the world *ruined* by Derek Walden.

Making a quick decision, she jumped from the chair. "Laykee, come here. Gather our things. We're going immediately to Palmer Oaks."

Derek counted himself extremely lucky to have lived to see Charles Town harbor. His experience on the pirate ship was as close to death as he cared to be. Now, on this brilliant summer morning, he was at last in a safe harbor, eager to be reunited with the settlers and ready to take possession of his land grant.

He had hoped to steal some time with Eden Palmer, but she hurried off the ship as soon as the gangplank was lowered. From where he stood on the deck, he'd seen her with a tall, dark-haired man who took her to his waiting carriage. And then he'd been swept up in the celebrations of his people and escorted to a meeting house where he had received endless praise and speeches in his honor. Women wept and men embraced him, their own eyes damp with tears. Katya clung to his arm despite his gentle efforts to ease her away. For the balance of the afternoon he listened to how the people had worried over the lateness of the baron's frigate, and how they seesawed between returning to England and staying in Carolina, in case their leader had been lost at sea. They explained that Governor Johnson had welcomed them cordially, but as yet, no one had been out to survey their wilderness acreage. The settlers had merely bided their time in the various boardinghouses in town, worked at mastering English and getting acquainted with the second and third generation descendants of the English and French Protestants who had immigrated before them.

The celebration went on till nearly dark. At last when Derek could break away, he held a private meeting in Dr. Messenbaugh's room over the bakery on Broad Street.

"Looks like we made it, Hans. All our people are together at last."

"A great day, I agree. Everyone in Charles Town was sending up prayers for our survival. And the adventure with the pirates is the talk of the town. Now you're a hero to the Americans, too."

"And Miss Palmer? Is she receiving proper credit for her courage?"

Hans was silent. "It's different with a woman, Derek. You know what the rumors are."

"Damn the rumors. She was unharmed and was as brave a girl as I've ever seen. I've told the Muellers that, but they still don't seem to accept her as their friend."

"I'm sure our people will forget in time. And Katya's just having a fit of juvenile jealousy."

"She's a bit worrisome. I've never encouraged Katya to think of me as anything but her friend, but she continues to have this infatuation. I realize it was a mistake to tease her with that kiss during the archery contest. She's sixteen now and should take a look at some of the young Swiss lads who would love to pay court to her."

"You may have to tell her what you've just told me. You should stop being so gallant and charming, for a change."

"Hell, I don't have time for such foolishness. I have a town to build."

"Nevertheless, you're a hero, Derek. And this new exploit with the pirates will only spread the legend of your valor."

"I don't want to be a hero, Doctor, only a planter. Charles Town is a fine city, but I'm eager to see our land."

"There's a letter for you on the dresser."

"A letter?" He picked up the envelope and tore it open. "From a man named Poinsett. He's inviting me to be his guest at River's Bend Plantation. Says he has a large and successful tobacco and rice farm which adjoins our property." He showed the note to Messenbaugh. "Fancy that. A friendly neighbor already. I believe I'll take him up on his invitation."

"You mean—now?"

"Why not? It's only seven o'clock, and I can ride the twenty miles in an hour or so. I'll take the survey map, and if it isn't too dark, I'll check the nearest boundary. I expect it will take a few days to locate the far corners of thirty thousand acres."

"I'll come with you," the doctor offered.

"No. You're needed here to help Karl organize for the move. My plan is for the men to come out first, stay in the tents or the three log cabins that are supposed to be on the acreage. Once we have adequate shelter, we'll have the women move in. The first thing we must do is secure a water supply, then we can take our equipment in by barge and start felling trees."

"What about the old plantation house—the one you said was near the center of the grant?"

"I'll inspect it right away. It fronts the river in the center of eight hundred prime acres, according to the map. It would make a good headquarters once it's made livable— and perhaps later a seat of government." He searched through several boxes until he found the rolled survey and a sizable iron key. "Here it is—the key to the front door. It was delivered to the king along with the death certificate of the former owner. Let's hope the place isn't in shambles by now or occupied by Indians."

"I'm not sure it's wise to ride alone at night in the wilderness," Messenbaugh said.

Derek clapped him on the shoulder. "After what I've been through this past week, I'll relish the feel of the good earth beneath a sturdy horse's hooves. I'll carry arms, of course, and head for River's Bend. But I'll return in a day or two to lead the men out to the land. Tell them to stock up on food and supplies. We'll work in six-day shifts and alternate crews to return to town for rest periods with their families. By God, Messenbaugh, this is the adventure of a lifetime."

Within the hour Derek was traveling west along the river road toward the Poinsett plantation. At first the Ashley was broad and wound past impressive mansions whose windows glowed like orange cat's eyes in the setting sun. But soon it narrowed as he traveled past swamps and thick stands of ancient cypress and oak groves. How good it felt to be in the saddle once more, to ride with the wind in a free land where his future lay before him like a waiting vision of heaven.

As he rode his thoughts drifted to Eden Palmer. Where was she now? he wondered. Was one of these beautiful houses her home? She had said she lived on the Ashley River. Poinsett would know, he was sure. And he was just as sure he would see her again before long.

It was nearly midnight by the time he arrived at what he believed to be the boundary of his property. The road was rougher than he'd expected, and he had been delayed once at an unmarked crossroad until he could determine which fork stayed closest to the river. He was starting to wonder if he'd been unwise to rush off like a youngster on his way to a fair instead of waiting until tomorrow and traveling in daylight.

Derek walked the horse along the path, which was obscure and roofed overhead by a tangle of tree branches. Maybe he wouldn't go on to River's Bend tonight after all, he mused. It would be rude to wake up the household at this hour just because of his childlike eagerness to see his own property.

Suddenly, a break in the trees between the path and the river revealed a surprising sight. There, silhouetted in the moonlight, was a two-story structure, its chimneys outlined against the night sky. He saw no lights in the windows, nor was there any sound but the wind drifting through the pines surrounding the house. Could this be the house that now belonged to him? It must be. It sat exactly where it was shown on the map, to the left of the road and fronting a narrow bend in the river.

What better place to spend his first night in the New World!

Derek found a rusty gate and led his horse through, then along a path overgrown with brambles and brush and untended flower beds.

As he made his way he thought he saw a flicker of light in the distance near some low structures that were probably old slave quarters. He noted that the orchards were extensive and the gardens appeared to be planted. Well, after all, the previous owner had only died last spring. A few plants would come up of their own accord. Or slaves might be living nearby and tending the garden. Or there was always the possibility of Indians.

He secured his horse at the back of the house and shoved his pistol into his belt. He walked onto the veranda and tried the door. It was locked. He tried his key but it didn't fit the keyhole.

He strolled around to the front of the house, mounted the broad steps and paused to admire the dark ribbon of water that flowed slowly and silently eastward under the pale light of the Carolina moon. The night air was heavy with the scent of jasmine, wild roses, and honeysuckle. His land. At last he was gazing across the property he had dreamed of for so many months. There, across the river, Waldenburg would rise out of the primeval forest. New generations would be born there. Free Americans. They would marry their neighbor's progeny and a new race would come into being.

He turned to gaze with satisfaction at the grand portico. At least the house was in good condition—just needed a little whitewash here and there. Heavy drapes covered the windows. Was the place furnished? This was far more than he'd expected.

This time his key worked smoothly. He turned the latch, pushed open the huge oak doors and stepped inside. With the moon shedding light into the interior, he saw he was in an entry hall and that the wood floor was highly polished and graced with a thick rug in the center of the area. A stairway led upward, disappearing into dark shadows. From near the wall, a grandfather clock ticked a throaty rhythm; beside it stood a chair and an umbrella stand. "Hell, it *is* furnished," he muttered, "and someone has recently wound that clock."

"Don't move—or I'll put a hole through your skull."

The hard cold barrel of a gun pressed against the back of his head. The voice was hard and cold, too, but it was definitely feminine. Damnation! He should have known there'd be some trespasser camped in the house. *His* house. His anger overcame any trace of fear. "I have no intention of moving," he said in a harsh tone. "This is my house and I plan to spend the night here."

"You're daft, sir, if you think that. Or you're as lost as a chicken in a swamp. This is *my* house. I don't want to kill you, so you can leave right now."

Slowly, he turned toward the doorway, hoping to get a glimpse of the woman who stood right behind him. From the corner of his eye he saw that she was quite petite and wearing a thin gossamer gown that did little to hide the outline of feminine curves. She kept her musket aimed at his head.

He took a step toward the door. For an instant the woman lowered the gun barrel.

He saw his chance, grabbed the barrel and wrested the weapon from her hands. He tossed it away, gripped her wrist and twisted her arm behind her, then drew her against his body.

She screamed shrilly.

"Stop that," he shouted. "I won't harm you—though you're a trespasser and God knows what else."

She struggled in his grasp, but he completely overpowered her.

She gave up and her small body became liquid against him. He wondered if she had fainted. With both hands gripping hers behind her back, and his fingers meshed in the silken tangles of her waist-length hair, he shifted toward a ray of moonlight to get a better look at her.

It was the last thing he remembered before a heavy blow to his head sent him to his knees, carrying her down with him. A second blow sent him into oblivion.

∾ 9 ∾

"Is he dead?"

Eden heard the question from far away. It was Laykee's voice; her own ears were buzzing and her senses were paralyzed. She was trapped by a thief who would surely do his worst any minute—only the man bore a startling resemblance to Derek Walden. Her terror must have caused her to hallucinate. As her mind cleared, she realized she was locked in the arms of the intruder, stretched facedown across him, her hands held behind her back.

Had she gone insane? Had her wayward thoughts, her fantasies about Baron von Walden, turned into an obsession? Or was this God's punishment for her forbidden desire for another woman's fiancé?

Finding the man's grip relaxed, she pulled her hands loose and rose to take a closer look. Her nerves were shattered; she didn't know what she expected—or hoped—to see.

In the flickering light of Laykee's taper she looked down at an unconscious Derek Walden.

"I hit him as hard as I could, Miss Eden. Maybe I killed him."

Eden's heart raced at the sight. With deep concern taking the place of panic, she removed herself from atop Derek's inert body and placed her hand on his forehead. He wasn't a ghost or a figment of her imagination. It was indeed the baron, and he might be seriously injured. A flicker of his eyelashes and a slight moan escaping his lips proved he was alive.

She set aside her amazement at finding him in her entry hall, and carefully turned his head to inspect the wound. His hat had been knocked off and she saw blood oozing from a gash in his scalp at the side of his head.

She looked up at Laykee. The Indian girl was standing calmly, holding the candle in one hand and an iron skillet in the other.

"Will he die?" Laykee asked with no sign of regret.

"No, thank the Lord. But he could be badly hurt."

"You didn't want him killed?"

"Don't fret. You did what you thought best. But our intruder is none other than the captain from the Swiss ship."

"Oh?" Laykee held the taper near. "So he is. But why did he sneak in?"

"We'll never know if he dies. Run to the kitchen and get a clean cloth and the ointment—and bring a needle and thread, just in case."

Laykee bent over to get a closer look at the unconscious man. "But what if he wakes? He could be plenty mad. He might—"

"Let's just pray he does wake up. And that his brains aren't damaged. Hurry, now. And leave the light."

Laykee placed the candlestick on the floor near Derek's head and hurried away, muttering to herself in Cherokee.

Gently, Eden fingered aside strands of Derek's hair and inspected the wound. The bleeding had slowed and the cut appeared to be only in the scalp. She discovered a second less severe cut near the first. He'd taken two hard blows.

He moaned again. His eyelids moved and his lips parted. Then he lay quiet, though he moistened his lips with the tip of his tongue.

Sitting back on her heels, she gazed at him and breathed a sigh of relief. He would be all right, she was certain. Guiltily she realized her prayers had been answered, though not exactly as she'd wished. Here was the baron once more in her life. But she hadn't expected to have him unconscious at her feet when she saw him again. As she watched, his color gradually returned to normal. What in heaven's name was he doing at Palmer Oaks—in the middle of the night— slipping into her house without the slightest warning? She remembered hearing her back gate rattle, then creak open; she'd glimpsed a man leading a horse through the moonlit garden and rushed downstairs, pausing only to take the musket from the wall behind the steps. As a child she had been trained in the defense of the house. It was necessary, her stepfather had said, when one's home was carved in the wilderness where there was little protection from bandits and savages.

But the baron's sudden appearance was a stunning surprise. Had he come in search of *her?* If he knew she lived here, why hadn't he paid a visit like any other gentleman? She doubted if a person of noble lineage would prowl at night and break into someone's home like a common thief. And what had he mumbled about the house being *his?* He'd been celebrating for hours in Charles Town; maybe he was intoxicated.

Eden looked at him closely. His eyes were beginning to open.

At last Laykee arrived with a cloth, a small pan of water, and the sewing basket.

"Put them here, Laykee, and light the big lamp. Then we'll see what needs to be done."

Derek coughed and lifted his head. With a groan, he pressed one hand to his scalp and clenched his teeth.

"Don't move," Eden ordered. "You'll start the bleeding again. If you'll lie still, I'll clean the wound—and stitch it, if necessary."

"Stitch?" he mumbled.

Eden ignored him and dipped the cloth into the water.

Derek lay back and stared at her. He blinked a couple of times, then said huskily, "This can't be real. I must be dreaming."

"It's real enough, my lord Baron. Now turn your face away and I'll bathe that cut. It's rather deep, I fear, but at least your skull isn't cracked."

Eden noticed that Laykee had retrieved the gun and sat in a chair close by. From there the solemn-eyed girl could watch the scene with the weapon ready if it should be needed. Eden had no objection to her maid standing guard, though she knew it wasn't necessary. But after all, Baron von Walden did have some explaining to do.

He didn't look away as she'd requested, but continued to gaze at her, his brow knitted with the effort to assess the situation.

"You needn't try to make me feel guilty, sir. You broke into my home. My servant, Laykee, has done her duty and laid you low. I'm sorry for your pain, but we did what anyone would under the circumstances."

He pushed to one elbow, startling her into sitting back on her heels.

Laykee aimed the gun at his back.

He stayed upright though his jaw tightened and his fingers were stained with blood when he removed them from his head.

"See there," Eden snapped. "You must let me tend you."

He reclined once more while keeping his eyes focused on

her face. "I'll be damned," he said, relaxing onto the floral-patterned rug. "It really is you."

"It is. Now turn your head while I clean that cut. I can see you've already left a spot of blood on my favorite Oriental rug."

He turned his head. "My apologies. I suppose this is all my fault."

"This unfortunate accident *is* your fault." She kept her tone curt to mask her rush of feeling. The man of her dreams was here—alive—calmly awaiting her touch. Her hands were shaking as she applied the cloth and carefully wiped away the caked blood. He made no complaint, which helped enormously.

"I hope you're not suffering," she said softly when he flinched.

"No more than I deserve."

"This is necessary, you understand. I'll have to cut some of your hair and sew the gash. Then I'll apply ointment to help the healing."

He tried to look at her, but she kept her hand firmly on his cheek. "Don't move," she ordered.

"Do you need my help?" Laykee asked.

Derek scowled. "Hell fire, is everyone gaping at me? I feel like a mutton on the cutting board."

"Only Laykee and I."

"Are you women alone here?"

"No," said Eden. "Our men servants are in the quarters." She took up the scissors.

Derek gave her a sidelong glance. "Could I inquire if you've done this before, Mistress Palmer?"

"Yes, I've done it many times—though usually for livestock."

"Did they survive?" he queried.

"Most did, as I recall."

"Then proceed."

Eden concentrated on clipping bloodstained golden

strands of hair from around the deepest cut and skillfully repairing the damage done by Laykee's skillet.

"You have a strong stomach, Mistress Palmer. Unusual for a gently reared lady."

Was this a compliment? she wondered. "I suppose I do, Baron Walden." She took another stitch while gnawing on her lip.

Derek said, "I thought we had agreed to use our Christian names."

"That was under unusual circumstances, as you recall."

"Isn't this an unusual circumstance?" he inquired.

"It is, indeed."

"Then why not dispense with the formalities—for good?" He reached out to touch her elbow, then his hand fell back across his chest.

With effort, she steadied her fingers. "One more stitch—Derek."

She felt his smile. "Thank you, Eden. After all, we're more than friends—we're neighbors."

She took the final stitch and snipped the thread with small sewing scissors. "There. Now that I've repaired your scalp, would you mind telling me what you're doing in my house in the middle of the night?"

"It was a mistake. I'm very sorry. My land grant is close by, and—" He touched his forehead. "I'd prefer to explain later, if I may."

She was instantly compassionate. "Of course. Where is your land grant?"

"Ah—just across the river." He sat up. "Thank you again—for your gentle nursing."

The impact of his blue gaze shook Eden to her core. She didn't want to feel what she was feeling. But he was sitting so close beside her, his eyes intense, his forehead dotted with sweat and a trace of blood. He forged a path to her deepest being.

Tearing away her eyes, she put the thread and scissors into

the basket. "I'm glad we'll be neighbors. I'm fond of your people. *Katya* and the others." She had to mention Katya, even at the risk of being obvious.

"I'm glad to hear that. I was afraid you and the Muellers had had a falling out. The Swiss have been known to jump to conclusions—and to be opinionated at times."

Falling out. She wanted to laugh at the understatement, but she had no sense of humor just now. She decided to plunge ahead, now that she'd opened Pandora's box. Looking directly at him, she said, "Katya has some ridiculous idea that I'm trying to steal her fiancé. I suppose that's only natural after our experience on the pirate ship."

"Her fiancé?"

"She told me the two of you are promised."

Derek shook his head and smiled wryly. "She's a sly one," he observed. "Full of youthful fantasies." He reached for her hand. "Eden, I am not engaged to Katya. Nor to anyone. On the other hand, *you* have a gentleman in your life. I saw him at the docks."

Flooded with joy, she barely heard his remark about Landon. "Oh, I guess I misunderstood," she managed breathlessly.

Laykee stood. "I suppose it's safe for me to leave now, Miss Eden."

She'd forgotten the girl was in the room. "Oh yes. But please prepare the guest room for Mr. Walden. I'm sure he won't be traveling anymore tonight. And Laykee, deliver his horse to the stable. Wake up one of the boys and have him feed and water it and bed it down until Mr. Walden is ready to leave."

"Yes'm." She drifted up the stairs.

"I'm a helluva lot of trouble, Eden."

Looking across at him, she felt her breath stop, the room disappear, leaving them in the eye of a velvet whirlwind. She was frozen in time, and felt as if her soul and his had been

94

united throughout eternity. This man was not a stranger, but the other half of her being. He had always been there, just beyond her vision, waiting for the right moment to join her as fate had always intended. In a whisper, achingly aware of his hand holding hers, she said, "No trouble at all, Derek. I'm just sorry you were hurt."

He drew her to him as she had prayed he would. He kissed her, teasing the soft flesh of her lips, then entering the recess of her mouth to find the tip of her tongue. Time didn't exist; the only reality was his touch, his latent strength, the feel of his heartbeat against her breast.

Her breast. Oh, dear heaven, she was wearing only her thinnest shift. She broke away and splayed her fingers over her bosom.

She saw understanding in his eyes, and something more: tenderness. Tenderness from this giant of a man who had fought across a continent to rescue his people from their enemies.

Slowly, he got to his feet and offered her his hand. "I have some explaining to do, Eden, but I think I should leave you and let you get some sleep in what remains of this night."

Shaken by a tumult of emotion, she walked beside him to the stairs. "The guest room is at the top on the left," she said. "Sleep as late as you like. And we'll talk tomorrow." When they parted, she felt a warm glow suffuse every part of her. Derek didn't belong to Katya. Maybe, after all, he did love her. Her, Eden Palmer. She swept into her bedroom and closed the door. How could she sleep when she was dancing on clouds, sailing over the moon, lost in a world of love? She swirled and pranced her way to her bed and flung herself over the sheets. Oh yes, she was in love. Nothing on earth could compare with this feeling.

But she did sleep. Sometime in the wee hours before daylight she rolled over and thought again of Derek. She adored him. Of course she did. But how odd that he'd broken into her house. He must have some reasonable explanation. He would tell her tomorrow. After that, she slept deeply until morning.

Derek didn't sleep at all. How could he when his head throbbed and he had just gotten himself into one hell of a mess? First of all, he knew he was in grave danger of falling deeply in love with Eden Palmer. Maybe it was the knock on his head, but his mind was fighting a losing battle with his heart. From their first meeting, the power of their emotions had forced them together. She had set off lightning inside him with a spark of her own—and answered fire with fire, passion with promise. He had loved Heidi as only youth can love, but he brought a mature man's love to his feelings for Eden Palmer. He had known many women, learned to compare and discard, and take what he wanted. He'd had no complaints. But little Eden, so full of life and warmth, courage and innocence, had captured his heart once and for all. He wanted her at his side, now and forever.

But dammit, he saw problems looming like the Alps of his homeland.

First, she had evaded his question about the man he'd seen her with in Charles Town. Who was he? His attire had been rich and impressive. If she had a wealthy gentleman seeking her hand, would she consider the suit of a struggling immigrant who didn't have a roof over his head?

And speaking of houses, why in hell did his survey encompass Palmer Oaks? He'd have to fabricate some lie tomorrow about why he "broke in," until he could get to the courthouse in Charles Town and discover why he'd been given property that wasn't his at all.

Thank God none of his settlers knew this house was intended to be theirs. None, except Hans. And probably Mrs. Messenbaugh. And she had probably told Mrs. Mueller—who must have said something about it to Katya.

He paced around the room with its fancy flowered wallpaper dancing beyond the candlelight. It was a grand house and Eden was right to be proud of it. He hoped beyond hope his survey was wrong. He could just imagine how she would feel if he told her that King George had granted *him* the plantation she loved so much.

He stopped in his tracks. The survey. Godalmighty, the map was in his saddlebag. At daybreak tomorrow he'd better make sure it was tucked away. The last thing he wanted was for Eden to discover on her own that he might be the new owner of Palmer Oaks.

❧ 10 ❧

It wasn't there.

Derek poked around in his saddlebag and kicked the hay scattered on the floor beneath his tack.

The horse snorted and stirred in the musty darkness.

Feeling along the shelves, Derek cursed under his breath. The survey map was nowhere to be found.

He let himself out of the barn and walked back toward the house. On the distant horizon a faint blue glow hinted at the day to come, and the predawn breeze felt cool to his feverish skin. Although he had finally dozed awhile last night, his head had throbbed incessantly and he had been much warmer than the temperature of the summer night.

I'll live, he told himself while wending his way past the gardens and entering the deep shadows of the house. Of greater concern than his head was the chance of Eden finding that bloody survey before he could get to the bottom of the conflict of ownership.

By the time he had washed and put on the clean shirt he'd taken from his saddlebag, the sun was flooding the quaint little bedroom with cheerful light. Maybe the map had fallen out somewhere along the trail, he mused. It could be lost for good. He could acquire a new copy of the original document from the courthouse in Charles Town. With luck, the one he had lost would blow into the next county.

The smell of bacon frying drifted from the kitchen. Would Eden be up this early? Thinking of her in her opaque gown, those pink ribbons tied at her slender throat, the suggestion of soft curves beneath the gauze, and the look on her face when she crossed her arms over her bodice, started a throbbing in his loins. None of that, he told himself. Eden was a lady, sweet and trusting and innocent despite her strong will and independent nature. Falling in love with her would be risky business. He'd been through hell when he lost Heidi. His heart couldn't take another loss, even a less violent one. Already he was in trouble over entering Eden's house in the middle of the night. If he had any hope of keeping her trust, and perhaps winning her love, he would have to walk on eggshells and solve this problem of who actually owned her plantation.

For starters, he would have to tell her the lie he had cooked up last night about how he gained entry to her house. He recalled saying the house was his. Would she remember that? She had been badly frightened and might have forgotten his words. Hell, he was a poor liar, and he hated to tarnish their relationship with deceit and fibs—but he had no choice. Gathering his resolve, he headed back down the stairs toward the inviting smells of breakfast.

Eden sent Laykee to the well house and busied herself in the kitchen. Soon, thick slabs of bacon were sizzling in the skillet which last night had been the weapon that rendered Derek Walden unconscious. She thought it appropriate to put the pan to use on his behalf. Humming a tune, she whipped up a half-dozen eggs, garnished them with onion and fresh ground pepper and set them aside. She expected Derek to appear right away. She had seen him returning from his early morning walk, noticed he carried a shirt, and assumed he was about to wash up and put on fresh clothing.

"Good morning, mistress," he said, strolling in the door. "Like a siren with her song, you lure me to your den."

Tingling delight swept through her at the sight of him. He filled the kitchen with his presence, stopped her breath with his broad smile, warmed her heart with the way he made himself at home.

"Not my song, but my cooking, I'll wager. I've heard a wounded man requires extra nourishment. I hope you will avail yourself of my simple fare."

"Simple? Bacon, eggs, a fresh loaf of bread on the counter—and peaches! Hardly simple, *fraulein.*"

Using a feminine wile, she untied the sash of her apron and laid it aside, revealing a lemon-yellow ruffled blouse tucked into full skirts of appliqúed linen. She had been up early washing her hair and brushing it till it glistened, selecting her attire for today, and planning exactly what she would cook for breakfast.

"We both need a hearty meal," she said, pouring fresh-squeezed orange juice into two crystal glasses. You will visit your land grant, I assume—and I will receive my indigo plants from Charles Town. We each have an important day ahead."

He took the juice and downed it where he stood.

"I've set the table on the back porch. The climbing roses are in full bloom, the azaleas and gardenias, too. It does smell delicious."

He was not thinking about the flowers. His eyes were

focused on her, heated with some private thought as he studied her.

In a husky voice he said, "I should claim a penance for the pain you caused last night." He stepped toward her and looped his arm around her waist.

She knew he was far too bold, but she couldn't find the strength to deny what her own feelings wanted so intensely. His lips possessed hers; his arms were strong around her. The kiss wasn't lingering, but oh my, it held so much pleasure and promise. Eden could think of nothing more heavenly than to start every morning of her life in just this way.

Releasing her, he picked up the kitchen fork and began flipping the bacon over in the skillet.

"I declare," was all she could say.

Within a few minutes they were seated on the back porch overlooking the lush gardens and the cypress groves in the distance.

"Cream—Derek?" she offered, unable to keep her eyes from his face. How imposing he looked in the shimmering morning light, like a Saxon prince from a picture book.

"Thank you." He poured the thick cream into his coffee and stirred it, his mind suddenly elsewhere.

"You must have much to think about," she suggested.

"Yes. But first I owe you that explanation I promised."

She took a sip of her own coffee. Touching her napkin to her lips, she said, "I must admit, I am curious."

"Naturally. It's a simple matter, really. I made a mistake. I was headed toward the Poinsett plantation, and saw a house through the trees. It looked deserted, completely abandoned."

She nodded. "I know it's not as well kept as when my father was alive. I haven't been able—"

He reached across the table and covered her hand. "You have nothing to apologize for. Your home is beautiful. Why,

I've never seen any place so charming, so inviting and pleasant."

"Especially *inviting,* it would seem," she said with a teasing lilt in her voice. "You actually claimed to own it at one point."

"No. I think I said I *wished* it were mine."

"Really? I guess I misunderstood. I was too upset to pay close attention."

"Forgive me, but I was a bit in my cups last night when I rode along the river. I had been celebrating with my people, and was ready for any adventure I might encounter. I saw the house so close to my own property and thought it was deserted. I walked around it—found the door ajar, and stepped in to have a look."

"The door ajar? But—that's impossible. Laykee always locks it before we retire."

He removed his hand from hers and picked up his fork and knife. "Maybe the wind blew it open. Please don't scold the girl." He began cutting his bacon. "We all make a mistake now and then. I've admitted mine already."

"Oh, I won't," she hastened. "But I will remind her to double-check the lock. Or I will do it myself." She gave him a satisfied smile. "I knew there was a reasonable explanation. And you paid dearly for your curiosity."

He didn't look at her, but concentrated on his plate. "Could have been killed, I guess. You might have shot me and been well within your rights."

The thought made her stomach turn. "You're right, absolutely. I've said a prayer already this morning for my hesitation to pull the trigger."

Now his eyes lifted to hers. Whatever had veiled them earlier had disappeared. "You don't have killer instincts, Eden. If you did, you would have disposed of me long ago."

She was still laughing when Laykee came running onto the porch.

"Miss Eden—Miss Eden, the barges are coming. I'll ring the bell."

Eden dropped her napkin and jumped to her feet. "Hallelujah. The indigo's here at last."

Derek folded his napkin beside his plate and rose with a smile. "Good luck, Eden. Is there anything I can do to help?"

"Everything's ready. My workers know exactly what to do. Even the children are going to carry pots to the beds we've prepared."

"Then I'll be going. I want to stop by Mr. Poinsett's, and then check the perimeters of my grant. Tonight I'll go back to Charles Town and organize the move."

"Please do stop by for supper before you go."

"If it's no trouble." His eyes crinkled as he gave her a devastating half smile. She would have kissed him then and there except Laykee was next to her elbow, waiting for instructions.

"None at all," she assured him. "Besides, I'll need to inspect my needlework on your scalp. I want to be sure there's no sign of infection."

"Then I'll be back in late afternoon. But please don't do any cooking. You'll be busy with your plants. We'll have a picnic on the river."

"Perfect. I have a favorite spot to show you." She thought her heart would burst with happiness. Her indigo was here; the day was divine—and the man she adored would share dinner at her side.

Within the hour Derek had been relegated to a special place at the back of her mind while she plunged into work. Three large flat-bottomed boats arrived and her hired hands moved the indigo pots into wagons for hauling to the prepared beds. The day flew by, and before she knew it, the late afternoon breeze was drifting in from the hills. Leaving a well-organized crew under the supervision of Joseph, she rushed to her room to bathe and to change into a fresh skirt and blouse. Derek was coming. He would soon be here. Her feet barely touched the floor.

He arrived at precisely six o'clock.

She was ready. Laykee was supervising an outdoor supper in the shade along the river for all the workers who had put in such a hard day. Eden was bathed and scented with her favorite rose water. Her picnic was in a sack waiting in the kitchen.

At the sight of Derek jogging his horse into her gate, she took a seat on the porch and picked up her embroidery. By the time he arrived at her side, she was looking relaxed, feminine, and busy with her handwork.

"Did your day go well?" he asked with a smile.

Keeping her voice friendly but nonchalant, she said, "Very well, thank you. The indigo is unloaded and much of it already planted. I expect it will be in the ground within two or three days. Did you meet Mr. Poinsett?"

"No, unfortunately he was away."

She took a stitch. "The Poinsetts are very nice people. They're extremely rich, of course. I expect they have nearly a hundred slaves, but they treat them well." She set aside her embroidery. "I have a present for you." She picked up a pouch from the table and handed it to him. "Indigo seeds. For your garden at Waldenburg."

"How kind—thank you." He grinned at her. "I know what a hard bargain Bull Hawkins struck with you."

"Joseph will tell you how to plant it. Do you feel like a picnic?"

"By all means. I've worked up an appetite."

In a short time they were riding side by side along a trail leading south from Palmer Oaks. Eden breathed deeply of the earthy fragrance and let her senses absorb the titillating presence of the man whose knee occasionally brushed her riding skirt. As the shadows lengthened, the night birds began their evening call. From the nearby swamp came the chug of frogs and the smell of dank vegetation.

Surely he loved her, Eden thought. How could he not when she adored him with every part of her being? She saw his feelings in his eyes, felt it in his touch. And he had won her trust. She knew she could put her life in his hands, and that was exactly what she had decided to do. If Derek Walden asked for her hand in marriage, she was prepared to say yes. They could marry at Christmas, perhaps, after she had brought in her indigo crop and owned Palmer Oaks. He would never know how close she had come to losing her home. And he would love her all the more when she gave him the title as a wedding gift. That was required by law, at any rate, but giving her plantation to such a man as Derek would be a greater pleasure than keeping it herself. Maybe someday it would be part of his town of Waldenburg. They would raise their children in the house and pass the years in love of the land and devotion to each other.

She interrupted her glorious fantasy when they reined in near a bluff on the river side of the road. "We'll have our picnic up there," she said. "I'd like for you to see the view—and if we're lucky, something very special."

"Sounds perfect."

Anticipation bubbled deep inside her as he reached up to assist her from the saddle. Their eyes met, and again she felt the exchange of a powerful force between them. Her hands slid along his shoulders and he brushed her forehead with his lips. She would love sharing with him the closing hours of this special day.

He secured the horses and tucked the sack under his arm. Taking his hand, she led him between the trees and up an embankment overgrown with golden fern and purple wampee. They arrived at a huge boulder with a flat surface at about Eden's eye level.

"We'll have to climb up," she said.

"I believe I can manage."

Putting his hands around her waist, he easily boosted her to the stone's lip and she scrambled to the top. She took the sack from him and waited while he found a handhold and pulled himself up beside her.

Sitting in the gathering twilight with her feet dangling over the edge of the boulder, she gazed at him, feeling like they were two children off on an adventure. She would have been happy to remain there for all eternity, lost in his eyes, only vaguely aware of the cacophony of the birds and the fresh scent of pine and wild bay, but the light was fading and she wanted to be sure he didn't miss the view.

"Follow me," she said, and led him to the far side of the rock outcrop. There, framed by two ancient magnolia trees, was spread a panorama so breathtaking, so peaceful, and so lovely in the evening's glow that he could only stare in silent awe.

Below them the hill dropped abruptly toward the Ashley River. The trees were widely spaced and the entire river valley could be seen: Palmer Oaks on the east bank, and beyond it, stretching endlessly like a dark green sea, the verdant new land of the Swiss settlers.

His arm draped over her shoulders, she looked up at him. He was studying the landscape, lost in thoughts of his own, his expression one of solemn pride and intense satisfaction.

She whispered reverently, "Your home, Derek—your future—it's there at your feet."

Her words broke into his musing and he smiled an apology. "Forgive me, I know pride is a sin, but damned if I can help it. My people have come so far, worked so hard, lost and gained so much."

"And you? Can't you spare one word of praise for their leader, Baron?"

"My praise goes to the English monarchs. Without their generosity, none of this would have been possible."

"Yes, it was good of King George—but he has much to gain, too, you know."

"Shall we toast him, then?"

"Gladly."

Derek shrugged out of his jacket and spread it on the smooth surface of the boulder.

She sat on the coat, her chambray riding skirt settling around her knees. She hadn't worn a hat, but only a silk lace kerchief confining her abundant hair.

He took a seat beside her and placed the sack between them. She opened it and pulled out a linen-wrapped package and a silver flask. Next she removed two small silver cups and watched him pour the red wine from the flask. Then she unfolded the napkin to reveal biscuits, thin slices of cheese and ham, two boiled eggs, and two raisin cookies.

"A feast for a king," he observed, smiling at her, reaching out to stroke her arm with great gentleness.

"No, for only a baron," she answered lightly. "How does his lordship's head feel this evening?"

"No pain at all. Only a few unanswered questions mulling around inside."

"Important questions?"

"Extremely."

"Anything I can answer?"

"You are the only one who can answer."

She paused. "Me? Then please ask."

He was silent for so long, she became uneasy. Something was troubling him, she was sure.

"The first question has to do with something I'm missing. I've lost or misplaced the survey map to my land grant."

She almost laughed with relief. But of course this was important to him and not a laughing matter. "If you're wondering if I've found it, I'm sorry to say I have not. Do you think it's at Palmer Oaks?"

Oddly, Eden thought he looked pleased at her response.

He said, "I'm not sure. Don't worry about it; I can get another."

"More questions?" she inquired and sipped her wine.

"Yes. One. Are you engaged to your cousin, Landon Palmer?"

◦❧ 11 ❧◦

"You've heard about Landon?" Derek's question caught Eden completely by surprise. She couldn't remember telling any of the Swiss ladies about her betrothal. And Derek had only been in Carolina for two days.

Some of the warmth of the past few minutes had faded from his eyes. They were guarded—waiting—uncertain. "I'm not usually so inquisitive about personal matters, but I'm particularly interested in your response. I saw a gentleman meet you at the dock. The incident piqued my curiosity." His tone was smooth, noncommittal, even casual if one missed a note of forced restraint.

"That was indeed my cousin Landon."

"This morning I had a brief talk with your maid, Laykee. She apologized for thumping me with her skillet."

"Oh. And then?"

"I'm afraid I intruded on your private affairs by asking bluntly if you had a commitment to a gentleman. I apologize for that, but I'm a blunt man at times."

"And what did Laykee tell you?"

"She said you were unofficially engaged."

"She spoke the truth. But there's more to the story."

Her announcement caused him to look abruptly at his cup, then take a drink.

"Derek . . ." She put her own cup down and touched his forearm, forcing his eyes back to hers. "On his deathbed, my father pleaded with me to marry Landon, his brother's son. Papa was very old-fashioned about family marrying family, and he was worried about my being alone after his death. At that time, I had no other serious liaison, and Landon is extremely eligible. Landon agreed to the match—and so did I."

"I see." His tone was distinctly disappointed, but he gave her a false smile. "Then we should drink to your future, to love and happiness. You are most deserving, Eden." He filled his cup to the brim, splashing some of the contents onto his coat. "To you," he said, and raised his cup, quaffing the liquid in one swallow.

"Derek—listen to me. I have changed my mind. Even before I went to Barbados, I was having second thoughts. I never loved Landon. I wasn't sure love was so important in marriage, not the storybook kind, anyway. But I know differently now. Landon doesn't love me either, I'm sure. I intend to tell him how I feel at our next meeting."

Derek covered her hand with his. "You said you know differently now. What exactly does that mean, Eden? What do you know now? What do you feel?"

She was lost in the intensity of his gaze. She knew what he wanted to hear—and she was prepared to say the words.

"Derek Walden—it's you I love."

"My God—my darling girl."

The picnic forgotten, he drew her into his arms, kissed her tenderly, then, with a moan, crushed her to him.

Her hands moved to his shoulders. His gaze was lighting fires in her deepest recesses. "Derek—I do love you. You are

108

everything a man should be. I never dreamed such a person could exist."

She felt his fingers tighten, almost tremble. He stroked her cheeks, her neck, paused at her throat as if he sculpted her from living clay.

"My lovely lady," he said softly, "you've given me back my life; I thought I was dead inside, but then I found you. I want only to teach you all the joy of love—and loving—now and forever."

She closed her eyes to receive his kiss. His lips were tender and warm as he kissed one eyelid, then the other. When her lips parted in a sigh, his mouth found hers, heated, demanding, searching. His tongue stroked through her lips, claiming her mouth with sweet invasion.

One arm encircled her back and he carefully lowered her to lie on the satin lining of his coat. He eased off her kerchief and combed her hair with his fingers. Leaning close, he placed a kiss on the throbbing vein along the tender flesh beneath her ear, then trailed to the hollow of her throat and stayed to brush the tip of his tongue into that sensitive depression.

Heat surged into her loins. A stray thought to make some resistance was instantly defeated by her body's response to his gentle exploring beneath the low-cut edge of her bodice. Lying across his forearm, she felt his muscle contract against her lower back; at the same time, he covered one breast with the palm of his hand. He had loosened the front ribbons and now he folded back the sheer fabric and bent to suckle the taut nub with infinite delicacy. He held it between his lips, nipped it with his teeth, then slowly circled the surrounding tissue with his tongue.

Gasping, she arched upward, her body dazzled with currents of desire.

He enclosed her other breast with his work-hardened hand, caressed it, then teased that pink tip with a kiss duplicating the first.

Her fingers curled around his neck. She rocked against him, gripping him, aware of the soft sounds escaping her throat. She wanted him—wanted him beyond reason or thought.

He kissed her again, deeply, as his hand strayed along her skirt covering her thigh. *"Liebchen,* my own true love, we're crossing the line. Is it what you want? Tell me, now, before we go further."

She had never wanted anything so desperately. She would have gladly died in his arms. "Please—yes," was her throaty reply.

"You won't be sorry."

Was he asking—or promising? She didn't know, nor did she care. "Love me, Derek. I want you to be the first—my only love." Her words were barely audible, but spoken from the depths of her being.

Rising, he unbuttoned his shirt. From half-open eyelids she saw his masculine beauty, the dull gold of his skin stretched over well-defined muscle, muscle honed from wielding a sword for the good of his people.

Her feelings were like twin vines, interwined with each other, physical and mental, barely conscious thoughts joined with desire, passion with admiration, longing with respect, touching with adoration.

With one hand supporting the small of her back, he lifted her while she unfastened her skirt and petticoats, then he drew them away and laid them aside. The cool night breeze on her stomach felt strange and erotic. He rested his hand over her and opened his fingers, which reached from hipbone to hipbone. As he moved his hand downward, his lips replaced his hand on her tender flesh below her navel, his tongue flicking in a circle, sending streaks of lightning to the core of her womanhood.

Instinctively she closed her legs; gently but firmly he parted them and caressed her inner thighs just above the tops of her silken hose.

"Relax, my darling. We'll go very slowly—you tell me to stop anytime you want. God knows, I want to please you."

She heard her own euphoric moan of urging. Words were unnecessary to show him her yearning need.

Again he sought her parted lips, then moved his body over her and placed his knees on either side of her hips. Straddling her in careful confinement, he lifted her arms over her head and leaned to nuzzle her breasts once more.

An agony of desire throbbed through her, moistening her in a place that demanded fulfillment of its own.

She gasped when his knowledgeable fingers discovered that hungry recess and caressed it to almost unendurable ecstasy. Writhing in his grasp, her blood pulsed furiously through her veins. She wanted more, more, needed something—the need forcing her to the edge of sanity. She heard herself pleading, but she was helpless to find the answer alone.

She felt him move away and strip his own clothing. He returned and held his weight on his forearms as he lowered his head to kiss her again. His bare chest touched her own heated flesh, his knees moved between her legs, easing them apart, leaving her vulnerable and open to his assault. His voice was husky and seemed to come from inside her head. "My sweet girl, I will hurt you. It can't be helped this first time."

"It's all right," she murmured, holding tightly now to his shoulders. She knew enough to expect some pain, but it would be far more painful to stop now when her need was so great.

With a groan, he pressed forward.

Her eyes opened, her breath escaped as the sharpness stabbed between her legs. She dug her fingers into his back, but she made no cry.

"My love—my love." His half-uttered words were accompanied by the slow ebb and flow of his fullness.

The discomfort was quickly overwhelmed with a new

surge of feeling. Her knees were bent now, her feet beside him at the edge of his coat, one on satin, one on stone. She heard him rasp deep in his throat, felt his muscles expand and contract with leashed power and agonizing control. Her body was accepting, responding, passion rising again with a newly won freedom of loving.

He shifted to reach for her calf, to massage it as if the pale gossamer hose didn't exist. Next her thigh, her hip, her belly, her breast. His whispered words were unintelligible, but she felt their meaning in the touch of his hand.

The waves returned, stroke after stroke, carrying her on crest after crest, pausing then swelling until she was breathless, clinging, begging to be broken on the hard shore of his passion.

Beyond control now, he carried her in a timeless beat, moving swiftly, possessing her fully, deepening, taking her to the precipice, then sweeping her beyond into star-filled spasms of flight.

For a time she floated in his arms, wracked with exquisite joy, spiraling in ever-widening circles as her heartbeat slowed and she drifted lazily as on a summer breeze until she rested in the shadows, secure in his embrace.

He kissed her with infinite tenderness, her forehead, her earlobe, at last her waiting lips.

"My God—my God—" He repeated his prayer as he held her naked body against his length. "Are you all right? Are you sure?" His voice was tortured, almost fearful, and certainly awestricken.

She gazed up at him now, and for the first time became aware of her tears. He was looking at her with such a mixture of love and despair, she felt her heart break with love for him. Smiling, she pushed back strands of damp hair that clung to his cheek. "I'm better than I've ever been in my life."

"But—you're so small, and I hurt you—"

She touched his lips with one finger. "Shh, Baron von Walden. I'm a woman, not a fragile bit of fluff." Her own words sent tingling pleasure to her heart. "A woman. Yes indeed. I *am* a woman."

He moved away and tried to pull the edges of his jacket over her to protect her from the rapidly cooling night air.

She rose to her elbow, stroked his chest and ran her fingers along the hard knot of his upper arm. "I'm so happy, Derek. I never knew such glory existed between a man and a woman." She captured his concerned look. "The pain was very little, and perhaps I've stained the satin lining of your coat. The pain is gone forever; the stain, however—"

"Nothing, nothing," he murmured, brushing her lips to silence her. Wrapping her in the coat, he pulled her across his lap and cradled her, covering her tangle of hair with kisses and speaking German phrases mingled with English.

The light was almost gone, leaving the sky a vast mauve pearl. She relaxed against him, thinking she should dress, but not wanting to move from his embrace. She heard a new sound beyond them, one which was special to her. If she was right, she could give him a gift to bring to a close this most profound experience. "Shh. Listen," she whispered.

He followed her eyes and stared overhead. "I see it—the first star," he murmured.

"Yes, but there's something else. Listen."

In the silent pause between dusk and nightfall there came a gentle rustle.

Now he heard it, too. A new sound above the breath of wind in the pines and magnolias—a whooshing sound, then a slow rhythmic flapping from somewhere beyond the treetops.

Eden whispered, "He's coming. I've seen him every time I've been here. Watch the treetops over there."

She gazed skyward, searching in the near darkness—and then she saw it and felt pure bliss in the sight.

A snowy egret, glistening in lily-white splendor, trailing nuptial plumes in its wake, was lifting above them, spreading its great wings in graceful majesty, circling, soaring, calling once, then swooping east toward its home in the cypress swamp. The grandeur of its farewell sent utter joy to the depths of her soul.

She felt Derek's eyes studying her and was embarrassed over her rush of emotion and unbidden tears just behind her lashes. She had seen egrets before, herons, too, and bald eagles, when they strayed from their nests in the swampland near the sea. But never at such an exquisite moment—nor had she shared the gift with someone she loved.

His hand caressed her face, his thumb stroking away the moisture along the corners of her eyes. "I see the beauty of your heart shining in your eyes—and I'm humbled by your sweetness."

She became aware of a deepening lethargy, a drowsiness that she couldn't prevent. The rightness of belonging to him was as clear as the evening star, as alluring as the gleaming river, as perfect as the graceful egret.

"Come, *liebchen,* you'll soon be asleep. I'd be content to hold you in my arms all night here in the moonlight, but you should be in your own bed."

Stirring, she allowed him to help her dress, even gave him a teasing grin as he awkwardly attempted to tie her head scarf. She finished the simple chore and received an admiring peck on the tip of her nose.

"We didn't eat our supper," she said, looking at the untouched food still in the napkin. "I'll leave it for the animals."

Dressed once more, they crossed to the edge of the boulder. She stopped to look one last time over her shoulder at the enchanted spot where her innocence had been given so willingly and with such delight. She would come here often, she vowed. And she would remember this night in her last moment on earth.

Mounted on their horses, they took time for one more lingering kiss.

"I'll be spending several days in Charles Town," he said, holding her hand. "There's so much to do before we move upriver. As soon as we arrive, I'll be working day and night to lay the groundwork for the town."

"I know, my darling. Don't worry about me; I'll be busy, too. Just don't forget I love you."

He shook his head. "I would be insane to forget such a thing. I won't worry, but I'll be thinking of you every minute we're apart."

"And I you, my love."

He drew her to him despite the movement of the horses, and kissed her passionately once again. "I'll miss your kiss, my sweet Eden, your touch, your smile. Wait for me, and I'll come to you."

"I'll wait. Forever, if need be."

Chuckling, he released her hand. "Not forever. That I promise. A week—perhaps two. Once I launch Waldenburg, we'll begin to make plans for the future."

"Yes—yes." She couldn't see him clearly, but she felt his smile, his pleasure, his love.

"Good-bye, sweetheart. *Auf wiedersehen.*" He spun his mount and put the horse into a gallop south on the river road.

In less than half an hour she was tucked into her own bed, yawning in the hopeless effort to stay awake and relive her surrender to love. Her last vision as she dropped off to sleep was of a simple wedding, she and Derek as bride and groom. She was sure Papa Charles would understand her not marrying Landon Palmer. From heaven, Papa would look down on her happiness and send her his blessing. It was deliciously cozy under her quilt—and her tomorrows held the promise of endless joy.

Four days later, as Eden sat on her porch having her

first coffee of the day, Laykee came up the steps to speak to her.

"Look what I found, Miss Eden. It's a map, I think. Must have fallen out of Mr. Walden's saddlebag. It sure got dirty in all that hay and dust, but you can read the printing."

❦ 12 ❦

"Eden Palmer's property is definitely part of the Waldenburg land grant." Derek looked at Hans across the table in the dining room of the Oyster Point Hotel. "I went directly to the governor's office today to search through the land records. I learned the truth about Palmer Oaks—and Eden Palmer's precarious position."

"How the hell did all this happen?" Hans demanded.

"Eden's stepfather, Charles Palmer, died last March while owing the Crown several back payments for the property. King George was given incomplete information, it appears. The king was told the property was in bankruptcy and the owner died without a direct heir—and that it was available for us—when in fact Eden has until November to make the final payment."

"Unfortunate. We're lucky it's only eight hundred acres out of thirty thousand."

"The records show Palmer brought in only one decent rice crop in the past three years. He made a little money out of tobacco and corn. He sold deer hides in the early days, but that tapered off with the Indian's increased habitation of the area."

"I thought the natives were friendly," Hans said before taking another bite of boiled venison.

"Some are—some aren't. I have yet to learn which tribes are hostile, but the Cherokee villages are not far away."

"So what do you plan to do? I thought a solidly built house would be of real use to the colony."

Derek studied his own nearly untouched plate. After a pause he said, "It would. But in all fairness, we must give the girl time to bring in her crop and make the payment."

"The indigo?"

"She insists it will thrive."

"I assure you it will not. Oh, she may harvest a few acres, but the process of oxidizing the substance to create blue powder is extremely difficult—even dangerous. Lime vats are required, and paddle wheels. It must be harvested at exactly the right moment, assuming it survives drought and pestilence until it's fully flowered. Why, the process would challenge the most skilled farmer—even if he knew the formulas, which are closely guarded secrets in the Indies."

"No doubt you're right, Hans. But I insist the lady have a chance. If she doesn't make the payment by November first, Palmer Oaks will be ours without question."

"Does she know about your claim?"

"No. Only that she must make the payment or the Crown will take the property. You and I alone know the details of our grant. I didn't mention the house to the others because I wasn't sure if it was habitable, or even remained standing. Now I'm doubly glad I didn't."

"You've seen it, I presume."

"Miss Palmer graciously entertained me there yesterday —tea on the porch, very nice." He thought Hans gave him a questioning look, but he ignored the implication. It was much too early in his relationship with Eden to make any sort of formal announcement.

117

"I assume it *is* habitable." Hans grumbled.

"Actually, it's a fine two-story structure, nicely furnished, quite attractive."

"Good. It will be part of Waldenburg before winter."

Derek lifted his tankard of ale and drank deeply, ignoring Hans's statement along with the ache in his head. He knew he could start foreclosure on Palmer Oaks based on the payments already overdue. Any shrewd businessman would urge him to do so. But he was in love with Eden and knew what that crop meant to her. On the other hand, wouldn't he be doing her a favor to save her from months of labor and expense which would be wasted in the end? He recalled how she confided that her home meant everything to her. She was prepared to fight to the last to keep it. How well he knew that feeling—and the agony and bitterness of defeat. He would not be the cause of Eden Palmer losing her home. Furthermore, he hoped to make Eden his wife. Likely that meant he would take ownership of the property when they were wed. What would the spirited young lady think about that? Damn, this entire business over Palmer Oaks had complicated everything. The biggest question in his mind was whether or not to say anything yet to Eden. She would certainly be upset. How could he bear to put more burden on that sweet girl who was working so bloody hard right now? No, he would wait to see how the indigo crop thrived. He wouldn't mention his own claim unless it looked as if the crop would fail. Perhaps if that happened, she would be relieved and happy that he would be the new owner—and she would marry him and remain the mistress of Palmer Oaks.

He replaced his drink on the table. "If she doesn't pay by the deadline, Palmer Oaks will be transferred to our grant. If she pays off the loan, the plantation is hers. Between now and then, no one is to know the situation."

"I have mentioned the house to Mrs. Messenbaugh."

"Very well, but please ask her not to say anything. Our colonists will be living in tents and wooden shacks at first. No use stirring up envy or hard feelings toward Mistress Palmer."

Hans nodded his agreement, but Derek saw a look of dissatisfaction in his eyes.

"I'd like to start the barges upriver tomorrow, Doctor. The bridge is a mile north of Palmer Oaks and will need some reinforcement before the wagons can safely cross."

"Karl has everything in readiness. Too bad you didn't see Monsieur Poinsett. From all I hear, the man's property is vast and enormously productive. I'm eager to talk to his overseer about soil conditions."

With a casual air, Derek pushed back his chair and stood. He had no desire to repeat his lies about how he'd lost his way on the road and spent the night in the woods after banging his head on a low-growing tree branch. *"Guten nacht,* Hans. I'll meet you at the loading docks at six in the morning."

"Have a restful night, Baron. You look as if you need it."

The morning after Laykee's discovery of the survey, Eden was dragged against her will from heavy slumber.

"Miss Eden—Miss Eden, I'se sorry to wake you, but Queenie is under the chicken coop. Them pup's comin' for sure."

It seemed only minutes ago fatigue had finally brought her sleep. She had tossed and turned all night trying to figure out the meaning of Derek Walden's survey map. She studied it for an hour after Laykee brought it from the barn. It was plainly the lost document he'd been concerned about. And no wonder. Right there, signed by the king, were the perimeters of Derek's land grant—and Palmer Oaks was *inside* the boundaries.

She had tried not to panic. After all, there must be some

reasonable explanation. Papa Charles wouldn't have lied to her about leaving her the property in his will. And she had read the mortgage herself where it said that the owner had until November first to pay the Crown.

But what upset her most was Derek Walden's subterfuge. He had asked her if she'd found the survey. After she said she hadn't, he pledged his love and given her the most ecstatic experience of her life. And she had given him her heart, as well as her virginity. Thinking back, she tried to remember his exact words. He had called her his true love. But he hadn't mentioned marriage, that she recalled. No, all those thoughts of a wedding had been in *her* mind.

"Miss Eden—the puppies. You better come."

It was all she could do to stir herself into consciousness. "What did you say, Dessie?"

"I'se sorry, miss, but you made me promise to fetch you night or day when Queenie's birthin' them pups."

"Oh yes." Blinking in the pattern of lacy sunlight playing across the bed, she forced herself to sit up and take the cup of coffee Dessie was offering. A sip of the strong brew helped jolt her senses into the present. "Where is Laykee?"

"She's in the orchard with the chillen. It's gonna be a fine peach crop this season. She wants to beat the birds to the ripe ones."

Remembering Queenie, she tried to push thoughts of Derek from her mind. "Under the chicken house, you say?"

"I heard her when I gathered the eggs a bit ago. Sort of whinin' and whimperin'. I tried to squat down and see how she's adoin', but it was too dark. I poured your coffee and come right up."

"Thank you, Dessie. I'll hurry. I promised Monsieur Poinsett's overseer one of the pups—and your little Vangie another. I expect this will be Queenie's last litter at her age."

After Dessie left, Eden washed her face and gave her hair a quick brushing. A search in the bottom drawer of her bureau produced a well-worn skirt and a blouse nearly ready for the rag bin. If she was to spend the day under the chicken house, she would dress for the occasion.

After several hours of encouraging Queenie, Eden relaxed and enjoyed the sight of five silky pups pressing tiny paws against their mother's underbelly in search of nipples. One little female did closely resemble Queenie. Suddenly, from her vantage point beneath the floor, she saw horse hooves stamping about outside her hidden niche. What now? She scooted along the packed earth, lay flat on her back and pushed her way into the sunlight. Looking up, she saw a sturdy chestnut stallion pawing the earth under the strong rein of its rider, Derek Walden. He wore a flowing white shirt and wide-brimmed felt hat; his broad thighs gripped the animal's withers as he brought it under control. Seated in front of the baron was the most beautiful child Eden had ever seen. The girl's smile was angelic beneath her perky nose, glowing rosy cheeks, and eyes the shade of morning glories. Her hair was the color of fresh cream.

"Good afternoon, Mademoiselle Palmer," said Walden, greeting her with an amused smile. "I thought I'd pay my respects as we passed by."

There Eden lay, flat on her back on the ground, her hair fanned into the dust, and wearing clothes that the ragman would disdain. Her face and arms were smudged, her fingernails broken and dirty, and she probably smelled of puppy and the chicken coop. If she could have disappeared, she would have gladly done so.

"I seem to have a habit of appearing at inopportune times," Derek said.

Heat flooded her entire being. She sat up and brushed at her skirt, only smearing more dirt across the shabby fabric. "I have a new litter of pups," she explained. She got to her feet and faced him with as much dignity as possible. "You do take me by surprise, sir. You can only expect an uncertain welcome."

The child swiveled toward Walden. He leaned near to

allow her to whisper in his ear. "Not now, *liebling.* Dogs with new pups are often unfriendly to visitors."

Eden smiled at the girl. "I'm afraid the ladies of Palmer Oaks are not prepared to receive today. But next week we'd be delighted. Could you come then? You see, the puppies were only born this morning."

"I see," said the child softly, her sweet smile still in place. "Could we, Dirk?" She again turned toward Derek.

"Of course, if you like. Oh, let me introduce Mistress Eden Palmer—owner of this lovely plantation."

Eden was enchanted by the exquisite girl. As eager as she was to question Derek, she couldn't possibly confront him in the child's presence. Stepping near, she reached to clasp her hand. "I'm happy to meet you."

Walden went on. "This is Anna Schaefer—a favorite of mine, I must honestly admit."

"I'm so pleased you and the baron stopped by. I apologize for my appearance. When you come back, I'll wear my prettiest dress for your visit."

"Merci," cooed Anna, but didn't take Anna's proffered hand. "I have a pretty dress, too. But I'd really like to see the puppies."

"And you shall. I expect they'll move to new quarters by then. Their mother, Queen Elizabeth, has a large box on the back porch, much handier to food and water. You can sit close by and watch the pups have their dinner."

For a fleeting instant the child's face clouded.

At once, Derek spoke. "We'll be camping under the stars tonight on our own land. Several boatloads of settlers arrived this morning."

As never before, Eden was devastated by Derek's presence, the intensity of his look, his air of confidence, the way he sat his horse. Knowing that he had held her naked in his arms, been intimate with her, possessed every inch of her body, shattered her emotions and made her cheeks flame with the memory. She couldn't help thinking that Katya's accusation may have had been right when she had written *Derek thinks Eden is a loose woman*. Is that what he believed after what had happened between them? What was he thinking? What did he truly feel for her? And did he secretly believe *he* owned Palmer Oaks?

She pierced him with an icicle look. "Please tell your people they are welcome anytime here at Palmer Oaks. My house is always available to you and your colonists."

"Thank you. That's very kind." He was looking puzzled. Good. She was puzzled, too.

"I hope you will visit our settlement as well," he offered politely.

"I will. *Tomorrow* if it's convenient." It was the opening she needed. She must find out as soon as possible the meaning of the survey.

"Excellent. I have no amenities yet, but we'll find a place in the shade for a cool drink. He smiled, but she could tell he was concerned over the emotional distance she had placed between them. "We'll be on our way, then. Good day, mistress."

"I'm pleased to meet you, Anna," she said, happy to divert her attention to the adorable child.

The stallion snorted and danced on its hind feet as Derek reined away.

For the rest of the day Eden spent hours on her knees clearing weeds from the indigo field and closely supervising the construction of the paddles to be used in the fermenting process after the plants were harvested. After dinner, exhausted, but freshened by a cool bath provided by Laykee, she sat on her upstairs veranda and watched the sun dip toward the western hills, taking the day's heat to earth and leaving behind the long azure twilight vibrant with the sounds of bird's evening calls, the prattle of crickets, and the occasional cry of a bobcat in the woods. Often a breeze drifted from the Ashley, adding to the humid earthy scent of the land mingling with the roses in full bloom and the lilies bordering the front of the house.

Normally she loved this time of day, this special place with its serene view of the river and the landscape. But tonight her heart was heavy as lead. She had given Derek Walden her love and her trust. Had Papa Charles been right after all when he told her to marry her cousin, Landon? Papa had always protected her, given her good advice. Now she had gone against his wishes and thrown caution to the winds. The result could be a broken heart.

As the shadows fell, she heard the sounds of music coming from the area where the new town of Waldenburg would rise from the wilderness. How wonderful Derek had looked this morning, holding that exquisite little girl whom he obviously adored. Could such a man be planning to steal her home? It seemed impossible, but tomorrow she would seek the answer. Unfortunately, she expected to have another sleepless night.

❧ 13 ❧

Carrying four jars of fresh peach preserves in her saddlebag, Eden rode along the river, crossed the wooden bridge, and arrived in Waldenburg in less than ten minutes. She found a tent city set up in the shade of trees bordering the open ground, and beyond that, corrals holding a large number of horses. Hay was stacked near the framework of a half-completed barn. The Swiss colonists were well-organized and moving forward rapidly in the building of their town.

But now on Sunday afternoon, work had been set aside, and the adults were visiting in groups under a leafy forest canopy while the youngsters raced and shouted and tumbled in their games under a brilliant summer sky.

Eden looked for a familiar face. As she walked her horse into the clearing, several of the settlers turned her way and nodded a greeting.

Then she saw Hans Messenbaugh approaching. "Good day, sir," she said, giving him a pleasant smile.

"Mistress Palmer, it's nice to see you again." His stern expression belied his polite words.

"Thank you, Doctor. I wanted to welcome you and the colonists to our valley. I've brought some peach preserves made from fruit from my orchard." She refused to be intimidated by this austere man. Neighbors were terribly important in the back country. Someday they might need each other to survive a crisis.

He assisted her to dismount.

"I was hoping to find Katya and Mrs. Mueller."

"Frau Mueller is packing for the return trip to the city. Katya is with Mr. Walden—telling him good-bye. The women stay in town during the week, you see."

Eden kept her smile though her heart sank like a stone in a millpond. So Derek and Katya were somewhere alone together, probably wrapped in an embrace. She had expected such a thing, but hearing it said was like a firebrand burning a path to her heart. She had made a fool of herself over Derek—and was paying a terrible price for her naiveté.

A matron wearing a white lawn cap atop her graying hair came to join them.

"This is my wife, Mrs. Messenbaugh," said the doctor.

It was all Eden could do to force words around the lump in her throat. "I'm glad to know you, madam. I'm your neighbor, Eden Palmer. That's my house on the river road."

"Yes. So I understand." Her tone was no warmer than her husband's.

Eden began to regret her decision to come. But there was the problem of the survey map. "I brought some peach preserves," she said with effort. "If you'll take them from the saddlebag, Doctor, I would be grateful."

"It's we who are grateful," said Mrs. Messenbaugh with restraint.

Eden wondered where she had gone wrong with the Swiss colonists. Maybe it was because she was carried off by the pirates. Well, she had tried, and that's all anyone could do. "Actually, I did have a matter to discuss with the baron. Is there a chance he might be here anytime soon?" She drew the rolled paper from a pouch on her saddle.

Dr. Messenbaugh looked around the area. "There they are now. Near the woods."

"Excuse me," said the doctor's wife. "I must return to my work."

"By all means," said Eden, barely giving her a glance. To her dismay, she saw Derek emerging from the trees arm in arm with Katya. His height was emphasized by the girl's small stature. The two were gazing into each other's eyes like any couple in love.

Katya walked with one arm comfortably wrapped around his belted waist. She looked as pleased as if she'd just won first prize at the county fair.

Derek looked pleased, too. While Eden watched, he stopped walking and playfully tweaked Katya's nose.

Their laughter floated on the summer breeze, and twisted a knife into Eden's heart. The ache swept through her like wildfire. The two were perfectly matched: both so blond, so fair, the ideal Swiss couple—the same heritage, the same language, the same memories of their homeland. She stared at them, envy and heartbreak searing through her insides.

She barely heard the doctor's voice. "Today Derek has been demonstrating to the men the proper way to plow a straight furrow, though where he learned it is a mystery. It's astounding to us all how a nobleman has taken on such menial chores. Why, he asks no more of others than he asks of himself. A wise and gallant leader, I must say."

"Indeed," she murmured, wondering if she could hold back her tears long enough to complete her important mission.

Derek and Katya chatted as they faced each other. Derek's hand rested on Katya's shoulder as she looked up adoringly at him.

The doctor said, "Everyone is expecting Derek and Katya to marry soon. The baron has led a lonely existence since his Heidi was murdered. He needs a wife at his side. And children. He can't live forever with a broken heart."

He didn't look lonely to Eden. Or heartbroken, either. Her unshed tears of pain began to change to anger and resentment. Of course, Dr. Messenbaugh had an idealistic view of the great Swiss *savior*. She knew differently. He had lied to her, tricked her, misused her in the worst way possible. With little effort, she could learn to hate the man.

Laughing, Derek pointed Katya toward the settlement, then retreated back into the trees. The girl hurried away and ducked into a canvas tent.

"I'll go speak to him now, if you'll excuse me," Eden said tightly. She remounted and rode toward the spot where she'd seen him disappear.

Leaving her horse, she pushing through the trees. When she found the clearing, she stopped to gather her courage. Derek was hitching himself behind the plow, picking up the reins and clucking to the waiting draft horse. He leaned into the work, the muscles across his broad back and along his bare arms straining under the effort.

The blade clanked against a buried stone. Derek planted his feet firmly, called encouragement to the horse and pushed with all his strength. The stone moved under the pressure, and the plow continued down the furrow.

If it had not been for the survey map in her hand, she would have left at once. The sight of his powerful physique, his hair loose around his shoulders, his earthy maleness as he expertly maneuvered the plow, made the pain of his betrayal even harder to bear.

But Palmer Oaks could be at stake. Taking a deep breath, Eden marched into the clearing. "Good afternoon, Mr. Walden," she said, with no hint of friendliness. "What a fine day you have for tilling your land."

When he straightened to face her, the horse stopped in its tracks. Derek eased the plow to the ground and wiped the back of his wrist across his forehead. His pleased look added more knife pricks to her already punctured heart. "Eden! I wondered what was keeping you. Take a look at my garden. I'll be planting your indigo seeds here in a day or two." He started toward her.

She took a step backward. "Nothing on earth would have kept me from seeing you today, Mr. Walden."

His smile faded, but he approached and stood close to her. "All right, Eden, what's wrong? You've been treating me like I had the plague ever since yesterday. If I've offended you—in any way—tell me so I can begin to make amends."

"Offended? That is hardly the way I'd describe what you've done."

His brow furrowed. "I can see you're upset. I should learn never to underestimate your temper."

"You needn't worry about learning anything at all about me—ever again."

"Eden," he said in a soothing tone. "Eden, for God's sake, what have I done? I thought—"

"This." She spat the word and handed him the rolled paper.

He took it but didn't open it. He just stared at it as if it contained his death sentence.

"I'm sure you're pleased," she said with acid sweetness. "I recall you were looking for it not long ago."

"You're right. I was looking for it. I was afraid this might happen if you found it before I could explain."

She put her hands on her hips. "Very well. Explain."

He knelt and unrolled the paper, then put his knee on one edge to hold it open. "Do you see this line?" He pointed to the perimeter of the Walden grant.

"Yes. And I see it encloses Palmer Oaks. I would like an explanation."

He let the paper roll together as he rose to face her. "The royal surveyors drew up the boundaries, but they were premature in one area—your eight hundred acres."

"Premature? What do you mean?"

"They knew the Palmer plantation was in default. They simply added it to the Walden land grant."

She felt as if he had knocked the breath from her. "No," she said in a whisper. Her breath and her anger returned simultaneously. "No," she cried. "I have until November to make the payment. I can prove it."

"Please, Eden, my darling," he tried to calm her. "Of course you do. I know that, too. I checked on it several days ago at the courthouse."

Oddly, that news only infuriated her more. "So you checked to see if you owned my home. Why didn't you ask *me?* Or did you think I was as stupid as I was naive?"

He was plainly agitated by her attack. *"Nein,* no, you're not stupid at all—and certainly not naive, well, a little perhaps, but I love—"

"Don't you dare speak to me of love. Now or ever. Just mark my words, Mr. Walden. You will *never* own Palmer Oaks. Never, never, never! I will bring in my crop and pay off the Crown. I will own my property, free and clear." Her voice rose shrilly, but she didn't care who heard.

"I hope so. I've always hoped so. When you calm down, you'll understand that, Eden."

"I do have one more question—assuming you have the ability for once to tell the truth."

His eyes registered defeat. "Hell, ask and you'll have the truth. I give my word."

"I can see it's a difficult task. But I would like to know how you got into my house last week."

He met her heated words with a cool response. "With a key."

"A key?" She was aghast.

"My key. Given to me by the king of England."

"Why, I declare—"

"I may be a liar and a blackguard, but I've not yet stooped to breaking into houses."

"Naturally I'd like to have the key. Now that you know the house is mine, you can return it."

"Naturally. But I hope you understand—"

"Understand? I do understand how you made a fool of me, sir. I'm sorry I met you. I hope I never see you again." She whirled away and thrust through the trees back to her horse. Wiping at tears, she threw herself into the saddle and cantered toward the bridge.

She was about to cross when a strange and beautiful sound penetrated her tortured thoughts. She paused briefly to look around and was suddenly hailed by a child's voice.

"Who's there?" came the cry from behind the cotton-woods.

A child so near the banks of the river. She had no choice but to see what was wrong.

She left her horse and parted the brush.

There in a tiny rocking chair sat Anna Schaefer. A small table was placed in front of the girl, and on it was a row of bottles of similar size, each one containing a varying amount of water.

"Who's there?" Anna asked again.

"Anna? Don't you remember me? It's Miss Palmer, the lady who owns the puppies."

Focusing on the voice, Anna looked toward her. "Oh hello. I was trying to plan a new song."

Eden had a dreadful thought. She looked closely at the pretty child. Was it possible the child was blind? Her eyes were beautiful, but—yes, there was no doubt. Obviously, Anna couldn't see her—and yet her face had an ethereal glow. Eden coughed to clear her throat and knelt beside her. "I didn't hear your song. Would you mind playing it again?"

"All right." Anna ran a plump finger along the sides of the bottles, then tapped them with her spoon. She counted softly, then stopped at the fourth bottle and picked it up, carefully poured a small amount of liquid from it and tapped again. Her lips bowed into a smile and she tapped out a bell-like tune, accompanying herself as she sang a French song. Her young voice was sweet and clear and on perfect pitch. When she finished, she looked toward Eden and waited for her response.

Eden was biting her lip, thankful that Anna couldn't see her tears. "Why, that was just beautiful, sweetheart," she finally managed. "You speak French and English and German. I'm amazed. And what a fine voice you have."

"My mother was an English lady from Leeds. Not a real lady, you understand, but she owned a shop . . ." Her voice dropped to a whisper. "Would you like to know a secret?"

Eden knelt on the ground beside her. "Oh, I love secrets. They're almost my favorite thing—next to the songs of little girls."

"Well, my mother was an actress before she bought her shop in Leeds. She sang on the stage in London."

"Is that a fact? Then I know where your wonderful voice came from."

"From her, I guess. My father was from Neuchâtel. He was a clock maker. He met my mother when he went to England with Dirk a long time ago." Anna paused. For the first time her expression showed a trace of sadness. It was as if a light had been dimmed behind her sea-blue eyes.

"Isn't your mother here?" Eden asked.

"No. She's in Heaven. I live with the Meyers, but Dirk looks after me. When I grow up, I might marry Dirk. He's very handsome, don't you think?"

She swallowed hard. "Yes. Very. You've seen him?"

"A long time ago. When I was a child. But he might marry Katya Mueller before I grow up. That's what Frau Meyer told me. Humph. I don't like Katya very much. But Dirk does, I suppose."

So even Anna knew about Derek's affection for Katya.

"I'm five," Anna announced. "Would you like another song?"

"Yes. Of course."

Anna tapped the bottles and sang:

"Rock-a-bye, baby, rock-a-bye, rock.
Baby shall have a new pink frock."

The brush parted behind Eden. She looked around to see Derek entering the bower.

"A new pink frock, and a ribbon to tie,
"If baby is good and ceases to cry."

He gazed down at her, his expression gloomy and guarded. She turned her back to him and focused her attention on Anna's song.

"What have we here?" Derek asked. His voice was light, but she knew the pleasant tone was pretense for Anna's benefit.

"Dirk," Anna cried. "Did you hear my song? Wasn't it nice?"

"Like an angel," he said, looking straight at Eden. "But

you shouldn't be alone so near the river. We've talked about that, *liebchen,* have we not?"

"But I'm not alone, Dirk," Anna piped. "My friend, Mrs. Palmer, is here. Don't you see her?"

"Yes. I see her."

"I must go," Eden said quickly, and rose from her knees.

Anna asked, "Please, may I come see your puppies? Next week, maybe, when they're bigger. Dirk will bring me. Won't you, Dirk?"

What could she do? She could hardly refuse the child. "Why, yes. That would be fine. Good-bye, Anna. I'll see you soon."

She tried to hurry by Derek, but he caught her arm. His touch sent misery racing through her to the tips of her toes. "Don't," she whispered. "It's only because of Anna."

He released her, but murmured, "For Anna, then. Until we meet again, *fraulein.*"

❧ 14 ❧

As his enemies closed in, Derek swung his broadsword with his last ounce of strength. Flaming missiles flew past, landing in the courtyard and crashing in exploding fire against the castle walls. He fell to the ground, paralyzed, unable to move or even cry out as the fire blazed around him and screams of agony pierced the acrid night air. He knew he was burning but he felt nothing, only horror and absolute outrage. He struggled for every breath, his brain silently cursing the French royalists who had brought destruction on his castle and his lands.

He jerked awake. How many years would he endure this recurring nightmare—a nightmare that had once been real? He hadn't burned to death during that terrible night in Switzerland, but his parents had. That sight would haunt him for the rest of his life.

Lying back on his cot, Derek stared at the stretch of canvas overhead and listened to the night sounds beyond his tent. He was here in Waldenburg, surrounded by people who loved him. He attributed his weakened mental defenses to exhausting work and heavy sleep induced by hard labor. And maybe the problem with Eden. It wasn't her fault. He didn't blame her at all for distrusting him, being hurt and angry, especially after the love they had shared, which meant so much to them both. Damn the bad luck to have lost the survey. And he cursed himself for not being open with her from the beginning. He would have to give her time to cool her temper, and then he could reason with her. She meant the world to him, but speaking his feelings was difficult for him. He pictured her proudly defiant, her eyes full of fire; and blushing shyly, tongue-tied and disheveled, prone in the dirt beside her chicken coop. He'd felt her compassion when she wiped blood from his head. Her mercurial moods intrigued him, her intelligence challenged him, and her beauty enthralled him. But seeing her yesterday, kneeling before Anna, his heart had turned over inside his chest. If he lost her, he wasn't sure he could deal with the pain.

He thought of Katya and the complications her feelings for him were causing. He had tried time and again to convince her he loved her like a brother, that he was a friend she could respect and depend on—but never marry. He hadn't yet been able to bring himself to be downright cruel to the girl. And now she was insisting he escort her to the soiree at Henri Poinsett's plantation two weeks hence. The party was in honor of the new Swiss settlers. Poinsett had invited all the Swiss ladies and their husbands or sweethearts. Some had declined, but most were delighted with the diversion after the months of stress and backbreaking toil. And Katya was the most excited of all.

Derek had hoped to be Eden's escort for the evening. She was sure to be invited, and he'd looked forward to sharing this pleasurable experience with her. But now he'd be lucky if she spoke to him. And what was worse, he would have Katya clinging to his arm. Would that upset Eden? He hadn't thought Eden would be jealous of the young girl; he'd told her he was not engaged to Katya. Was it possible Eden believed he lied about that, too?

He turned onto his side and gazed through the open flap of his tent. Yes, it was possible, more than possible. Women did have the damnedest way of getting themselves upset over nothing. He stretched on the hard, uncomfortable cot, feeling his muscles ache from the day of plowing. Time. That's what Eden needed. Time to cool off and think things through. He wouldn't visit her again before Poinsett's party. He would find an opportunity to speak privately with her, find out if her fury had abated. It was like wading into a maelstrom to tangle with Eden Palmer. Especially where her plantation was concerned.

Eden pulled on her black lace gloves and took one last look in her mirror. Landon was downstairs waiting for her, and she would have to make the best of it. Tonight was the first time she'd seen him since her arrival from Barbados. He'd taken her at her word that she was too busy with the indigo to have time for social engagements.

Nor had she heard anything from Derek. Not that she expected to after making it plain she never wanted to see him again. But Anna had asked to come see the puppies.

That would have made a perfect excuse for him to visit had he really wanted to. She hated to admit her disappointment that he hadn't bothered to call.

She put on her black wide-brim hat and tied the ribbon. Her pearl-gray gown of moiré camlet suited her somber mood. She had purposely avoided wearing mourning for Papa Charles because he disapproved of the practice. But tonight she felt like mourning. She had failed to tear Derek Walden from her heart; she was being escorted by a man she disliked, and she'd be forced to appear merry so the Poinsetts would know she appreciated their invitation. The only lift to her spirits was the knowledge that the indigo thrived. In two months she would sell her crop and pay off the mortgage—and her secret debt to Bull Hawkins. Holding that positive thought, she went down to meet Landon.

"My darling Eden. I have missed you terribly." Landon met her at the bottom of the stairs and escorted her outside to the boat.

Taking a seat by his side, she tried to hide the disdain she felt for his appearance: his satin suit, knee hose with silver buckles at his shins, and especially his pompous powdered wig. It was impossible not to compare his foppish appearance with the ruggedly handsome looks of Derek Walden.

She listened to his dull chatter about the social life in Charles Town, and wondered how she could ever have considered becoming his wife.

When the boat was moored to the landing at River's Bend Plantation, Eden set her chin and prepared to endure the evening. Derek was certain to be present. After all, he and his settlers were the official guests of honor. She would avoid him if possible and leave for home early if that could be arranged.

As she entered the reception hall, Eden was impressed as always by the enormity and elegance of the home of this second-generation French family who were her nearest neighbors. For Henri Poinsett to open his house for such a gala occasion was further evidence of his sincere pleasure at the arrival of the Protestant settlers from Neuchâtel, Switzerland.

Eden rested her hand on Landon's extended forearm. Henri Poinsett, always the gracious host, greeted them warmly and explained that the Swiss colonists were expected to arrive by barge at any minute.

A minuet was in progress as they were escorted into the grand ballroom, with its arched mahogany ceiling and walls lined with soaring mirrors. It was already crowded with dancers: ladies in brilliant dress, their hoops swaying gently as they moved on the arms of gentlemen in formal attire— all revolving in an endless reflection of billowing satin and silk.

"Eden, my dear. Would you join me on the dance floor?" Landon bowed before her and offered his arm.

With a false smile she followed him as he began the maneuvers of the elegant dance. Already she was thinking about escape, but knew she would have to wait until later and then plead a headache.

Several of the matrons gave her smiles of recognition. She presumed Landon had been able to hide her escapade with the pirates from these prim ladies. Otherwise she could have expected the same cold shoulder that she received from the Swiss. The daughters of these ladies had been her friends— and now all of those girls were wives and mothers. Two years ago she had danced the night away while fending off the advances of every eligible bachelor in Charles Town. Little did they know Papa Charles was fighting a losing battle with bankruptcy, or they might have found her less appealing. Charles had told her she should choose a husband, but she had been happy to remain single and stay at Palmer Oaks.

Now she was nineteen—and would probably spend her life as an unmarried woman. She wouldn't marry Landon if he were the last man on earth. And the one man she desired, even if he were a cheat and a cad, was in love with another girl. Her mood darkened as she forced herself to nod and smile to the tittering ladies.

At the end of the dance, the orchestra sounded a fanfare, and applause broke out in the ballroom.

"Oh, they're here."

"Yes, the brave dear souls."

"Let's greet them properly."

Eden was swept along through the wide doors leading into the reception hall. The Swiss colonists had indeed arrived, and were being received like royalty by the descendents of their fellow settlers of a generation past.

It was like a family reunion. Eight Swiss couples in charming native dress were being hugged as if they were long-lost relatives. The conversation slipped easily into French, the common second language of one and all.

Derek Walden stood a head taller than anyone present. His striking figure dominated the room. Despite his request to the contrary, he was addressed as "Baron" by everyone who greeted him.

From her vantage point in the corner, Eden watched the proceedings. It intrigued her to see how easily Derek impressed the Huguenots with his sophistication and natural grace. If they had expected a country bumpkin or illiterate Bavarian, they were quickly enlightened. She found it less interesting to watch an adorable Katya, her white-gold hair in braids, her ruffled blouse and embroidered skirt and vest extremely flattering, clinging to Derek's arm.

"Your heroic Hun is quite impressive," came a voice at her elbow.

Without looking at Landon, she replied, "He's not *mine* —that's quite obvious—and he's not a Hun."

"But he *is* a hero." His voice held a cutting edge.

"I suppose so." She couldn't deny the truth about that.

"Pardon my bluntness, Cousin Eden. But it does seem

odd that such acclaim be awarded to a man who owes everything he possesses to the English Crown."

"Money isn't everything, Landon," she said sharply, then wondered why she should rush to the defense of a man she despised.

She knew the instant Derek spotted her from across the room. She felt his look like the leading edge of a storm. Snapping her fan, she nodded slightly to acknowledge him, then turned again toward Landon, only to find he had left her side to freshen his drink once again.

Feeling awkward and uncomfortable, she fanned her feverish cheeks and wished she could sink through the floor. She shouldn't have come, but it would have been dreadfully rude not to appear at the welcome party of her new neighbors.

She saw Derek making his way through the crowd, coming toward her. Surely he wouldn't dare address her after she'd ordered him to leave her alone.

But he did. Looking elegant in black, his hair neatly bound, he grasped her hand and placed a fleeting kiss on her fingertips. She noticed he wore a massive crested ring on his right hand. She'd been under the impression he had given all his family jewels for his cause. Another lie, perhaps.

"Mistress Palmer," he said smoothly, absorbing her with his eyes. "How nice to see you again."

She wanted to slap him for being so bold, defying her wishes, making her blood rush to her head and her heart leap in her breast. "Good evening, Baron." She pulled away her hand and fanned her cheeks.

"Would you care to join me in the next dance?"

"No."

His eyebrow lifted as she became aware that all eyes were on the two of them.

"No, thank you," she said, and flashed him a smile before retreating again behind her fan.

He leaned near. "I've missed you," he said. His words were no sooner spoken than Katya arrived and took hold of his arm.

"Hello, Mistress Palmer," she purred with eyes like a tigress. "How lovely you look. So—mature—in your gray dress. I suppose the pirates ruined your yellow one."

"My God, Katya," Derek snapped. "Why bring that up?"

Katya looked up at him with innocent eyes. "Oh, I'm sorry. She was just so brave, being carried aboard the pirate ship by that awful man. Do you suppose the Hardys have been hanged yet?"

People were eavesdropping. Eden prayed for the musicians to begin playing, but they were fumbling through their music. She hated herself for caring what anyone thought about her, but she heard herself say, "I was locked in the hold immediately. Then rescued by the English with no harm done. And I don't know or care about what has happened to the Hardys."

Derek touched her shoulder. "You don't have to explain, Eden. You were heroic. I was there and saw everything that happened."

Someone called, "A toast to Baron von Walden. A toast to the brave Swiss colonists!"

The music swelled and the gathering launched into applause. Derek and Katya turned to acknowledge their accolades. They were surrounded by well-wishers and drawn into the crowd.

Landon ignored the festivities and returned to her side.

"I have a headache, Landon. I'm going to the garden for a breath of air."

"Certainly, my dear," he said without concern. "I'll dance a turn with Mrs. Wilson."

"Dance all you like. I'll see you again at dinner."

She escaped to the veranda, then strolled down the broad steps to the rose garden.

The night air was heavy with perfume from the surrounding bushes in full summer bloom; overhead, the moon was rising in golden splendor above the far hills; the song of crickets vied with the splash of a fountain centered in the grassy courtyard. At the far end of the manicured grounds, the Ashley River glimmered in the moonlight as it flowed toward the sea thirty miles to the east. Drifting from the mansion, the music added its own romantic charm to the bounties of nature.

Breathing deeply of the soft, scented air, Eden wished fervently she could leave the party. Tonight she was unwanted and unnecessary and only in the way. And Derek's presence and the way Katya doted on him was unendurable. The only thing left was to break her engagement to Landon. He might protest, but he would not be heartbroken.

She took a seat on a marble bench, relieved to be alone with her tumultuous thoughts. Seeing Derek had completely unnerved her. Would she ever be free of his power over her, free of the dizzying response to his haunting smile, free of the ache of knowing he belonged to someone else—never to her? Sitting there, surrounded by serenity and loveliness, she steeled her heart and took a solemn vow. She would never marry until she found true love, and if she upset Landon and caused a scandal, so be it. She would make a life for herself at Palmer Oaks and remain a spinster for the rest of her days.

"Are you well, Mistress Palmer?"

The low voice, the unmistakable accent, sent her newly born strength whirling into oblivion.

She looked up at Derek. His face was shadowed, but his wide shoulders and broad chest were ribboned with moonlight. She felt a shiver of excitement race along her spine. "I'm quite well," she answered, proud of the casual tone of her voice.

Moving, she kept the bench between them. "I didn't mean

to be rude to your people, but I felt the need of some air. I expect to greet everyone at dinner."

"I met your *friend,* Landon Palmer."

"My friend—and my cousin," she pointed out.

"As a matter of fact, he informed me he was your fiancé."

"He said that?"

"He was very sure about it."

"Oh. Well, as you know, we've had an understanding."

"You implied otherwise."

"Circumstances were different then."

"They've changed now?"

"Perhaps. Don't let it concern you." She prayed she had interjected the right amount of arrogance.

He put a booted foot on the bench and rested his forearm on his knee. Now the light played across his features. "You have accused me of falsehoods, Eden. It seems you, too, can play that little game."

He was right, of course. She had told him she was not engaged to Landon, knowing full well Landon believed otherwise. "I don't care to discuss it," she said defensively. "You should return to Katya. I'm sure she's looking for you."

"The last time I saw her, she was dancing—with your *fiancé.*"

"How nice," she said archly. "And pleasant for Landon. I've been poor company for him tonight."

"I'm grieved for him." He looked down at her for quite some time. "Eden. This conversation is ridiculous. You know how I feel about you. After what happened between us—"

She jumped to her feet. "How dare you bring that up. It was a terrible mistake. I was merely carried away by the romance of the setting and—"

"The setting? You're sure that's all?"

"Completely sure."

In the next moment, he was around the bench and grasping her hands, pulling her against him. "Tonight the setting is equally beautiful. Since you're so easily influenced by such things, I should take advantage of the moonlight." His arms enclosed her, his lips crushed hers. Her body responded with unleashed desire, fired by the memory of their previous intimacy. She clung to his upper arms, unable to resist, then giving in to the hurricane engulfing her emotions. Time stopped, then spun again as she melted into him, accepted his mouth, his body, his masculine power staked against her.

Abruptly he stepped back, keeping his hands on her shoulders. "Call your fiancé, if you like," he said huskily. "I'll give him whatever satisfaction he demands for the pleasure I just experienced."

"I should. Yes, I should call him at once," she gasped, her nerves skittering, her knees so weak she wondered if she might fall.

He smiled down at her, but it was a smile laced with bitterness.

"But you won't," he said. "By the way, Anna and I will call on you soon—if we're still invited."

"Of course." She couldn't think clearly; her mind was a jumble.

"One more thing." He removed an object from his pocket and pressed it into her hand. Her house key. "Good evening, Mistress Palmer." He pivoted and strode back toward the party.

Words were beyond her. One kiss and all reason had flown. Where was her pride, her vows to hate Derek Walden, her pledge to end his influence on her heart? Gone. Shattered. With one kiss he had destroyed all her resolutions. She threw the key into the nearest flower bed. It wouldn't do for Landon to see her carrying it.

When her senses returned, she slipped into the ballroom

and whispered to Landon that she was ill and must leave immediately. She could tell he was annoyed, but he agreed to take her home.

On the way, she turned to him and said quietly, "Landon, I'm ending our engagement."

- He gaped at her. "What's this?"

"I said, I'm ending our engagement. I have decided not to marry after all."

"But that's impossible."

"Not impossible. I'm sorry, but I don't love you. And I don't think you love me."

"Love? Oh, of course I love you. Politely, of course, which is the way it should be."

"Courtesy isn't enough for marriage. At least, not for me."

"But you promised your father on his deathbed."

"I regret that. But I don't think he would want me to be unhappy."

"Are you suggesting that I can't make you happy?"

"I appreciate your effort, cousin, but I'm afraid not. I take the blame entirely."

"This is just a mood you're having, dear. Women are like that. And they do love to play hard to get."

Eden wanted to scream. "Landon, this is not a mood. I'm not going to marry you. Please don't make this more difficult."

He squared his shoulders. "I've told everyone, discreetly of course, that we're to be married. I will not be made a laughingstock in Charles Town."

The small craft rowed by one of Eden's servants bumped against the dock. "We're here, Miss Palmer," the man said with a note of relief.

Eden got out and walked briskly toward the house. Landon trailed behind her. She faced him at the door. "Your horse is at the stable, Landon."

"But—I thought I would be your guest tonight—here."

"That won't be convenient."

"Very well, Eden. I'll go. But say what you please, our betrothal stands. You'll find a solemn pledge is not easily tossed aside."

After he was gone, she leaned against the door frame and stared across the river at the lights of Waldenburg. She was in a fine mess now. But she was sure beyond any doubt that she would never be the wife of Landon Palmer.

ᏽ 15 ᏽ

For two weeks following Poinsett's ball, Eden worked from dawn till dark. As much as possible, she tried to put Landon from her mind—and Derek, as well. It was easy to forget Landon, but she could not keep Derek from her thoughts.

Had she been too harsh with Derek? Had she misjudged his relationship with Katya? True, she'd seen them together, but that didn't prove they were planning to marry. He'd told her he wasn't engaged to Katya. Only Dr. Messenbaugh and little Anna had indicated otherwise. She should be willing to trust Derek above anyone. She would have—if it hadn't been for the subterfuge over the boundaries of her plantation. The more she considered that problem, the less she blamed Derek. King George had made the mistake, not the leader of the Swiss colony. Derek had hidden the problem from her, but maybe he was trying to spare her feelings.

As each day passed, she rationalized more and more,

finally deciding she had been too hasty to ban Derek from her life. And she was finding it impossible to ban him from her heart.

September brought the steamiest weather of the year. Queenie's puppies were six weeks old. In the garden, the indigo reached above Eden's waist. But there had been no word from Derek.

The second week in September, shortly after a cooling rain, he arrived unexpected and unannounced with Anna perched on his saddle in front of him.

Eden had just walked from the area where vats were being constructed and had poured herself a lemonade. Her private delight at seeing Derek was undeniable proof she was still deeply in love with him.

He rode up to the steps and smiled his heart-stopping smile.

"Hello, Derek—Anna. I'm so pleased to see you." She meant it sincerely. For today, at least, she would forget about her concern over the survey, try to make a new beginning, take control of both her temper and her passion.

She hurried down the steps and reached for Anna. "Come, darling. I'll take you to the pups. Laykee is feeding them. My, you'll be surprised at how they've grown." She glanced at Derek and received a nod of approval.

Once Anna was seated by the puppies' box, Eden led Derek across the lawn toward the indigo.

He was quiet, introspective, the perfect gentleman.

"It's a beautiful sight," he said, looking across the sea of gently waving greenery.

"Yes, it is. The plants are growing like the beanstalks that belonged to Jack in the fairy tale."

"Beanstalks?"

"An amusing story. I'll tell it to you and Anna someday."

They stood at the edge of the forty-acre indigo field. From there to the farthest tree line stretched row after row of hearty green plants, flourishing in the hothouse warmth and humidity of the Carolina lowland.

"Messenbaugh is surely mistaken this time," Derek noted.

Eden reached down to pick one of the leafy fronds and hold it up for his inspection. "It really is like a bean, you see. It's called a legume."

"I'll tell Hans. He'll be impressed with your knowledge." His eyes expressed his own admiration as he smiled at her.

Looking up at him in the dazzling sunlight of mid-afternoon, she felt the familiar jolt to her senses, enhanced by the remembrance of his lips against hers, his body close, the daring and dangerous manner in which he had swept her into his arms—and taken her to the stars.

She cocked her head and adjusted the wide brim of her hat. "I know all there is to know about indigo, Mr. Walden. With Bull Hawkins's strong plants, and the knowledge of fermentation, I'll produce a crop to raise eyebrows in Charles Town. I expect to get five shillings a pound at market."

"When do you plan to harvest?"

"When it's in full bloom, probably in late October. The drying sheds and vats are under construction. The barrels for shipping are arriving next month. Once the dye stuff is extracted and cut, it's an easy matter to haul it to market. The difficult part is the fermentation process. The plants must be watched day and night; limewater—but there I go, giving away all my secrets."

His eyebrows arched and he feigned dismay. "Ah, I had thought to trick the secrets from you. But you're too clever by half, *fraulein.*"

Tearing her eyes from him, she stooped to pick up a handful of dark, pungent soil. "Here is the real secret," she said. "It's been waiting a thousand years to nourish my plants this very summer. Just think, the lovely blue dye will color silk from the Indies to Ireland, maybe even France and China."

He cupped her hand displaying the soil and held it near his nose, as if to check the quality of the earth. But his lips strayed to the tender flesh of her wrist. She felt the feathery touch down to the tips of her toes. Releasing her hand, he nodded in agreement, as if unaware of the kiss.

"Derek—I'm sorry for the way I acted at Poinsett's ball."

His smile was warm, understanding. "Apology accepted, my lady."

Despite her turmoil, Eden was determined to keep her emotions carefully in check. "Thank you. So—how are things at Waldenburg?" I see constant activity on the river and hear hammering in the forest."

"Going well," he said. "We'll soon start the church on the commons."

"Why, it won't be long until you'll have houses to compare with mine, or even Henri Poinsett's." She was immediately sorry for her words. They sounded vain and officious. "I mean, it does take time to build an entire town. If there is anything at all I can do to help, please don't hesitate to ask."

"I'll keep that in mind," was his polite response.

As they walked back toward the house, he slipped his arm through hers. The gesture was simple, the kind that any gentleman would have offered. But the implication of renewed friendship, a truce of sorts, filled her with deep satisfaction.

Arriving at the back of the house, she and Derek discovered Anna seated on the ground in the shade, her skirts full of roly-poly brown and white puppies, squirming and whining, their eyes recently opened to a strange new world. Opposite her, capturing the occasional stray, sat Laykee.

Eden relished the sight, then enjoyed it doubly when she saw the look on Derek's face.

He squatted on the ground beside Anna and talked

foolishly to the puppies, holding up first one, then another, describing each one while carefully concealing any pity he felt for the blind child.

Eden signaled to Laykee to stay seated, and she pulled up a nearby lawn chair for herself. For several minutes all was wonderfully serene, then suddenly one pup made good its escape by crawling beneath Derek's boot and heading straight for the duck pond.

Eden jumped up and ran after the creature, but was too late to prevent it from tumbling into the shallow water. Disregarding her skirt and her gossamer sleeves, she knelt in the soft mud, plunged her arms above her elbows into the water, and held up a streaming and decidedly startled puppy.

Rippling with laughter, she carried the mischievous pup back to the shade, where she was greeted with applause from Derek and Anna, a smile of approval from Laykee, and a grateful wag of Queenie's tail.

"The female, wouldn't you know," said Eden.

"Independent women seem the rule at Palmer Oaks," Derek noted with a grin. He placed a hand on Anna's curls. "We should be going, darling. Put the pups in the box there beside you. Queen Elizabeth will want to feed them soon."

"I'm sure they're hungry," Anna said with the voice of authority. "They've been sucking on my fingers."

"Anna," Eden began gently, "would you like to have one of the pups when it's old enough to leave its mother?"

"Oh, I surely would, Miss Palmer. Could I, Dirk? I think I could take care of it myself."

"You can ask Frau Meyer, *schatze*. If she agrees, you may certainly have one."

Laykee cleared her throat. "Excuse me, Mr. Walden, could I speak privately with you?

Eden couldn't have been more surprised. Servants never asked for such privileges, and Laykee was as quiet and reserved as anyone she'd ever known. But she was sure the

149

Cherokee girl wouldn't have been so daring unless she had a very important reason. "I'll take Anna to the kitchen for a lemonade," Eden offered. Her reward was a most appreciative look from her servant.

A short time later, with Anna's hand securely clasping hers, Eden returned from the kitchen to find Derek headed her way. Curiosity nibbled at her, but she had to wait until either Laykee or Derek was ready to reveal their shared secret.

He lifted Anna in his arms and kissed her cheek. The little girl rested her head in the crook of his neck and closed her eyes with a sigh.

"She still gets tired," he explained. "The trip was hard on her. But her strength is returning rapidly."

"Please come again, Derek—any time." Eden meant it with all her heart.

"We'll be back. After all, we must keep an eye on the puppies' progress. One day, Anna may want to choose one for herself. Thank you for your offer, Eden."

The tender look he gave her, the way he caressed her Christian name, made her feel soft as heated honey. He mounted and placed Anna in the saddle before him. Riding near, he leaned down to take Eden's hand. She had rolled up her wet sleeves, and his eyes strayed along the smooth, fair skin of her forearm. Then his look shifted to her eyes. "Very kind of you, Eden, very kind indeed. Thank you."

"You're more than welcome," she answered while drowning in his indigo gaze.

Straightening, he released her hand and encircled Anna's chubby waist, then reined toward the gate. Looking back at the last minute, he called, "Tell Laykee I appreciate her suggestion. She'll explain."

As soon as they were gone, Eden rushed to the house, her curiosity now bursting out of control. "What's happening, Laykee? Mr. Walden said you would explain."

"It's not a secret from you, Miss Eden. Only from Anna. I didn't know how else to speak in private to Mr. Walden."

"It's all right. But I'm very curious."

"I spoke about Anna's blindness. I've seen such a child before in our village. A boy whose sister was tortured and killed by our enemies. He saw it all, then became blind for many months."

"Did he regain his sight?"

"The shaman prepared some herbs and held a special ceremony. Afterward, within a few weeks, the boy could see. Some said it was the herbs, some said it was the boy's faith in the shaman."

"That is fascinating. Do you suppose it could work on a white child?"

"I don't know. But I could go to the village and get the herbs. I know the ceremony, too, though I'm no shaman. I asked Mr. Walden about it and he said he would be willing to try anything to help Anna. But he won't tell his people, he said. They might think it's evil."

"It's a wonderful idea, Laykee. Could I go with you to your village? I haven't been to Congarees in years."

"Of course, but no one else. Especially not Mr. Walden. The young warriors wouldn't like to have a foreign man staying in our camp."

"I'll ask Joseph to act as escort. He can leave us there and return later to guard us on our way home. We'll go as soon as possible. If there's any hope at all for Anna to see again, it's certainly worth a try.

Derek stared across his two acres of experimental indigo and wondered if he should feel guilty for taking time to grow the rare crop, even though the seeds Eden had given him had sprouted and produced healthy, vigorous plants. Preparing the garden had taken several days of backbreaking work, time he could have used to help raise the log walls of the

151

village church. Nothing he could say would convince Hans Messenbaugh that planting indigo wasn't a complete waste of effort. Furthermore, he suspected Hans was annoyed because he hadn't yet taken steps to claim the Palmer house and lands. Hans was sworn to secrecy on the matter, and Derek had explained the complicated legal circumstances. But Derek knew Hans was suspicious of his friendship with Eden Palmer—and would not approve of the famous leader of the Swiss enterprise becoming involved with an outsider. This was a narrow-minded view that he expected Hans to revise before long.

Kneeling, he tugged a determined weed from the dark earth. He loved Eden, and nothing would ever change that. She was the first woman since Heidi to touch him deeply, to not only inflame his desires, but to reach his mind and spirit, to dwell continuously in his thoughts, to make him dream again of sharing life with a woman, of having children of his own, of spending his future in the warmth of her smile, the joy of her embrace.

Waldenburg was now a reality. His people had taken hold and made the land their own. Their spirits were high, and their individual cottages were occupying the town site he'd plotted months ago. The women had made friends in Charles Town, where they were accepted and respected by the English and French settlers; his own importance had waned; he wasn't needed as before. Of course, he'd been elected mayor in the first free vote in their town council meeting. He had duties, important duties, but the heavy cloak of responsibility, the guidance and protection of their very lives, had fallen from his shoulders. He was relieved to have left the pedestal he'd been placed on and become an ordinary member of the community. Pedestals were not only false, they were lonely places to inhabit.

He actually felt old sometimes, older than the young couples, several now with babies on the way, babies who would be the first generation born in Waldenburg. And he felt centuries older than Katya, with her childish tantrums and constant possessiveness. Maybe he was just tired, he decided. Physically and mentally drained after all he'd been through this past year. Thank God he was making progress with Eden. At Palmer Oaks last week she'd been warm to him at last. He would call on her again soon—and Landon Palmer be damned. He refused to believe she would marry that fop. They hadn't taken any vows, and he wouldn't let Palmer hold her to some vague commitment.

He would have to wait, of course, until she returned home. She had sent him a note a few days ago saying that she and Laykee were going upriver to Congarees for the feast of the full moon. He knew they were going to try to get help for Anna. If only they could help the child. Derek had strong doubts about their prospects, but if they could convince Anna she would be able to see, she might truly regain her sight. There was nothing he wouldn't trade or sacrifice for that darling girl's happiness. Lately he'd seen her smile again, even laugh that day with the puppies. If only his prayers for her were answered, he'd never ask God for anything again.

"Derek! Walden!"

He saw Hans rushing through the trees. "What's wrong, Hans?"

"I just came from town. The Indians are on a rampage, burned an outlying settlement. I was told to alert our settlers of the danger."

Walking briskly toward the commons, Derek put his hand on the doctor's shoulder. "Stay calm. What tribe was it? How far away?"

"I don't know. I admit I panicked. But aren't the Indian villages just west of us?"

"The Cherokee villages are there. Congarees is the closest —about an hour's ride. But there are other tribes: the Yamassee, Choctaw, Savannahs—I've heard of many. And we know nothing of these people, how they live—and fight."

"Verdammen! I'll study the savages' habits later, Derek. Right now we'd better get our weapons and send the women to Charles Town."

"Of course. Alert Karl and Hilda. Take an armed escort into town. I'll make sure we're well-defended. What about Palmer Oaks and the people at River's Bend? Have they been warned?"

"I stopped long enough to alert the hands at Palmer Oaks. Didn't see the lady. One of the men headed toward Poinsett's with the news."

Derek stopped in his tracks.

"Come on. We've got lots to do," Messenbaugh urged.

Eden had gone west to Congarees. The thought of what might happen to her turned Derek's blood to ice.

"You go on ahead and follow my orders."

"What about you?"

"I'm riding west alone as soon as the men are ready."

"West! Hell, that could be suicide. Why would you do that?"

"To find the truth. Search the forests for signs of hostiles. If I see anything, I'll bring a warning." He couldn't tell Hans he would leave his settlers, take any risk, to find Eden.

Hans shook his head. "Insane. You don't know these woods like the natives. This isn't Neuchâtel, Baron. If they catch you, you'll be killed without mercy."

"We don't have enough information to know what's really happening. Go now and rouse the others. There's every chance it's a false alarm."

Hans gripped his forearm. "Take care, then, Derek. Arm yourself well."

Derek turned toward his tent. He kept pistols ready, ammunition, his sword. His intention was to ride west, then snake through the woods on foot toward Congarees on the upper Ashley. If he encountered Indians on the move, he'd have to abandon his search for Eden and slip back to warn his people and fight if necessary to protect them. As much as he loved Eden, he couldn't let hundreds of his colonists die while he searched for one woman.

His concern deepened as he headed for the pen to get his horse. His darling Eden was on an errand of mercy for Anna. Had she traveled into the teeth of a revolt by vicious natives? She could be dead by now—or cruelly used, a prisoner, taken God knows where in this immense American wilderness. No, this wasn't Neuchâtel—but here as in his former homeland, there was danger, cruelty, and death. Man's fate, he thought, while putting cartridges into his saddlebag. To be born, to fight, to die. He'd had one love snatched from him by mindless killers. He'd risk his life to prevent a second tragedy. He loved Eden Palmer. Surely God wouldn't take her from him—not when he'd just found her.

At midday he approached the Cherokee village of Congarees. He heard the sound of talking and laughter, and carefully parted the brush to peer into a clearing dappled with sunlight and shadow.

The sight he saw was as astonishing as it was lovely. There, gathering wild strawberries, were half a dozen Indian maidens, their chatter gentle and happy, their raven-black hair flowing around smooth shoulders and hips, their lovely young bodies gleaming and fully exposed to view. They wore innocent smiles and baskets draped over their forearms. They wore nothing else at all.

He had expected warriors, armed savages, vicious killers. Instead he was witness to innocent beauty, lovely girls picking fruit on a serene fall afternoon.

He started to back away when limbs crackled behind him. He whirled to face a stocky copper-skinned native wearing buckskin breeches and a leather headband around his forehead. The Indian was the first native he'd seen in the wilderness. And the man was fighting mad.

Another Indian crept out of the brush on his right, another on his left; six, ten, twelve or more. He heard screams behind him. The girls must be frantic. He didn't understand exactly what was going on, but he knew furious looks when he received them. With no chance to escape, he pulled his gun from his belt. Too late. A stealthy savage grabbed him from behind, bringing him to the ground, then hit him with a club.

He struggled. More Indians clubbed him, beating him nearly senseless. He expected to die, but they only brandished their knives and didn't stab him. He was half conscious when they hauled him to his feet and bound his hands.

Pushed and shoved through the forest, he thought what a fine defender he was of his people, of Eden, or anyone else. He had walked into this trap like a lamb on its way to be slaughtered.

∽ 16 ∾

Eden sat cross-legged on a woven hemp rug, her skirts resting across her knees and her hands folded quietly in her lap.

Beside her sat Laykee, looking quite at home in her natural surroundings. Across from them sat Chief Tahchee and Oowatie, the shaman.

Once the brief journey from Palmer Oaks had been completed and both ladies were welcomed warmly to the

Cherokee village, Eden had sent Joseph home to continue his critical work in the indigo fields.

That was two days ago. Today, Eden and Laykee would have their final meeting with Chief Tahchee and Oowatie. She had been treated like visiting royalty, housed with Laykee in an attractive, if not entirely modern, log house where she had been provided with every comfort.

During the day yesterday, Eden had been allowed to walk freely through the community of fifty or sixty private dwellings, pick fruit from the orchards near the town house, and most important, pay a call on Oowatie, the shaman whose herbs were the real purpose of the visit. Last night, she and Laykee had been dinner guests of Chief Tahchee, his timid wife, and his rotund daughter Wurteh.

Now she sat in the cool town house and listened closely to Oowatie's instructions to Laykee for the rites and herbal treatment to be administered to Anna Schaefer.

A commotion outside interrupted Chief Tahchee's farewell blessing.

An Indian brave, clad in loincloth and moccasins, his head shaved, his clamshell collar clattering with every step, rushed into the dim interior. His startling message was quickly translated by Laykee.

"A man—a white stranger—has been caught spying on the maidens in the forest. He's being dragged into the village."

Eden looked in alarm at Tahchee. The chief rose to his considerable height. He made an impressive figure in the glimmering firelight—his skin like rich coffee, his head smooth except for a thick lock at his crown. The news of the capture barely ruffled his calm demeanor. But it was plain that his guests were now dismissed from his presence.

Blinking in the afternoon sun, Eden followed Laykee into the square in front of the town house. She was anxious to leave as soon as they could saddle their horses. Despite the very pleasant time they'd spent here, she knew that she was an outsider, that these people were fierce warriors, and that the white man's laws had no meaning in this untamed land. She noticed with increasing concern that Laykee was as eager to be away as she was.

"Are you frightened?" Eden whispered as they walked toward the enclosure where the horses were kept.

"I'm sure *we* wouldn't be harmed," said Laykee, "but I'd rather not see what they'll do to the intruder."

"Why would anyone spy on the girls?"

"I doubt if he was spying at all—probably just stumbled onto the maidens gathering berries. You see, because of the heat, they often enjoy disrobing when they're alone in the woods."

"You mean they were naked?"

"I think so. Otherwise, I don't believe the men would have been so upset. White strangers are usually welcome, once they explain why they've come."

A band of a dozen warriors emerged from the nearby forest. Proceeding them walked six young women, clad demurely in white deerskin shifts, their eyes downcast, their baskets carried in their hands.

Eden and Laykee stopped in the shadows, where they could watch without being seen. From every corner of the village women and children and barking dogs descended on the approaching group. Only when the maidens walked close did Eden notice their dark eyes were dancing with excitement, their lips clamped in the effort not to grin. One actually kept her hand over her mouth as her shoulders shook with embarrassed giggles.

"These are the berry pickers?" Eden asked in a whisper.

"Yes. They hastily pulled on their dresses after they were seen. It's no shame to them, but it will likely be fatal for the man who saw them."

"But if it wasn't his fault—"

"He saw them. That's enough, unless he has a very good excuse for being in the area."

The braves marched by: tall men, well-built, their beads and shells rattling, their faces set in anger. In their midst, half a head taller, a man with a shock of golden hair walked stiffly, his jaw locked against anger and pain.

"Derek!" Eden said in sudden horror. Her heart flew into her throat as she recognized him. A captive, perhaps doomed to a terrible death. She was unable to move, but Laykee rushed out to fall in step with the maidens. After a minute she returned.

Eden grasped her arm. "What did they say?" she choked.

"Just as I thought. The baron came upon the girls gathering berries; I'm sure he was as surprised as they were. Their screams brought the warriors. Mr. Walden was subdued after a brief struggle."

"Oh dear heaven! But what is he doing here? What will happen to him?" Eden was frantic. She felt she must be to blame somehow for this dreadful circumstance. Had he followed her here for some reason? Why else would he suddenly arrive at Congarees?

"I don't believe he'll be killed," Laykee said softly.

"What did the girls say?"

"I spoke to Wurteh, Chief Tahchee's daughter. She's such a silly girl." Laykee shook her head in disgust.

"But what of Derek Walden?" Eden's nerves were stretched to the breaking point.

"We must wait and see."

"No, we must do something. We'll go to the chief, explain that this man is our friend—*your* friend, Laykee. Tahchee seems like a reasonable man. Surely he will see the whole thing is an accident; Derek meant no harm."

"Perhaps. From the way Wurteh rolled her eyes, I don't think *she* wants harm to come to the 'most handsome white man I've ever seen.'"

159

"She said that?" Eden sagged with relief. "That's good, very good. Tahchee will listen to his daughter." She paused to collect herself. "Do you think we could manage a word with Derek? He knows nothing about the Indian people of America and must be terribly confused. I want him to know we're here to help him. If we explain his innocence to the chief, maybe Tahchee will release him."

"Come. We will try. They're taking him to the town house."

The square resembled a beehive poked with a stick. Buzzing and bustling, the villagers crowded the area, taking turns peeking through the single opening of the meeting house.

Laykee left Eden at the back of the crowd and spoke to a warrior guarding the door. Returning, she explained, "That man is called Chota. He is the most angry of all. Wurteh is his promised bride, which is a great honor for him. He told me the white man dishonored her by seeing her disrobed. He wants to kill him."

"No. Oh no."

"But Wurteh says the white man must not die."

Eden felt like she was being ripped apart, torn first one way, then the other. Was it possible Derek Walden's life depended on the outcome of a lover's quarrel? "Can we see him? Please help, Laykee. I must talk to him."

"Follow me. We'll speak to Chota."

With racing heartbeat, Eden followed Laykee through the low door of the town house and into the dim, smoky interior. After the heat and confusion outside, the lodge was cool and orderly. As soon as her vision adjusted, Eden saw that Derek had been bound to the center post and was being surveyed by Chief Tahchee and his daughter. Her heart twisted inside her at the sight.

In the dancing light of the holy altar fire, Derek was a golden lion caught in a trap of twisted rope. He was not at all resigned to his fate. His jaw was clenched in anger; his feet were planted as though he hoped to uproot the post; his muscles strained against the bonds confining him. His earlier struggle was evident in his torn shirt and traces of grass and dirt and blood clinging to his clothing and exposed flesh. The thong around his neck, by which he'd been pulled through the village, was wrapped around the stake. Along his throat his skin was chafed and bloody.

Swept with fear and pity, she watched him struggle briefly, then, with a curse, lean against the post. His left eyelid was swollen and blood seeped from a wound in his right thigh. Had they shot him? Was he seriously injured? She had to do something—but what?

Laykee gave her a look of warning, then walked calmly to the chief. After a lengthy exchange in the Cherokee tongue, she signaled for Eden to come forward.

"You may speak to the captive," said Tahchee solemnly. "Laykee tells me you are his friend."

"Yes," she said quickly, averting her eyes when she heard Derek's grunt of recognition. "I'm sure he's very sorry— that it was all a mistake. It's possible he was trying to find me, deliver an urgent message. This man is the guardian of the child your shaman has offered to help, the blind child." She paused for breath, then hurried on. "And he's a stranger in our land. He's from across the sea and has no knowledge of Cherokee customs . . . why, very little of English customs, either." She risked a glance at Derek. "He's really quite harmless, sir, I assure you. He wouldn't think of causing trouble or bringing shame on your innocent maidens." She tried to think of anything else she could say in Derek's defense.

"He doesn't look as helpless as you say," noted Tahchee. "Chota says he fought like a bull once he recovered from the surprise of the braves' attack."

"Oh, but he's not a warrior at all. He and his people are

161

gentle farmers. And he loves the poor blind child very much." Her throat constricted and her eyes burned with unshed tears of frustration. Was any of this making sense to the stony-eyed chief? What words could she use to gain his sympathy and understanding?

From her shoulder Derek's voice came low and heavy with feeling. "Eden—thank you for trying, but I'd prefer you get safely away."

Tahchee raised his hand and addressed himself in English to his daughter. "Wurteh, come with me. We'll speak to Chota. He is demanding this white man's death."

Wurteh shook her head vigorously, sending her gleaming hair flying around her moon-shaped face. Her words were Cherokee, but her objection to the death sentence was more than plain.

Tahchee led her across the room to a stiff-backed Chota standing near the entrance.

Laykee threw a hopeful glance at Eden and followed the chief and his daughter at a respectful distance.

Doing her best to control her emotions, Eden turned to look up at Derek. She knew he was suffering, possibly even in severe pain. He no longer struggled, but to her surprise, was regarding her with a hint of a smile at the edge of his lips. Just a brave front, she thought. No one in his right mind would find such a situation amusing.

His muttered voice held no hint of weakness. "You paint a fine picture of me, Miss Palmer. I almost didn't recognize myself. Let's see—gentle, harmless, rather a simpleton drifting through the forest admiring the flora and fauna. At least you were correct about my feelings for Anna."

She was astounded at his cool impertinence. "I was trying to help. Surely you can't object to my saving your life."

He shifted his weight against the post. "Naturally I'm appreciative. But I suppose I'm guilty as charged. It's embarrassing enough to die for such an idiotic reason, but even worse to have a woman describe me to my captors as an empty-headed bumpkin with little intelligence and no fighting skills."

"Would you rather I told them how fierce you are, what a dangerous fighter, a brave leader? I understand your pride is damaged, but 'tis better to be humble than staked over a slow fire." Her sharp words hid her relief. He must not be suffering as much as she'd feared if he could manage to criticize her. After a quick look at the conference taking place at the far end of the room, she moved nearer. "Are you badly hurt, Derek?"

"A minor wound in my leg. My head pounds like hell. Someone clubbed me before I knew what was going on. When I could stand, they brought me here."

"They said you spied on their maidens."

His brows lifted. "I saw them, I'll admit. A lovely sight, but not worth dying for."

"But what are you doing here?"

"I came looking for you. There were rumors of an Indian uprising. I knew you had traveled west to get help for Anna. I couldn't let you walk into a band of hostiles."

"You mean, you're here to save me from the Indians?"

"That was my intention. My attempt at heroics appears both foolish and unnecessary.

"Indeed," she sighed.

He started to chuckle, but winced instead.

Instantly she moved close and stroked his shoulder. "Derek, forgive me. We stand here bantering like we were at a picnic. You risked your life to help me. You're hurt—and in grave danger." Looking closely at his scratched face, the blood caked along one side of his head and staining the bridge of his nose, she ached with pity.

His eyelids lowered; his mouth softened. "Odd, isn't it, how frequently we meet under such adverse circumstances? The pirates' ship, a darkened hallway, now an Indian stake. You must find my repeated blunders somewhat boring."

"I would hardly call your effort to save lives a blunder. You were first described to me as very brave. I must agree that is accurate." She hoped the deeply felt compliment would make up for her earlier belittling of his nature.

"I retained some dignity with the pirate. On this occasion, I feel like a fool. The report of danger was obviously an error. And now I'm brought down for the crime of gaping like an idiot at a group of frolicking young ladies."

"Laykee says it's the custom in the summer. And from the faces of the girls, I don't think they were terribly upset."

He moved again, his muscles tightening as he pulled against the ropes.

"Oh Derek, this is insane. We have to get you released right away." She reached up to touch his forehead. It was heated and damp. Tenderly, she stroked his temple and attempted to wipe away some of the dried blood from his hairline. Struggling with conflicting sensations, she whispered, "Thank you for coming, even if—"

"No," he said gently. "You have no need to thank me."

Her hand moved along his exposed upper arm. "I wish I could take away your pain," she said in a voice so low she barely recognized it as her own.

She caressed his arms, his neck, forgetting her surroundings, losing herself as if drugged by his courage, his rugged beauty, the awareness that his own longing was engulfing her like an ocean wave on welcoming sand.

He leaned his head down as best he could.

She saw the rope tighten around his throat. Her words of protest for his pain were lost as his lips found hers, holding them softly, allowing the arousing touch to join them in a union as fragile and doomed as butterflies wafting on a midsummer's night.

Parting on a sigh, she stepped back and absorbed his dark gaze.

"I love you, Eden Palmer," he murmured in a voice laden with sadness. "If I don't survive this, remember my words."

Words that meant so much to her—given to her now in this desperate dilemma. How could she ever forget them? Overcome with feeling, she rested her open palm on the rise of his chest. She felt the swell of sinew, the moist stretch of skin, the throb of his heart. His words penetrated her soul, but all she could think of was the danger he faced. "Derek, you cannot die."

"Psst . . . Miss Eden," came a voice from behind her.

Like a sleepwalker awakening, she turned to stare at Laykee.

"There's hope. Tahchee will have him released."

Eden went weak with joy. "Thank the Lord. We'll take him to Waldenburg. He needs his wounds tended. He needs—"

"No, you don't understand. He *will* be tended by the medicine man, but he can't leave here."

"Medicine man? Oh, but when he's healed, he can leave."

"I don't know. Maybe he won't ever leave Congarees."

"But—why not?"

"Wurteh, the chief's daughter—is going to marry him."

17

For a moment Eden was too stunned to respond.

"It's a great honor," Laykee said.

"Marry him? I don't understand."

"The chief's daughter holds much power in the tribe."

"But Laykee, she can't force him, can she?"

Laykee turned to Derek. "I must explain, sir. Wurteh, Chief Tahchee's daughter, is very taken with you. She wants you for her husband."

"Godalmighty," he rasped and rolled his eyes upward.

"I'm sorry, Mr. Walden. The chief's commands must always be obeyed or—"

"Or what?" he blurted.

"Or you will die," Laykee said softly.

Eden felt faint. "No," she stammered. "Derek, your people will come for you—surely." Panic dulled her brain. "Laykee, tell the princess that he's spoken for—by me—by you—someone." Her voice rose shrilly.

"It doesn't matter," Laykee said flatly. "She wouldn't care even if he had a wife. He is now the possession of the Cherokees. And Wurteh has claimed him."

"What if I refuse?" Derek interjected.

"You will die for sure, sir. Burn, most likely. My advice is that you do whatever you have to for now; maybe later you can escape. She might let you go if you prove unsatisfactory."

"Verdammen," he growled.

They were interrupted by the approach of Tahchee, with Wurteh and Chato just behind him.

Eden's head cleared as her first shock subsided. Surely something could be done. They weren't entirely removed from civilization. They could go for help. Derek must stall for time. She took a close look at Wurteh, whose adoring eyes were fixed on Derek. The girl's linen shift, the layers of beads and shells, the massive silver broach adorning her blue-black hair, showed plainly that she was a princess. Unfortunately, no amount of finery could turn her into a beauty, at least not by the white man's standards.

Wurteh grinned hungrily at Derek, dimpling both fat cheeks as her eyes sank like raisins buried in pudding. "White man pretty," she cooed.

"No!" came Chota's guttural objection.

Eden jerked her attention to the warrior. Maybe this was help from an unexpected source.

Tahchee scowled at the brave, then questioned him in Cherokee.

Laykee tossed a glance at Eden, then looked at Derek and placed one finger over her lips to recommend silence.

Chief Tahchee spoke to Wurteh, whose grin had become a pout.

Eden held her breath. Was Chota insisting that Derek must die? Would Chota's wishes outweigh those of Wurteh's? She began to pray the girl would have her way, after all. Gazing back at Derek, she gave him a look of absolute sympathy. He was suffering physically and his life hung in the balance. Yet she saw more anger than fear in his expression. She reminded herself he was a fighter, despite her recent claims to the contrary. He was a legendary baron, a warlord who had fought battles and was held in great respect by the Swiss. To have his life, his future, bandied about as if he were a prize stallion, must be demeaning as well as threatening.

Tahchee raised his hand and addressed the group. "Chota, the leader of his clan, has been promised Wurteh as his wife. I have reminded Wurteh of that promise. She has agreed to allow the matter to be settled with a contest between the two suitors."

Eden spoke without thinking. "You mean, if Mr. Walden wins, he will be free to go?" She knew instantly she'd said the wrong thing. Laykee was frantically shaking her head, but it was too late; the chief's eyebrows met in a swift scowl.

In a tone of brittle authority, Tahchee announced, "The *victor* will have the hand of my *daughter.*"

"And the loser?" Laykee ventured while Eden bit into her errant lips.

Instead of answering Laykee, the chief addressed Eden. "I was told by Laykee that you have a claim on this man. Is this true?"

She swallowed hard and tried to think. She realized she must choose her words with care. Looking at Laykee, she prayed for a signal, but her maid only shrugged her shoulders in a gesture of helplessness.

Derek broke the silence. "Miss Palmer and I are engaged to be married, sir. I'm sure you know the importance of that custom in English society."

Her heart sank. Didn't Derek realize he could be condemning himself to burn at the stake if Wurteh couldn't have her way?

He went on. "I would, however, be honored to set aside that engagement and marry your daughter—once I have bested your warrior at whatever competition he chooses."

Eden's lips parted in astonishment. She had gone from engaged to rejected in a matter of seconds. She wondered what Derek was thinking. For certain, he was gambling with his very life.

Wurteh was smiling again, her huge hips swaying under her loose skirt. Her beads popped and crackled as her eyes danced in excited rhythm. "My white man win. I have him first." She gave Chota a victorious smirk. "You will lose, Chota. The golden man is very smart—like all whites."

Chota looked daggers at his fiancée.

Her smirk softened into a smile of pity. "Maybe I'll marry you, Chota, later, when I'm tired of this Englishman and put him away." She then made a comment to him in Cherokee which appeared to be an apology.

Wurteh's conciliatory words were entirely wasted on the furious Chota. He stamped one foot in anger and pointed at Eden. His heated remark required interpreting.

Tahchee said, "You, Miss Eden Palmer, will be given to the *loser* of the contest. If your white man marries Wurteh, I will see that you're taken in and cared for by Chota. This way, you will not be abandoned and disgraced. You will have a husband—one man or the other."

Words failed her. To her utter amazement, she would swear she heard Derek chuckle deep in his throat. Dear heaven—and she'd thought he had no sense of humor. If he thought this was amusing, he would find humor in a grave-digging.

Eden stared from one to the other. Why, everyone looked satisfied with this absurd arrangement. Content with his decision, the chief was turning to leave. Wurteh was drooling again over Derek, who returned the girl's look with something resembling a friendly overture. Laykee appeared relaxed and resigned, while Chota—Chota was now eyeing *her* with a predatory glint.

Two stout Cherokees released Derek from the post. Two Indian girls motioned for Eden and Laykee to follow them outside.

When they all emerged into the metallic brilliance, Eden tried again to communicate with Derek, who was held by the braves.

One of the maidens took hold of her arm.

"Derek," she cried. "Please be careful."

He was able to give her one quick, encouraging smile. "Take heart, *liebchen*," he said as he was prodded away. "Trust me." He emphasized his words with a wink that turned her knees to jelly.

Guarded by the Indian maiden, Eden considered all that had happened. She realized now that Derek intended to *lose* the contest, and he had shown great cunning by planting the idea that *she* should be handed over to the loser. This ensured he would be allowed to take her away afterward. Another amazing thing was the way Tahchee had assumed he was doing her a favor by making certain she had a husband—either Derek or Chota, it didn't matter which. Either man was good enough for an underweight pale-skinned woman with questionable skills as a wife. Derek didn't know Indian ways, but he certainly knew human nature. No wonder he had winked as he was led away.

All he had to do was lose the contest to Chota.

Water drums throbbed their deep-throated rhythms as Eden and Laykee waited in front of the town house. The area was packed with onlookers in a festive mood; anticipation filled the air, children laughed and screeched and played games under the increasingly warm sun under a cloudless sky.

Derek was soon returned to the scene by his captors. His wounds had been cleaned, his damaged clothing replaced with snug buckskin pants and a beaded sleeveless vest. He was feeling much better, strong and certain of his plan.

Wurteh occupied the place of honor at her father's right hand. Her dress was lavish with beadwork and wampum shells. She held eagle feathers in each hand and lifted them in acknowledgment of the cheers of friends and well-wishers.

Chota strutted like a rooster for Wurteh's benefit. Though

he was far less imposing a figure than Derek, he vied for the princess's attention with loud chanting and a spontaneous dance.

Eden maneuvered close enough to Derek to speak to him. He was unfettered, relaxed and confident.

She stood beside him, but kept her eyes on the commotion in the square. Without looking at him, she said, "Are you all right?"

"Yes. And you?"

"I'm frightened to death."

"You don't look it. I'm proud of you. Whoever wins your hand today will be a most fortunate man."

She cocked her eyes at him. *"You, of course."*

"As I've said before, nothing is certain in life, is it?" His tone was mildly sardonic.

"Don't be foolish. We must plan our escape."

"Shh. Time for that later. First I must decide how to lose to that arrogant creature stomping around like a buffoon."

"Of course you must lose," she hissed between clenched teeth.

"Then you understand my plan?"

She gave him a withering look. "Certainly."

"Clever girl," he quipped. He lifted an eyebrow. "I could yet change my mind. I've been told by a Cherokee who speaks English as well as the queen that I'm extremely fortunate to be chosen as Wurteh's consort. Princess Wurteh is next in line to be *chief* of the Cherokees. I might enjoy being the husband of a chief." As always, he took pleasure in teasing her. And maybe his banter would help ease her fear.

"You wouldn't dare."

"Think of it, chief consort of seven clans, ruler of a dedicated army of fine warriors, freedom from mundane chores—just hunting, fishing, riding through the mountains—"

"And *husband* to Wurteh," she snapped. "Her slave, her

plaything—until she tires of you, as she's already suggested."

"I was just giving it some thought."

He ended his bantering when he glanced at Wurteh. The princess was sending Eden a look that would pierce a buffalo hide.

Eden said crisply, "I'd better rejoin Laykee before someone suspects we're planning mischief. I pray you perform at your lowest level of skill."

"It won't be easy. Losing to a lesser man goes against the grain."

"Do try your best."

"I'll have to settle for *second* prize."

"This is no time to jest, Baron."

"Perhaps I'm serious."

"Just please get us out of here and I'll find you most amusing."

"And will you retract your betrothal to your cousin?" He altered his tone.

"Why bring that up now?"

"Perhaps you will *have* to refuse Mr. Palmer. After all, you wouldn't want a polygamous relationship."

"Polygamous? But this wedding won't be real. Not like holy bonds."

"Are you certain of that, my lady?"

"Yes, of course," she murmured.

He had no chance to say more, as he was called forward to begin the competition.

He listened closely to the English-speaking Cherokee in charge of the proceedings. Derek figured losing would be a simple matter—only requiring that he swallow his pride and appear to try to win. He had spent the past hours silently despising himself for causing this predicament. He'd been far too hasty in rushing off to the village in pursuit of Eden. Fear for her safety had replaced his usual clear thinking. He should have made an attempt to confirm the rumors of an uprising before racing like a lovesick fool to rescue his lady—a lady who had no need of rescue, it turned out. He had certainly put both of them in danger, and now he must act out this foolishness to gain their freedom. He had no fear for himself. If he had been forced to marry Wurteh, he could have resigned himself until managing his escape, hopefully before his countrymen arrived here and caused a real battle. But Eden's situation was quite different. If she were handed over to Chota, he knew he would have to intervene at once, and God only knew what the result of that might be.

His musings were interrupted by the bilingual brave. "We will begin now, white man. The choice of the weapons for the contest will be made by Wurteh."

He felt a trickle of alarm. All could be lost if she made up the rules of the competition.

"I'm ready," he said solemnly. He would have to remember the Cherokees had invented these contests, and could reinvent the rules to suit their purpose.

The brave who was officiating came to his side. "We will go into the town house for the contest. After the winner is decided, we will have the two marriage ceremonies."

Derek didn't like the sound of it. What sort of competition could be held in the dim interior of the lodge? He had expected knives, archery, spears, a horse race. If this was a trick, there would be little chance of an easy escape. Somehow, whatever it cost him in personal shame, he must *lose* this goddamned contest.

When all were gathered inside the meeting house, Chief Tahchee led Wurteh to a seat of honor; beside her, he seated Eden. Then he raised both hands skyward and spoke a few words in Cherokee. Following this invocation, he spoke directly to Derek.

"You, white man from a faraway land, have been looked upon favorably by my daughter, Wurteh. You have shown your willingness to become her husband."

Gazing at the gray-haired chief, Derek wondered if the old man really believed he wanted to marry the girl, or if the fact he would otherwise be burned at the stake might have something to do with his decision.

Tahchee continued, "The husband of a future chief must be a thinking man as well as a strong man. The contest Wurteh has selected will prove who has the greater mind—Wall Done or Chota."

Hell, an easy loss, Derek thought with some relief. It must be plain to Eden that he was an imbecile; soon he could appear to be a blathering idiot to everyone present.

∞ 18 ∞

Derek learned the worst as Tahchee explained the competition. "A story will be told. My daughter, Princess Wurteh, will decide the winner."

His hopes plummeted. If Wurteh was to decide, she would surely choose whomever she wanted—regardless of what happened in the "contest." Still, he must try. He concentrated on the instructions being given by the Cherokee brave.

"Each man must tell the exact story of how the world was made. The best storyteller will win Wurteh's hand. Chota will begin."

The story of creation? His mind whirled. There must be dozens of versions. Maybe he should plead ignorance and refuse to compete. Not good enough, he thought quickly. Not with Wurteh staring at him like he was the Christmas turkey. Somehow he had to find a way to be much less appetizing.

Chota stepped into the firelight. He was plainly an angry and determined combatant. With great flair he raised both hands skyward, then pivoted to face the four corners of the earth, each in turn. He crossed his arms over his chest and began speaking in his Cherokee tongue in a voice as dramatic as the most skilled Thespian.

At Derek's elbow, the translator spoke in English as the story unfolded.

"The earth is a great island floating in a sea of water. It is suspended at each of the four points by a cord hanging from the sky vault, which is solid rock. When all was water, the animals lived beyond the arch above in Galun lati, but they needed more room. At last, Beaver's Grandchild, the little Water Beetle, offered to go see what was below the water. It dived to the bottom and came up with soft mud, which began to grow and spread until it became the island we call the earth. It was fastened to the sky, but no one remembers who did this."

Pausing, Chota bowed toward Wurteh, who was clearly impressed. Then he went on. "The Great Buzzard made the mountains by roughing up the earth when it was still soft and wet. Wherever his giant wings struck the earth, there was made a valley, and where they turned up, there was a mountain."

Derek studied Wurteh. Yes, she was caught up in the story, her attention fixed on Chota. This was a hopeful sign.

Chota's voice rose. "The world was cold until the thunders who lived in Galun lati sent their lightning and brought fire into a tree. The raven tried to recover the fire from the tree and was scorched black. The eyes of Hooting Owl became ringed with ashes. There were many bad affects on animals, reptiles, and birds living there in Galun lati. But

175

the Water Spider spun a bowl for her back and caught one little coal of fire, and so brought back fire." Again he bowed to Wurteh, whose eyes were wide and glistening.

"That is the beginning," Chota said proudly. "I will tell more at some future time."

Derek's opinion of Chota was definitely heightened. Hell, the man could top Aesop, and he'd been clever enough to leave his audience in suspense and eager for more.

"Now it is Wall Done's turn," announced the brave. "You may speak in your native language and I will translate."

He had an idea. He prayed it would work as he stepped into the light and bowed to Wurteh, whose brow was now knitted in confusion. He felt Eden's eyes on him, but not for all the king's riches would he look at her and muddle his thinking.

"Here is my story," he began in English. "Before everything, there was a great king up above." He waited for the translation and saw Wurteh nod in approval. "This king saw only water below, and all was emptiness. So . . ." He put his hand over his chest. "He pulled out a bone from his side and said: 'From this rib bone, I will make a woman.'" After this translation, Wurteh no longer smiled.

He continued. "The woman wanted to create many more people, so the king allowed her to plant seeds in a huge garden." He made a large circle with his arms. "But her seeds would not grow until the king ordered the rain to fall. Only then did the seeds become men and women. All the new men and women were happy until the first woman decided to abandon the garden and take everyone away in her boat. She had become evil from eating a fig, you see, and she disobeyed the king." He noted Wurteh was frowning after this was translated.

"So the woman reached the middle of the sea and tilted the boat until all the new people drowned, with the exception of two strong men who then had to go and save all the animals."

Even the interpreter now looked confused. "Animals? What animals?" he asked.

Again Derek made a circle with his arms. "All the animals in the world."

The interpreter shook his head. "But you didn't have animals yet."

"Just repeat what I said," Derek insisted.

Wurteh was definitely annoyed. Did she find the story stupid? Offensive? His ploy must be working. He would move in for the kill. "As I said, the woman brought much evil to the world. She was helpless to do anything right without assistance from the king. The king made her a slave and taught all men that women must be ruled with a strong hand, especially when they become a wife. This worked much better. The plants flourished, the new people growing from the seeds were happy, the men were glad to be like kings, and the women were happy to be the men's slaves. So it is to this very day." He folded his arms across his chest and awaited the reaction.

Derek's prayers were answered when Tahchee quickly consulted with his grim-faced daughter, and then addressed him. "You *lose,* Wall Done. You are not a good storyteller. You have lied—and you have insulted Wurteh. She does not believe all women must be slaves, and she does not think your white man's king ordered such a thing. My daughter will wed Chota. You *must* take the white woman, Eden Palmer—if she will have you. If she does not want you, you will die. Tahchee has spoken."

Chota and Wurteh's marriage ceremony took place at once; it was extraordinarily simple. The couple exchanged gifts and left the town house to join in the feasting outside.

Then Derek was prodded to stand beside Eden and Laykee, in front of the chief.

Tahchee surveyed the bride and groom with an air of indifference. "Eden Palmer," he said, "I heard your sad story of the blind child and I have provided herbs to help her, is that not so?"

"Yes, Chief Tahchee. I do appreciate your kindness. The herbs are with Laykee and will be taken to the child's village."

"Laykee will travel with you and Wall Done tomorrow, after the dancing and feasting are finished. It is important you have a husband, but I will not force you to become this man's wife."

Derek looked at her, but to his surprise, she avoided him and kept her eyes on the chief.

At last she spoke. "What if I *decline* to marry him? What if I don't wish to be his—slave?"

"That is your choice—to be made freely like all Cherokee women. We do not believe women must be slaves like Wall Done has said."

"If I refuse to marry him, I request his freedom so he can return to his home."

"No. He must leave here as your husband, Eden Palmer. I can feel very sorry for you if you marry him, so you do not have to do that, after all. But if you do not, he will die at the stake, which is a good end for him, in my mind."

She barely blinked. Slowly, she turned to look up at him. Was that a hint of teasing in her eyes? She studied him at length, as if trying to decide whether to purchase a chicken at the market.

Almost imperceptibly, he shrugged his shoulders. "Take your time," he said under his breath. "I only face being burned alive." He watched her lashes flicker as she suppressed a smile.

"I will marry him," she announced with no enthusiasm whatever. "He might prove useful, though certainly not as a storyteller."

"Very well," Tahchee agreed. "Since you and he have no gifts to exchange, you can say the words, then spend the night in the bride's lodge. At dawn tomorrow you are both free to go. But if Wall Done spies again on the maidens, he will be put to death in a most cruel manner."

Derek rolled his eyes, but remained silent.

"What words are necessary, Chief Tahchee?" asked Eden.

"You say—'I give you corn.'"

"I give you corn," she muttered, not even glancing his way.

"Now, he must say—'I bring you meat.'"

"I bring you meat," he said with a perfectly straight face.

Tahchee waved his hand. "Now you are married. The lady will go with the maidens to her bridal lodge. Wall Done will go with the men to bathe in the river—then he will be allowed to join his bride."

At sunset bonfires blazed and the dancing began in earnest. Derek's patience was at the breaking point when several warriors conducted him to the river just beyond the town. He was more than happy to bathe in the cool shallow stream, a bridegroom's traditional cleansing, he learned from the few words of broken English. He was given a loincloth, beaded vest, moccasins, and a thong to tie around his forehead. Feeling foolish, he was grateful his Swiss countrymen couldn't see his humiliation at the hands of American "savages."

At last, well after midnight, Chota was blessed by the shaman Oowatie and the group snaked out of the lodge to the beat of a single muffled drum. Derek received no blessing, but was marched along to a nearby hut and handed a torch.

Oowatie was smiling when he pushed open the door and motioned for Derek to enter.

"I'd like my own breeches and boots," Derek demanded. "And untie my hands," he said to Oowatie.

"Not now, Wall Done. You will have your old clothing returned by sunrise—here, outside the door when the latch is released. Also, those of your wife."

"Very well, but at least release my bonds."

"No. She will do that." Ootawie grinned and added, "Maybe."

"I see. In other words, I'm to be delivered to my bride like a trussed-up ram," he grumbled.

"She is a woman. She has great power. She will decide." Another condescending grin.

"You people have strange ideas. So be it. Farewell, Ootawie. Please accept my deepest thanks for supplying herbs to help my little girl. Oh—by the way, where is Laykee?"

"She wait. Till sunrise. Go in now. We must take Chota to his bride."

Holding the torch in both hands, Derek entered the dark hut. The door was latched behind him.

He had to stoop until he moved to the center of the small circular room, where he had enough head room to stand. As far as he could tell, the place was deserted.

"Dammit," he cursed, and held the torch high to gaze around the enclosure. Where the hell was Eden? Swinging back to the door, he shouted at the sound of the retreating drumbeat, but received no response.

He was considering bludgeoning the crude wooden door when he heard movement behind him.

"Derek?"

At the sound of Eden's muffled voice, he spun around and raised the torch.

"Derek . . ."

She was in here someplace—but where? The torch cast dancing shadows around the unfurnished hut. Lowering his gaze, he saw an assortment of clay pots sitting near the central fireplace, laid with branches but as yet unlit, and a distinctive lump beneath one of the bear rugs in the far corner.

The lump moved. It spoke. "Derek, I'm here."

He crossed to the speaking rug. "Eden . . . for Christ's sake, are you all right?"

180

"I'm fine." A sob.

"Eden—"

"I thought you weren't coming," came the ragged voice.

"What are you doing under there? Are you sure you're not hurt?"

"Yes, but—"

He knelt beside the bulging furry rug. "What is it, sweetheart? Let me see you."

Small fingers appeared at the edge of the skins, then moist curls, then a damp forehead, limpid eyes, and a delicate nose. "I don't have—"

"What did you say, *schatze?*"

Her pink-rimmed eyes gazed up at him, widened, then were swiftly covered by the rug.

"Eden, look at me," he ordered, as if speaking to a wayward child. "I realize I look absurd in this garb, but I had no choice in the matter. Now, tell me what's wrong." She seemed all right, and his patience was fraying. It had been a godawful day; he'd been beaten by hostiles, been forced to play the complete fool, and robbed of his clothes and his dignity. Now, the girl he adored was hiding under a bearskin and refusing to communicate.

She folded down the rug from her face. "Your attire is very odd, but at least you're a man. I'm a woman and—I have only the same tiny scrap over my body. I don't even have a vest. Please put out the torch."

He chuckled and sat beside her. "Is that all that's wrong? After all we've been through, after your courageous stand on my behalf, after being captives of dangerous hostiles, you're worried about maidenly modesty? You may recall, sweetheart, I've beheld your lovely body once before. And sooner or later you'll have to come out from under that rug."

Her cheeks flamed. *"Later,* sir. Tomorrow. Laykee said my clothes would be left outside at dawn. She promised."

Looking down at the pretty little face with its mouth turned into a pout, eyelashes shimmering on pale cheeks, her hair a tangled halo around her head, he felt an over-whelming rush of tenderness. The last of his defensive wall so carefully constructed over the years since Heidi's death crumbled into dust.

Moving away, he laid the torch on the central fire until it crackled into life. He crawled to the pots and found a jug of water, tilted it to his lips and drank deeply. Over the edge of the jug he saw her open her eyes and twist her head to look at him.

She studied him. "Your hands are tied," she said softly.

"I can manage," he answered, putting down the jug. "Here is a basket of strawberries," he tempted her. "When have you last eaten?"

"I don't remember."

"I'll make you an offer. If you'll come over here by the fire and untie my hands, I'll give you all the sweet plump strawberries you can eat."

She sat up while gripping the bearskin over her breast.

"You'll need nourishment before we leave in the morning," he said. "I hope to be out of here at the crack of dawn."

A silence followed, broken only by the wind rustling the oak leaves outside the hut and the call of an owl on its nightly hunt.

Finally she said, "You could *hand* me something to eat."

He arched his eyebrows. "Oh? I'm the one who's bound. Why don't you come over here and help yourself."

"Because we are *not* married. You lit the fire against my wishes—and I am practically naked."

"Oh, that." He took another bite and chewed thoroughly. "Hm. I could close my eyes, I suppose."

"I know what you're doing, Derek. You're getting even because I took my time about deciding to marry you. Besides, I don't trust you."

"Rightly so." He put down the berry and looked at her. Her face was pale and her eyes swollen. She must have truly been worried about him. But they were safe now, and perhaps a little friendly teasing would ease the tension he felt between them. "On the other hand, you may have to trust me. Despite what you say, I *am* your husband." Hearing her catch her breath, he pursed his lips to hide a smile.

"We're not married, and you know it!"

"I thought we exchanged gifts, verbal ones anyway. The holy man blessed us, and we've certainly been the cause of lengthy celebration—along with the princess and her groom, of course."

"But I'm a Christian—and so are you."

"True, but does that mean our vows were false?"

"But we didn't say anything—just traded nonexistent corn and meat. I don't call that vows."

"There are quite a few souls just outside who would disagree with you."

She smoothed back her hair. Her rug slipped a bit, revealing a smooth shoulder and the upper swelling of one creamy breast. "We're Christians in a pagan land," she said righteously. "Besides, after hearing your story today, I think Wurteh made the right choice."

"Oh really? Then you're disappointed you're not in Chota's honeymoon lodge tonight?"

"Oh no, I didn't mean that." He could see she was upset and flustered. She folded her arms over her breasts and held the rug firmly in place. "I'm referring to that part about a wife being a slave. It's odd because . . ."

"Yes?"

"Because I said almost the same thing once to Laykee."

"Really? You said a woman should be a slave to her husband?"

"Of course not. But she usually *is* a slave—regardless of how nicely she's treated. When I said that to Laykee, I was thinking about what it would be like to be married to Landon."

The man's name speared him, destroying his teasing

183

mood in a heartbeat. "Yes, your fiancé. Forgive me, I'd forgotten your betrothal."

"I—forget it, too. More often than not. Derek, I will be honest with you."

"I would appreciate that."

"I have made it perfectly plain to Landon that I will not marry him."

He absorbed this for a moment. It was what he'd prayed for, but did this mean the engagement was officially ended? "I'm glad to hear that—more than glad." He studied her as she sat half concealed by the bearskin. She was irresistible. "I'm sorry, Eden. You've had a bad time these past few hours." He scooted near her, held out his bound wrists. "Untie me and you may have all the strawberries you want. No more bargains."

She began working on the ropes binding his wrists.

To please her, he closed his eyes until he felt moisture on his hands and heard a sniffle.

Cracking one eye, he peaked down at her. She was bent over his wrists, tugging at the ropes. Her hair tumbled over her bare shoulders and back, curling along her spine. Just below her narrow waist, a thong held a square of white leather that barely concealed her bottom. The soft swell of her hips was exposed at either side. He could see she was trembling; her words seemed washed with tears.

"I've nearly got it loose. One bit more." She sniffled again.

The ropes gave way.

She raised a tearstained face to gaze up at him. One arm lay over her bare breasts; one hand was knotted in her lap. She whispered, "I was so frightened tonight, Derek. I thought they'd killed you after all, and it was my fault for saying what I did about not wanting to be your slave. Wurteh hated your story. So did everyone else."

He used his thumb to gently wipe her cheeks. He was painfully aware of the pressure in his groin, and prayed she couldn't see what was happening. "And you hated it, too?" His voice was husky, not nearly as casual as he'd hoped.

"I thought it was brilliant. Horrible and blasphemous, of course, but brilliant."

Cupping her chin between thumb and forefinger, he leaned to kiss her. He hadn't planned to, but to resist would have taken more strength than any man possessed. He couldn't contain the desire driving through him.

To his surprise, she rose to her knees and slipped her hands behind his neck, taking his kiss with sudden fierceness, parting her lips, clinging to him, the tips of her breasts brushing against his bare chest in sweet abandon.

"Eden, my darling girl," he murmured, holding her close, feeling her shaking, her broken sobs, her tears. "You're safe now, little one, and so am I." He stroked her hair, the curve of her back, her delicate neck. He was sure these past hours had drained her of her strength, leaving her vulnerable and frightened. Her youth and lack of worldliness had replaced her usual abundance of spirit and fortitude.

She looked up at him with adoration shining from her eyes.

She might not be his slave, but tonight he was hers.

❦ 19 ❦

Derek tipped Eden's chin and gave her a light peck on her lips. "I'll stoke the fire and get the strawberries."

She nodded gratefully. "I'm sorry I've been such a weakling," she murmured as he bent over the fire. "I'm better now."

Carrying a pot of berries, he scooted back to her. "You're entitled to a few tears, Eden. It's been a strange and difficult time."

His gentle words caused more tears to spill from her eyes. "Shh, hush now. It's over." He moved near and encircled her shoulders and drew her into his lap. When she settled against him, he said as if to a child, "I'll tell you a secret—if you'll promise not to ridicule me."

"Ridicule you? Of course not."

"I was more than frightened yesterday; I was on the verge of panic."

She looked at him in surprise. "You? That's hard to believe. You appeared quite calm during the whole ordeal."

"I was angry and humiliated until they threatened me with burning. But then my blood ran cold. I don't fear death, but to die by fire, after what happened to my family in Neuchâtel—it sends horror to the depths of my soul."

Eden touched his cheek with her fingertips. "I know what this admission has cost you, how hard it must be to face

186

those terrible visions from your past. You made that effort so that I wouldn't be ashamed of my own lack of courage. I appreciate that, Derek, more than I can say."

She slipped a hand around his neck and snuggled into his chest. He was pleased her shyness had disappeared. Here in the firelight she was exquisite, her pale skin opalescent, her breasts soft and inviting, with traces of blue vein beneath the graceful spread of her fingers.

"I've never known such a woman," he whispered with his lips brushing her temple. "Part child, part firebrand, wise and delightfully naive. You've given me renewed life, as surely as you've given life to your indigo, and hope to Anna. I love you, Eden."

He put his hand under her chin and raised her face to his. He covered her lips and kissed her, demanding, forceful, pressing her lips apart, sweet-tasting, exploring. His tongue found its way, as a hundred tiny fires ignited within him, fires he knew could consume him if left unchecked.

He eased her to the rug. When the kiss ended, she studied him through heavy lids; he saw her open desire, her willingness to go further, her own awakened passion ready for him.

"And I love you," she whispered on the wings of a sigh.

Leaning near, he stretched his hand wide and captured both tips of her breasts, one beneath his thumb, the other with his little finger. His lips touched an earlobe, then trailed downward until he suckled a rosy nipple and moved slowly to the valley between her pliant mounds.

His need spiraling, he stretched out full-length beside her and pulled her close. "I wish our wedding today had been real," he murmured. "Binding and forever. You remind me of a flower in my homeland, the edelweiss, pale and lovely and open to love." Despite the growing pressure he felt, he allowed himself the pleasure of beholding her beauty, revealed to him unashamed, a woman who had given him such priceless gifts, first her love, then her lovely body and, just as important, her trust.

Passion overcame thought. He quickly untied her breechcloth and moved it aside. While bending to kiss the rise of her stomach, he slipped one knee between her legs and parted her, opening her to him as her arms encircled his back. He throbbed in response to her touch, his body eager to search out and claim the center of her secret place.

Slowly, slowly, he reminded himself. He wanted her to have as much pleasure as he could give. He lifted her hand and kissed her palm, then used his tongue to moisten her fingertips. His lips found her wrist, then the inside of her elbow. Her sighs told him her body was responding to his caress.

Trapping her hands at her sides, he lowered his chest just above her, then rested lightly against her, massaging her breasts with a slow rotation, feeling her writhe in growing passion, her eyes closed now, her breath coming in quick gasps as her desire flamed.

His fingers explored her feathery softness. She was ready, eager, moist. He held back, lingering at the waiting entrance, hesitating, exploring, stroking her until she cried out for him to claim her.

Her fingers dug into his shoulders. Sweat dotted his brow, a few drops falling to her breasts. He clenched his teeth in an effort to go slowly.

Waiting was no longer possible. He wrapped one arm beneath her waist and lifted her to deepen his possession. He groaned and thought he heard her matching sound. Her head was laid back, her hair a pale cloud floating as she moved in perfect rhythm with him. She had learned how to magnify pleasure for both of them with her own eager response. Her lashes fluttered on her flushed cheeks, her lips open, damp with longing.

He arched his back, keeping his hands on her hips and possessing her deeply. No longer could he control the spasms of his ecstasy. She held him in a living vise as they moved in tandem toward fulfillment, climax, her raging passion meeting his on every level.

At the moment of release, Eden cried out, her body trembling, intense as he gripped her in the most profound of life's natural joys—satisfying, beautiful, the ultimate union of two of God's divine creatures.

Exhausted, gasping, he leaned on his palms and trailed kisses from her throat, across her shimmering breasts and then to her welcoming lips.

Without leaving her, he carefully rolled to his back, carrying her to lie along his body, her head resting over his heart, her hair fanning across his chest, her slender hips cradled between his thighs. Never had he known such utter contentment, such unsurpassed happiness, such inner peace.

It was a while before they parted.

Together they lay back on the fur. Holding her against him, Derek softly kissed her cheeks and each closed eyelid.

Beginning to doze, she turned her face upward and lightly kissed his chin. "I love you, Derek Walden—now and always."

His lips brushed the tip of her nose, trailed her cheek and touched her mouth. "I love you, little one." After a pause he said, "You didn't eat any strawberries." He waited for a response, then realized she was asleep. He held her close as the fire died, leaving an afterglow of light and shadow on the curved structure around them. He loved her—and for the first time felt humbled by another human being. She was more than he deserved. But God, how could he live without her? There were problems to solve, especially the ownership of Palmer Oaks, but if she would have him, he would make her his wife as soon as possible. From this time forward, every night without her in his arms would be a night lost to longing.

Just before dawn he roused her by bringing her the dress

and undergarments that had been left outside the door. "We're free to go," he said gently.

Awake at once, Eden took the clothing.

"I'll change outside," he offered.

"You have new clothes?"

"Breeches. The Indian vest will do for a shirt. I guess my own clothes were past salvaging."

She threw off the bearskin. "Turn your back."

Smiling at her sudden modesty, he obeyed. "Please hurry, sweetheart. We don't want to risk our Cherokee friends changing their minds." He ducked out of the hut, leaving her to dress.

Eden needed no further prodding. It felt good to slip into her own clothes, though they were dreadfully wrinkled. At least they had been washed and smelled of soap and sunshine. Before leaving, she glanced around the hut. The central fire was cold now, only black embers on the ground. The pot of strawberries had been dumped over and the berries were scattered and crushed. She wanted to remember the Cherokee lodge where she had truly been a warrior's bride. Whatever the future held, she would treasure last night and the joy of her fulfillment as long as she lived.

The ride home was swift and silent. Laykee wasn't ordinarily inclined to conversation, and today kept her thoughts to herself.

Eden rode astride in front of Derek, his arm wrapped protectively around her waist. Her mind was refreshed and her thoughts churning. The entire experience in Congarees was like a dream. Reality was rushing toward her with every beat of the horse's hooves.

They rode past Henry Poinsett's stately mansion, where ochre smoke spiraled from several chimneys in the first pink glow of early morning. The roosters' crowing drifted from the coops beyond the stables.

With the horses holding a steady canter, they covered the

last mile to Palmer Oaks. Eden saw no sign of alarm as they approached. Smoke rose above the servant's houses. Already several hands were headed toward the indigo fields. They waved a welcome as she rode toward the house. Joseph and his people would assume her trip to Laykee's village had been safely completed. Obviously there was no further concern of Indian attack in the area.

Arriving at the back veranda, she allowed Derek to assist her to dismount. Before he left the saddle, she spoke to him for the first time since they'd left Congarees. "Keep my mare for now. You can return her whenever it's convenient."

But he swung to the ground. "It's a short walk to Waldenburg. If I arrive on your animal, it could raise questions."

Questions? She realized she hadn't concerned herself with what he would tell his settlers about his adventures in Congarees. "Go along, Laykee," she said to the woman, who waited nearby. "Take both ponies to the barn and see that they're tended. I'll check the kitchen for anything that might serve as breakfast. Please come in, Derek. We'll have a cup of coffee."

Congarees seemed increasingly unreal as Eden led the way up the steps, across the porch, and entered the familiar back hall of the house. She felt Derek moving behind her, though the moccasins he wore made no sound on the oak floor.

The kitchen was shadowed and cool at this hour. She found matches and started a fire in the grate beneath the coffeepot.

Turning, she saw Derek filling the doorway, leaning against the frame. The sight was startling. Until now she hadn't been completely aware of the incongruous mixture of Swiss and Indian. Although Cherokee men were notable for their height, she wondered where they found breeches which so perfectly fit the baron's hips and long, well-formed legs.

The beaded ceremonial vest appeared out of place against the rippling gold of his flesh, the massive breadth of his shoulders, the suggestion of burnished hair in an hourglass pattern trailing from his chest into the waist of the snug deer hide. And his eyes—no full-blood native ever owned such a pair of azure-blue eyes. To complete the contrast, of course, was his hair, flowing loosely in yellow-gold strands along his cheeks and brushing his shoulders. Sometime since dawn, he'd discarded the leather headband. He did, however, have a distinctly primitive appearance, though more like a Viking than a Cherokee.

"I shouldn't stay," he said solemnly. "But I wanted to talk to you privately for a moment."

Swiftly, she crossed to him and held out her hands.

He grasped them, but she sensed he felt uneasy, either because of his peculiar attire or—uncertainty over what had transpired between them. Plainly, the intimacy of the honeymoon lodge no longer existed. "Of course. I know you're anxious about your people. What will you tell them?"

"I'd prefer to say as little as possible. It's not that I mind looking foolish myself, but I don't want to compromise your reputation. I'll say I searched for hostiles between here and the village, stayed there to witness their ceremonies, then returned home. If Laykee says nothing, I don't think our misadventure will be discovered."

Slowly Eden withdrew her hands. His plan was practical, necessary to prevent scandal, but must he approach it with such cool pragmatism? She wondered if he was already regretting his words of love spoken at a time of mind-drugging enchantment—in another world, another time, a faraway kingdom where Indians reigned in primitive splendor.

"Misadventure," she repeated woodenly. "Of course, you're right. In fact, we can pretend none of it ever happened." Eden turned back to the coffeepot to hide her disappointment. "It was really quite amusing when you consider it. A harmless episode—very funny." She threw him a false smile over her shoulder.

His silent scrutiny gave her no hint of his thoughts. She fumbled with the cups and saucers, thinking how unkempt she must look wearing clothes that appeared slept in, and with no chance to even run a comb through her hair since yesterday.

His voice held an almost imperceptible touch of aloofness when he said, "Thank you for the offer, but I must decline the coffee. I need to get to Waldenburg."

"Oh?" Her heart sinking further, she set down the cups and forced her expression into polite indifference. "Yes, I do understand."

"I hope you will come to the village next Saturday for the dedication of the town."

"Certainly. And thank you again for trying to help me—even if—"

"Eden." He rasped her name.

Something was bothering him. They had been so close last night, as close as two people could be. Her throat was thick with tears, but she refused to let them reach her eyes. She coughed and lifted her chin. "What I'm saying, Derek, is that we could forget the entire experience. Considering the circumstances, we were both carried away—well, just because we traded some corn and venison—"

He crossed the room in three quick strides. His arms went around her. One hand cupped the back of her head and his fingers meshed in her hair. His look was so solemn, so fierce, so laden with passion, his eyes blazing with blue heat, she felt shock waves race through every part of her body.

"You may forget what you like, Mistress Palmer. But I will never forget what we experienced yesterday. Whatever decisions are yet to be made, wherever the future takes us—for one night you were mine—and I meant every word I said." He crushed her along his length, lifting her to her toes until he claimed her mouth in a kiss of raging urgency. His tongue found its way between her lips, scattering her thoughts and sending liquid fire to engulf her senses.

Her legs turned to butter as she clung to his bare shoulders, her fingers clamped along the tense muscles. She willed the kiss to last throughout eternity as her own desires were released in waves of unrestrained ardor.

As swiftly as he'd embraced her, he ended the kiss and stepped back. "I love you. Remember that." His tone was ragged, almost harsh. "And remember that the Swiss are not frivolous with words. *Auf Wiedersehen*. I will see you again soon—with your permission, of course."

Speechless, her breath gone, she watched him pivot and walk with purposeful steps from the kitchen.

Her knees buckled and she sank onto the kitchen stool. Whatever else Derek Walden might be, he was a man of decisive action—a man with an inclination to take what he wanted—comfortable in the assumption his prize was eager to be won. Heaven help her, she found that quality as captivating as the mystery lurking behind his stunning indigo eyes.

∾ 20 ∾

Derek crossed the wooden bridge and made his way to his half-finished house as if returning from a stroll in the woods. Several early risers saw him from a distance, but no one made a fuss over his sudden reappearance or his odd clothing. He was grateful for a few minutes of peace to pull together his fractured nerves and get control of his mind and his emotions. He would have some explaining to do to Messenbaugh, but it was reassuring to see that life had returned to normal after the scare over the Indian uprising.

He must do some serious thinking. He had told Eden he loved her—it was absolutely true. He was not a man to play games with words, especially about this most powerful of emotions. But did she believe him? She had certainly given him her love, her trust, at Congarees. But in the cool light of dawn, their experience in the Indian lodge took on an unreal quality. The truth was, they had problems to face. And he was uncertain about the outcome.

Inside his small cottage he shed his vest and removed the moccasins. Comfortable things, but hardly suitable for the leader of his straitlaced Protestants.

While dressing, he mulled over the problem with Landon Palmer. He was convinced Eden didn't love Palmer and would never marry him. Why was the man being so difficult? Any gentleman would accept the rejection, heartbreaking as it might be, and bow out of the picture without upsetting the lady and making a fool of himself in the process. He'd only met Palmer once, at Poinsett's gathering, but he'd taken an instant dislike to him. Landon Palmer was overtly arrogant, and plainly prejudiced against the Swiss newcomers. Not only that, he had a reputation in Charles Town as a roué, with an eye for the ladies, especially an actress from the newly formed theater. Derek himself had seen Palmer openly flirt with several women at the party while claiming to be engaged to Eden.

Derek considered another complication, one he'd never encountered in his life. He was practically destitute. He couldn't help comparing this rustic, simple cottage with the magnificent forty-room castle of his youth. That castle was now a burned-out shell and belonged to the past. He had been prepared to live austerely for years, but now he wished for riches to lay at Eden's feet.

He had few possessions of any value. All that was left of his family heirlooms were the two rings. He picked up the velvet box from the dresser and opened it. One ring was massive, emblazoned with the baronial arms of Walden— three onyx lions with ruby eyes on a shield of solid gold— the other was a smaller lady's version bearing the same crest. Everything else had been destroyed in the fire or sold to raise money for the immigrants. He had not expected to love again after Heidi, but if by chance he decided to wed, he had assumed his choice would be one of his Swiss settlers who would understand his position. To lose his heart to a lady of property, a woman with a fine home and with important social connections in the town—it was a twist of fate he'd never anticipated. He remembered how she had tossed her head the day they'd met and said, "Miss Eden Wentworth Palmer, of the Carolina Palmers." She was certainly no snob, but all he had was a half-finished shack, a patch of garden, a close-knit community that might resent their leader marrying a foreigner—and a future dependent on hard work, the whims of nature, and endless sacrifice. Hell, she'd just been through all that in the creating of Palmer Oaks. He couldn't carry her across the Ashley and expect her to start over. If they married, she would bring her plantation to the union—while he had little more than the clothes on his back. All he could offer was his undying love—and potential. True, it was thirty thousand acres of *prime* potential, but it would be years before he could provide a home equal to the one she already owned.

Eden's husband, whomever she chose, would take possession of her property according to the law of the English colony. She had made it more than plain that she intended to own her property and never relinquish the title. She would have to when she married, of course, and this was where Landon Palmer had the upper hand. Palmer was her cousin; to sign over the deed to him would be keeping her home in the family. Derek didn't blame Eden for wanting to hold on to her land, but it complicated the hell out of his suit for her hand in marriage. She had accused him once of coveting Palmer Oaks. How could he convince her he desired only the *mistress* of Palmer Oaks, and would marry her even if she were an orphan from the alleys of London? In fact, things would be much simpler if she were.

Two days after her return from Congarees, with Indian summer holding sway over the land, Eden received a note from Derek and the settlers of Waldenburg inviting her to attend the celebration of giving thanks and feasting at Waldenburg—an all-day party with the highlight to be the formal dedication of the town, the blessing of the cornerstone of the church, and the joyful reunion of families who were moving into their newly built homes surrounding the central commons.

For several weeks she had seen wagons and boats laden with household goods and supplies for winter arriving at the dock at Waldenburg. She was eager to share in their excitement—and more than eager to see Derek again.

Wearing a rosy chintz dress with ruffles at the elbow, and a perky straw bonnet tied with a pink ribbon, Eden rode her mare across the wooden bridge adjoining the two properties. She was greeted by a welcoming committee of several men and women, and guided to the commons, where mandolins and fiddles and flutes played a lively tune, and a feast was laid out under the shade of immense oaks and cottonwood trees. Folk dances were under way on the wooden platform set up near the meeting house.

Within minutes she spotted Derek. He was dressed in a grenadier green suit, traditional of his Swiss homeland, and had just finished dancing a polka with Katya Mueller. Katya was looking up at him, catching her breath and laughing with delight. A tug of jealousy nibbled at Eden's heart, but she suppressed it quickly, reminding herself of all she had shared with the baron of Waldenburg.

He saw her across the crowd and headed her way.

She watched his approach—her heartbeat wildly out of control. Baron von Walden looked every inch a noble lord, handsome as a conquering hero ought to be. A smile played on his lips—and Katya Mueller continued to grasp his arm.

He bowed and doffed his hat. Katya was forced to release his arm and smile a welcome, a smile which was blatantly artificial.

"Welcome to Waldenburg," said Derek. "We're honored to have you join us."

"I wouldn't have missed it," Eden said brightly. "Our lands adjoin, after all, and we share the Ashley; our futures are intertwined." It was a speech she had planned well in advance. "I've brought a gift in my saddlebag. It's for your new church."

"Then if Katya will excuse us, we'll get it at once." He offered his hand.

As she took it, he turned to Katya, whose smile had

disappeared. "I'll see you after the ceremony, dear," he said firmly. Despite Katya's obvious annoyance, the dismissal had been final.

Together, Eden and Derek crossed the commons toward her horse, tethered near the stable.

"You look lovely, Eden," he said with a glance in her direction.

"Thank you, but I'm sure you exaggerate."

"You must learn I always say exactly what I mean."

She shifted her eyes and noticed his were intense, but friendly. "Then I stand corrected. I *will* try to remember." As always, his touch sent sparks along her spine. And his words were titillating. Did he refer to his recent declaration of love? It seemed likely, and that thought sent her head reeling.

Reaching into her saddlebag, she removed a package and handed it to him.

As he unwrapped it, she noticed again the impressive ring he displayed on his right hand. Today he was a baron, after all. No one would deny it.

From the wrapping he withdrew a cross made of carved oak and polished to metallic fineness. Its base was made of cherrywood decorated with shells with centers of mother-of-pearl.

"It's magnificent," he said, obviously touched.

"My stepfather made it for our chapel when I was a child. The wood came from trees on our land, the shells from the seacoast above Charles Town. It symbolized for him the most important gifts of our new home—from land and sea. It's a humble gift, not of great value, but I hope it will bring blessings and luck to Waldenburg."

As she made her little speech, she could see he was moved, and also that he was not likely to express his deepest feelings. It didn't matter. She felt his pleasure and appreciation reaching out to her.

He lifted her fingers to his lips, then continued to hold her hand. "My dear Eden, let me be the first of the Swiss colonists to say thank you, for the cross and for being our friend." His eyes were cobalt as she gazed up at him. Nothing would have pleased her more than to embrace him, but that wasn't possible standing here in plain sight of the villagers. She had felt more than one pair of eyes on them since they'd walked toward the stable.

Instead, she retrieved her hand and said, "Your people idolize you."

"I hope they'll soon forget I was their liege lord and think of me as simply Mr. Walden, a settler and a farmer, the same as they are."

"They shouldn't forget what you've done, Derek. You risked your life and sacrificed everything for them."

"Call it noblesse oblige—my duty, my obligation, and my pleasure. It's a burden to me that some of my people still think of me as "Lord"—as some heroic figure who can do no wrong."

"Like Moses—or William Tell?"

He smiled at her. "When one is very high upon a pedestal, perfection is assumed. I've left the pedestal—and am far from perfect."

She might have argued that point, but he led her back toward the commons, where speeches and prayers were about to begin, and seated her on the front row of observers. Her heart was so full of love, she only half listened to the succession of speakers, the minister, the comments from the village hierarchy, and the hymns sung by the children's twenty-voice choir. She was especially pleased to see Anna Schaefer, dressed in a white pinafore, performing in the front row of the chorus. But she found it impossible to concentrate when her mind was filled with Derek Walden.

She paid closer attention when a city elder awarded Derek special acclaim. She listened, but her mind was drugged by his presence, his proud bearing, his grace, his rugged features. Could such a man truly love her? If so, nothing would prevent her from finding her way into his arms, becoming his wife if he so wished. Whatever problems might arise, they could weather them together.

At the close of his modest remarks to the people he'd once ruled as lord, Derek held up the cross and explained the gift to the audience.

Eden's face flushed. She was acknowledging the settlers' applause when she felt a hand on her shoulder—masculine, cool, and possessive. Startled, she looked up into the face of Landon Palmer.

The shock of seeing him turned her thoughts into chaos. Had he been invited today? She had heard that Henri Poinsett had received an invitation, but was leaving for England and unable to attend. Landon could have considered himself included in the general invitation to the townspeople of Charles Town issued in appreciation for their hospitality these past months. Not that he had lifted a finger to help them. In fact, only a few of the city folks were here.

She tried to smile politely, but knew her effort was less than convincing. He squeezed her arm and took up a stance beside her chair. She wondered how he could feel comfortable in his elegant satin suit and full powdered wig here in the outdoor freshness, among the plainly dressed people from Europe. Folding her hands in her lap, she looked hesitatingly at Derek. With every passing second she grew more annoyed and embarrassed.

Derek was addressing the gathering, but she was certain the tone of his voice had changed from relaxed pleasure to a distinct hint of tension. Did anyone else notice how he was affected? She wished frantically that Landon would at least remove his heavy hand, but he kept it firmly in place. That he was staking his claim must be apparent to everyone, most especially to Derek Walden.

Landon leaned down and slipped his arm around her shoulder. How could he make such a display of possessiveness—here in front of everyone, and in the middle of Derek's speech? Suddenly it occurred to her that was exactly what he had in mind—to prove to everyone that he *did* possess her, that he would barge into their celebration to prove it to everyone.

Anger swept over her, white-hot and uncontrollable. It was all she could do to keep her seat until Derek was finished speaking, then she jumped up and walked briskly toward a quiet spot under the trees. Landon followed her closely, as she knew he would.

She whirled to face him. "You were extremely rude to cause a scene during Mr. Walden's speech."

His smirk told her he couldn't care less.

"What do you want, Landon?"

"I want you to leave with me. Immediately."

"I will not. You can leave or stay—but I'm not leaving the party."

His smirk turned into heavy annoyance. "I have told you I consider us betrothed. You shouldn't be attending social affairs without me. You didn't bother to see if I was invited and would act as your escort."

"It never crossed my mind," she snapped. *"I* was invited. These people are my neighbors. I'll come here anytime I please."

"They are immigrants, nothing but poor farmers and common shopkeepers—without even their shops as assets. You are a Palmer, with important family connections in England, the daughter of my dearly departed uncle. I consider it my duty to save you from romantic fantasies."

"You have no obligations whatever to me, sir. I manage Palmer Oaks and I can take care of myself."

"You think you know everything, cousin. Hasn't it occurred to you that your devoted baron is a fortune hunter? He could live here in a hut—or he could marry you and *own* Palmer Oaks Plantation."

She wanted to strangle him. What a pompous fool he was.

Of course she had considered that possibility at first. But now she was sure Derek loved her. She refused to believe otherwise. With great effort she controlled her voice. "Listen to me, Landon. I am not leaving the celebration. I will, however, agree to see you in Charles Town. Tomorrow, if that's convenient. We absolutely must settle this matter of our engagement."

His face relaxed. "Very well. I suppose no harm will come to you in the shadow of your own home across the river. I'll be in my office tomorrow. What time will you arrive?"

"I don't know. Hopefully late morning. As you know, I'm extremely busy with the indigo."

"Not too busy to waste time with these foreigners. Calm yourself, my dear, I'm leaving." His lip curled in disdain. "Give my congratulations to the Germans. They have stolen by some means the best and largest land grant in the region, land that should have gone to Englishmen." He turned on his heels and marched to his carriage.

Shaking with fury, she walked back toward the commons.

Derek soon gained her side. His expression was veiled and distant. "Your cousin left without you, it appears. Or must I still consider him your fiancé?"

"I apologize for Landon."

"I hope he didn't upset you."

She strolled beside him as he avoided the crowd and walked toward the cottages. "Landon is a difficult man. But soon I expect to put him out of my life—except for the courtesy due a family member."

"I'm very glad to hear it."

They stopped in front of a log house. "I'm furious with him," Eden said fiercely. "He came here only to humiliate me. I'm going to Charles Town tomorrow to end my engagement."

She saw satisfaction pass behind Derek's steel-blue eyes. "Then I'm glad he came," he said. "Though he stirred things up a bit at the dedication."

"I was mortified. Your people must think I'm dreadful."

He stroked her sleeve. "They will learn to love you—as I do. And they are deeply touched by your gift of the cross."

She dwelled on his words—he loved her. She wanted to believe him, more than anything in the world. But he had lied once before, or rather, hidden the truth about his survey including her land. And he had everything to gain by marrying her—not just an adoring wife, but the title to Palmer Oaks. Which one was most important to him? Or was it all one tidy package? Worse, how would she know unless she married him, and then it would be too late if she made a mistake.

"What's wrong, Eden?"

Damn his perception. He always had the power to see through to her thoughts, to her heart. "Nothing. I'm just upset about Landon's behavior."

"I do love you, my darling. I pray I've regained your trust."

How could she resist him? Her doubts fled as she gazed into his eyes and let his words seep like balm into her soul.

"Wait here," he said. "I have a gift for you."

He stepped into his house and quickly returned.

Cupping her hand, he placed something hard and cool inside it. When Eden looked, she saw a ring, a smaller, exact duplicate of the one he was wearing. Stunned and thrilled, she looked up at him. "But—this is exquisite. I—don't know what to say."

"Say that you love me—that someday you will be my bride."

Biting her lips to stop their trembling, she stared at him. She felt he had just laid the world at her feet. She loved him, wanted him too much to let foolish doubts spoil her happiness. "Yes," she whispered. "Oh yes, I will marry you, Derek Walden. And I will make you a good wife, I do swear."

His arms encircled her as his lips claimed hers.

She wrapped her hands behind his neck and leaned into his hard body. She held back nothing, but opened her lips and gave herself up to the lightning of his touch, the thunder in her mind, the fire inside her soul.

After a time they parted and he smiled the smile that had entered her dreams night after night for months. "Should we make the announcement today? I can't think of a better occasion."

She wanted to with all her heart. But first she had one matter of honor to clear up. "Not yet, Derek. I wouldn't feel right to announce our engagement until I've spoken to Landon. I must make him understand, once and for all, that I won't marry him, that I belong to another."

Derek looked disappointed, but quickly recovered. "Soon, my darling Eden. Soon."

∞ 21 ∞

Eden didn't arrive in Charles Town until nearly five o'clock. She had spent an exhausting day in the indigo fields, and then had taken time to bathe before her visit with Landon. Her fatigue was forgotten as she approached the office he kept in the center of town. She was ready to do battle, if necessary. She was not leaving here until he agreed to release her from her pledge to marry him. She would get it in writing so there would be no legal problems in the future.

His door was unlocked, so she entered and crossed the

marble entry to his private office. Looking inside, she found it deserted. How odd. Of course, she was much later arriving than she had planned. He might be taking a walk on such a nice afternoon—or maybe he had gone to tea. She removed her bonnet and took a chair. She would wait for him to return. She was sure he wouldn't leave his office unlocked overnight, and she didn't care how long she had to sit here; she would settle things with Landon before this day was over.

Muffled laughter from the adjoining suite caught her attention. So someone was here, after all. Without a second thought, she crossed to the door and opened it.

A woman screamed.

Landon jumped up from a chaise and tugged up his breeches.

Eden stared in disbelief.

"Eden—well, I do swear . . ." Landon found his voice as he buttoned his pants. His shirttail was only partially tucked into his belt, and his chest was exposed to view. His face was beet-red, but his expression was now amazingly composed. Behind him on the chaise, clutching her gaping bodice with both hands, knelt a disheveled girl, her cheeks bright pink beneath gaping eyes.

"I didn't mean any harm," the girl squeaked in the voice of a three-year-old. "I mean—Landon—we weren't re-ally—"

"Hush, Fanny," Landon snarled.

Still in shock, Eden looked from Landon to the girl, then back again at Landon. Collecting her wits, she put her hands on her hips and searched for words. She might have expected such behavior from Landon—but right here in his office?

The girl called Fanny had worked her arms into her sleeves and clambered off the chaise. Barefooted, her hair in shambles, she announced, "I'm Fanny Picket, an actress at the new theater. I'm not just anybody, you know. So—who are you?"

"Shut up, Fanny, and get dressed," Landon snorted.

Fanny scurried to the Chinese screen in one corner and ducked behind it.

"Now Eden," Landon began, "you can't blame me—"

"Hold your tongue, Mr. Palmer. I'll have my say and then I'm leaving." She discovered that suddenly words came glibly. She was neither distraught nor heartbroken, but disgusted to the tips of her toes.

"Please, my dear—"

"Don't address me in familiar terms—ever again. I have considered our betrothal ended for some time past, so your tryst means absolutely nothing as far as I'm concerned. Just acknowledge our engagement finished and I will go. Later I'll get your word in writing. If I see you in Charles Town in the future, which I suppose is unavoidable, I will be civil to keep tongues from wagging, but that's all."

To her astonishment, Landon crossed to her and took hold of her upper arms in a bruising grasp. "No, Eden. You can't dismiss me like a naughty child. I admit I was tempted beyond control by this whore."

"I'm not a whore!" Fanny screeched from behind the screen. "I had a lover, but only one, and we were to be married. Landon said he was engaged, but he said he would break it off, that you didn't want him anyway."

Glaring up at Landon, Eden wanted to slap the haughty look from his face. He had been raised with every advantage, never turned his hand at honest work, had a fine education and opportunity for a gentleman's style of living —but he was spoiled and egotistical, lazy and downright dishonest. "At least you guessed right about that, Fanny," she said, staring daggers at Landon.

"You don't mean that," Landon said, his fingers digging into her shoulders.

"Let me go," she said with a voice like granite. "How dare you!"

"I'll tell you why I dare, Eden Palmer. Because I will never release you from your promise made to your stepfather on his deathbed. Fanny is a tramp who means nothing to me."

"Landon!" cried Fanny.

He ignored her completely. "What does it matter if I have a romp with her? I'm not going to marry her."

"Landon!" Fanny howled again.

He went on, his grip tightening until Eden winced in pain. "She means nothing to me, do you understand that?"

"She's exactly what you deserve, cousin. Why *don't* you marry *her?*"

She felt his hands loosen slightly. Her insulting suggestion had made an impression.

She went on. "Consider what it would be like to have Fanny as your wife."

His eyes narrowed. "I won't have another man's used goods."

"Is that so?" Eden asked. She could taste disgust on her tongue.

"It's *you* I want, Eden Palmer. You're a woman to tame and treasure—a woman of virtue whom everyone in Charles Town respects and admires. There is power in respect, my dear girl—and you have Palmer Oaks. Someday it will be equal to Poinsett's plantation. Oh no, my lovely fiancée, I'll not lose you over a tumble with a mindless little vixen like Fanny."

Eden heard Fanny curse. She almost felt sorry for her. She must have been an easy mark for a man such as Landon. Eden glared at him. "Let me go, Landon. Our betrothal is ended."

He released her and yanked his coat from the back of a chair. "A betrothal is a serious matter, not easily broken, especially by just one of the two parties involved. I know you're upset, rightly so. No doubt you're jealous, as well. I apologize, but you were supposed to be here this morning. I insist we discuss it later when you've had time to think it through—and you'll realize I'm right." During this speech, he tucked in his shirttail and drew on his coat. "Good-bye, Eden. I won't see you out."

Without a backward glance, she marched from the room and slammed both doors behind her.

A headache unfurled behind her eyes and she felt slightly woozy. Jealous! What an egotistical boar. Would she never rid herself of that man? He seemed obsessed with her—or with obtaining her plantation. Well, she had done all she could for now. She would eat a bite at her town house and get a good night's rest. At first light tomorrow she must hurry home to begin the last preparations for the indigo harvest. The problem with Landon would have to wait.

Eden knelt in the pungent damp earth between the rows of six-foot-high indigo plants. It was getting dark and she was about to quit work for the day. She broke off one small bud and sniffed it, then rolled it between thumb and forefinger. Then she pressed it open and inspected the interior. Yes. Perfect. Less than a week and the plants would be in full bloom with orange-colored blossoms and ready for harvest. Just in time, thank heavens. Her best estimate was the last week in October for shipping to market. She would arrange for barges on that day. The barrels were stacked and waiting.

Laykee sauntered up behind her. "Miss Eden, there's a message from you. A young Swiss lad brought it."

She got up and brushed her hands, then took the note. It said, *Meet me right away at the indigo field at Waldenburg. Urgent.* She would have been pleased if the note had come from Derek. But she recognized the scrawl of Katya Mueller, identical to the two messages Katya had sent her on the boat. Katya's notes meant trouble, but Eden decided to answer the summons. Curiosity? Perhaps, but she couldn't resist going to see what Katya had up her sleeve.

She rode across the bridge at a canter and skirted the edge of the village. Luckily no one saw her in the ebbing twilight. She rode directly to the grove of trees where she had tied her mount the last time she'd seen the small field of indigo. This time she led her horse just inside so it wouldn't be seen. She asked herself why she was being so furtive, but she had no real answer. Only that where Katya was concerned, she felt it wise to exercise caution.

She entered the clearing and found Katya waiting. "Good evening, Katya," she said pleasantly. "I came right away."

"You knew *I* sent the note?"

"I recognized your handwriting."

"Then I'm surprised you came at all."

"I want to be your friend, Katya. I know you're hurt and angry over Derek's attentions to me, but sometimes these things happen and can't be helped."

"And sometimes they *can* be helped."

She tried to see Katya's expression, but it was growing dark. "What do you mean?"

"I mean I want you to know the truth. You'll be angry now, but you'll be glad later. You'll thank me, I know."

"And what is the truth?" she asked gently. She couldn't imagine what fibs Katya would come up with next.

"The truth is, Mistress Palmer—Derek doesn't love you at all. He never has. He loves me."

Eden sighed. She was sorry she'd come. If only Derek had found the courage to end Katya's obsession with him, regardless of how much pain it caused the young girl at the time. "I'm afraid you're mistaken, dear," she said with sympathy in her voice. "Derek does love me. We plan to marry before long."

"I'm not surprised he asked you. That was part of his plan."

"His plan?"

"You see, I know all about the survey map which includes Palmer Oaks. And I know you'll lose your land if you don't pay the king what you owe."

"You do?" Eden was appalled. Had Derek shared this most private information with Katya? Why would he do such a thing?

Katya answered the burning question. "Derek tells me everything—because he loves me. He doesn't want to break my heart, but he always puts Waldenburg first—even if he has to suffer."

"What are you saying?" Cold dread took hold of her.

"I'm saying that Derek believes you will bring in the indigo crop. And the only way he will own the plantation that was meant to be ours—is to marry you."

Her heart stopped. The suspicions, doubts, and fears that she had buried inside rose to choke off her breath. "No. He loves me. I have his ring." She tightened her hand around the ring he had given her just yesterday.

Katya laughed a mirthless laugh. "I know. He told me he had hooked you into his scheme. He had planned to marry you and move into your house." She lowered her voice. "He was heartbroken, naturally, because he would have to give me up. But I promised to wait—forever, if necessary. I promised to be here for him always—right across the Ashley."

"You're—lying." Her heart screamed a denial, but her mind told her it might be true.

Katya's tone became low-pitched and cutting. "But now Derek doesn't need to marry you to get your plantation."

"What do you mean?"

"I have more bad news for you."

What else could Katya say to tear out her heart?

"Look." Katya held up her lantern to spread light around the field.

Eden looked closely, then felt horror engulf her. The once

211

flourishing plants were brown and brittle—dead in their furrows.

"Oh my God. What happened?"

"Locusts!" Katya grinned at her, her pale beauty taking on a ghostly quality in the swaying light.

Eden sank to her knees and ran her hands through the dead plants. When she raised her palm, she saw two green locusts clawing across her flesh. She threw them down in disgust. It was true. A plague had destroyed Derek's young indigo.

It was her worst nightmare. She saw them now—the green insects lining the lithe stalks and munching away at the last of the succulent leaves. There would be no way to stop their invasion. Eden saw the large profits she had expected in the years ahead being eaten alive before her very eyes.

"Terrible, isn't it?" Katya snickered. "It means that Dr. Messenbaugh was right. Indigo will fail in the Carolinas. And more important to me—it means Derek will get Palmer Oaks when *your* crop is eaten."

Stunned, Eden rose to face Katya. The young girl's gloating look sickened her, but beyond her despair over the indigo, Eden's greatest pain was Derek's betrayal. He must have told Katya everything. She realized that she didn't hate Katya—it was *Derek* who had lied to her and broken her heart.

"I'm going now," Katya said. "It looks like I win after all."

"One question, Katya. Does Derek know about the locusts killing his crop?"

"Not yet. He's been in the forests all day with the men. But he'll find out by tomorrow. And then you can give back that ring, Mistress Palmer—and he can give it to me. Soon Derek and *I* will be living at Palmer Oaks." She walked from the clearing, leaving Eden alone in the dark—the most complete blackness she had ever experienced.

She was standing in the furrow, shocked and miserable,

when she heard someone approach. As a slice of moon lifted above the treetops, she saw Derek coming toward her. She wanted to run, hide, protect her heart from the pain she knew was coming. But it was too late.

"Eden? Is that you? I saw Katya running toward her house."

"Yes, Derek. I'm afraid I have bad news."

He hurried over and started to embrace her. "What's wrong? Did you see Landon? My God, I'll thrash the man if he continues to—"

"Not Landon," she said, avoiding him. "It's your indigo. Look." She reached down and scooped up a handful of soil, dead leaves, and a gorged locust.

"What the hell—"

"Locusts have eaten your crop. I expect the plague is only delayed by the river from arriving at Palmer Oaks."

"Jesus—you'll lose everything, Eden."

"No. I won't. I'll harvest tomorrow. It's only a few days early and I can still get this one crop to market."

"My darling, it's a severe blow to you," he said quietly. "It means the future of indigo in South Carolina is very uncertain." He started again to embrace her, but she pulled away. "I'll help you with your crop. I'll come tomorrow," he added, confused by her reaction.

"That won't be necessary."

"I would like to help."

"No, Derek. I'd rather not see you tomorrow. I'll be very busy—and I must do some serious thinking once I've sold the crop."

"Thinking? About what?"

"About us. Our future together." With a heart like lead, she slipped the ring from her finger and handed it to him. Thank heavens it was too dark to see his face, his eyes, his lips.

"Eden—why are you doing this? If you bring in your crop, we can marry as we planned."

"I love you, Derek, but I'm unsure of your true feelings toward me. I'm afraid you have betrayed my trust."

"I don't know what you're talking about. Forget the crop. Let the locusts have it. I don't know why you're so set on it anyway. You're driving yourself to exhaustion, taking risks with the lime—forget the damned indigo, and the payment to the Crown."

Her blood froze. "And lose Palmer Oaks—to the king— and thus to you? Is that what you're suggesting?"

"Hell, Eden, what difference does it make? I will own the plantation and it will belong to you, as my wife."

"You don't understand, do you? When, and *if,* I marry anyone, sir, I will come to my husband as a property owner. I'm not married yet, and I may decide never to marry. I may give Palmer Oaks to my husband as a wedding gift, as is his right, but I will never *lose* it by default."

"Damnation, Eden—you still don't trust me. Why can't I prove my love to you?"

"I believe I have the truth from Katya. So much has happened in such a short time. I'm tired and unsure of myself, and of you. Katya swears you love her—she knows about my debt to the Crown, and Landon swears you only want Palmer Oaks."

Abruptly, he wrapped one arm around her. A shard of moonlight highlighted his eyes, the bridge of his nose. He kissed her, smothering her mouth with almost cruel abandon. When he released her, he said harshly. "So it's Katya you believe. And Landon. Go home, Eden, and bring in your indigo. Marry Landon, if he's your choice. But I swear to you—no one will ever love you as much as I do."

He stalked out of the clearing and disappeared through the trees.

She stood there shaking in the cooling night breeze. She had lost him—no, she had thrown him away. Did he really think she would marry Landon? Derek didn't know her at all if he thought she would go to another man's bed after all she had shared with him. His parting words rang in her ears, but did he really mean them? She felt all hope for future happiness swept away, smothered by a blanket of deathlike ennui. The end had come too quickly for her to absorb. Later, she thought, she might weep and wail and scream in misery, but right now she hadn't the strength to whisper. Numbly, she found her way to her waiting mare and started toward home.

Derek strode toward the Mueller's cottage. As angry and upset as he was with Katya, he also blamed himself for her continued interference. He remembered Hans's accusation that he was cowardly not to make his feelings clear to the girl. He dreaded the scene, but Katya had gone too far—and he was much to blame.

Before he reached the house, he heard a rhythmical creaking coming from the nearby trees.

He followed the sound and discovered Katya on the children's swing created from a board suspended by two ropes. As she swung higher and higher, tipping up her feet, her skirts lifted in the breeze, she hummed a tune to herself. Such an innocent, childlike vision in the broken rays of moonlight—but the girl's manipulations, eavesdropping, and lies had nearly wrecked his chance for happiness.

"Katya!"

"Hello, Derek," she cried as she hopped off the swing.

She started to embrace him, but he firmly gripped her shoulders.

"Derek, I'm so sorry about your indigo. But we don't need that crop, do we?"

"Katya, forget the indigo and listen to me."

"Don't frown like that." She pulled away from him. "I said I was sorry—"

"Young lady, I have some questions for you."

She tilted her head. "Very well."

"I have just spoken with Eden Palmer."

"I spoke to her, too." She ran her fingers along her thick blond braid.

"Did you send for her to come see my indigo field?" he demanded.

"I thought she should see it. It means her crop will fail and we will get her plantation."

"How did you get that information?"

"Oh—I heard my parents talking about it."

"Just as I suspected. You poked your little nose into other people's affairs. Frankly, I don't believe you summoned Miss Palmer out of concern for her welfare."

Katya pursed her lips and said nothing.

"You were wrong, Katya. Wrong to tell Miss Palmer that I loved you—wrong to threaten her with the loss of her home."

Katya's eyes flashed in the moonlight. "You *do* love me, Derek. And I love you."

It was all he could do not to shake her. But he remembered her youth—and his own part in all this. "Katya, I've watched you grow up—and I care deeply for you. But I am not in love with you. Furthermore, you don't love me, not in an adult way."

"I do—I do! How can you say that?"

"Because if you did, you would consider my happiness— what I want, not just what you imagine or wish to be true."

"I—I want you to be happy."

"Good. I was sure I could count on you being sensible once you understood my true feelings."

She looked at him, her lips curved downward, her chin starting to tremble.

"The truth is, Katya dear, I am in love with Eden Palmer. I have asked her to marry me—and my happiness depends on her accepting my proposal." He hated to hurt the girl, but his honesty to her was long overdue.

Tears rolled down her cheeks. She covered her mouth and began to sob.

Dammit, he wanted to comfort her, but he firmly held his ground. "Katya, do you understand what I'm saying? I will not marry you—not now—not ever. Miss Palmer is angry and hurt, and may refuse my suit for her hand. If so, I will accept her decision and respect her wishes, no matter how hard it will be. I expect you to accept *my* decision regarding you—in the same courageous fashion."

She shook her head, her pigtails flying.

"You must, child. You're a lovely girl, beautiful and bright. I've seen Max Schriner sending you admiring glances. Other young men, too. It's time you turned your attentions to someone more nearly your age. You'll be surprised how quickly you'll recover from your childhood infatuation with me."

"Never—never," she choked.

"At sixteen, your life is only beginning. Hate me, or forget me, whichever works best for you. But you must promise *never* to interfere again in my private affairs."

Suddenly she clenched her fists at her sides. Between sobs she snapped at him, "All right, Baron, I'll leave you alone— forever. I'll never speak to you again—ever! And if I die of a broken heart, you'll be sorry!" She whirled away and ran toward her house.

Derek took a deep breath. Then he muttered, *"Nein, schatze.* You won't die. You have a strong Swiss spirit. You'll live—and find someone else to receive your passionate devotion."

⤜ 22 ⤛

Riding at full gallop, Eden raced beside the river toward home. Her pain and shock were so intense, she felt as if she'd been hauled from a lovely dream to find herself drowning in quicksand.

She had given Derek her deepest love, her body, and her total trust. He had betrayed that trust, taken her love and hypnotized her into a state of mindless euphoria. He had said he knew how important Palmer Oaks was to her, and yet he suggested she let it revert to the Crown as if that meant nothing. And if she did, would he marry her? Or did he plan to take the plantation and marry Katya instead? How surprised he would be if Bull Hawkins showed up to exercise his lien and right to purchase. It seemed impossible that a man she loved and adored could be so greedy and devious. She admitted she was naive—how many times had Derek called her that? Well, she was learning. But the lesson was excruciatingly painful. She couldn't help loving him, probably always would, but at the same time, she couldn't trust him after he first concealed the truth about his claim to her land, then took advantage of her attraction to him, and now belittled her efforts to hold Palmer Oaks free and clear in her own name.

Sadly, she equated Derek with Landon. Just like her cousin, Derek had planned to marry her, then take control of her property. The only difference between them was that Landon was stupidly obvious, while Derek used his abundant charm and devastating good looks to lure her to the altar. And, worst of all, Derek must have thought that the best way to ensure her pledge was to seduce her.

She reined up at her barn and flung herself out of the saddle. The horse was lathered, and she called to the stable boy to cool it down.

Tears might have helped, but she was beyond them as she marched to the area beside the river where the indigo would be prepared. For a time she stared blankly at the crop, lush and serene in the dim light of the moon and stars. Tomorrow she would start the harvest, and the indigo leaves would be gently cut and deposited into the water, where they would decompose into the substance called indoxyl. For the next few days every step in the process was crucial. She would get little sleep, but she doubted if she could sleep anyway after today's dreadful events. Damn all males, she thought bitterly. Each one was greedier than the next. Thirty thousand acres wasn't enough for the baron. He wanted her eight hundred, and the roof over her head to go with it.

In her agitated state, Eden ignored the contradictions seesawing in her head. It was perfectly clear to her that she had suffered terrible humiliation at the hands of the authoritative Swiss nobleman. Humiliation and heartbreak. How eagerly she had flown into his trap. Luckily, Derek had overplayed his hand just in time for her to discover his duplicity. Now he would never own Palmer Oaks.

As soon as she got to her room, she fell across her bed and lay with one arm across her eyes. After her day of labor in the fields, her dress was ripped and stained with dried mud. She would throw it away as soon as she was able to move again. The room was stuffy, but she hadn't the strength to get up and open the window.

Lying quietly in the dark, Eden felt her depression and misery spread throughout her being. She sobbed once and covered her face, fighting to keep anguish from engulfing her. She knew if she let the tears start, she would soon drown in unhappiness and self-pity. She was to pay a high price for going against Papa Charles's last wish that she safely marry Landon and be done with it. But she loved Derek Walden, to her regret, and would find it agonizing, if not impossible, to tear those feelings from the depths of her soul.

She rolled to her side and gazed at the moon framed in its blanket of dark velvet beyond her window. Despite her torment, she felt herself growing drowsy. There was so much to do; tomorrow the tall flowering shrubs would be cut. By this time tomorrow night she would be stationed at the vats to watch the process and check the plants every hour. Then the yellow liquid would be drawn into the containers with the paddle wheels that would throw it into the air to facilitate oxidation. That process was even more critical. At exactly the right moment, the limewater would be added to stop the fermentation. Only she could make that decision— and she must be on a twenty-four-hour vigil to ensure success.

She was sleeping deeply when the alarm was shouted. She stirred, then drifted back to sleep. A minute later she popped open her eyes.

"Fire!"

Had she heard a shout? Fighting a fuzzy brain, she moved to the side of the bed. Her eyelids were heavy, her lips swollen and dry. She wore the soiled garment of yesterday.

"Fire! Fire! Help!"

This time there was no mistaking the cry.

She moved to the window and opened it. A cool breeze from the river washed over her, helping to clear her head. Eden saw that the moon had traveled to the opposite horizon since her last observation. Leaning out, she glimpsed Joseph running toward the back of the house. He was illuminated by the torch he held aloft.

."Joseph!" she screamed. "What's wrong?"

He stopped and called up to her. "The indigo! The east corner is blazing, ma'am. I saw a glow and went right over. Already lost half an acre, I reckon."

"I'm coming." Fear scattered the last of her grogginess and she rushed from the room and ran down the stairs to the kitchen. Joseph was waiting to meet her, his eyes wide with alarm.

"Get everyone—everyone!" she commanded him. "We'll use the buckets from the barn. Line up at the river. Send me all the men you can. If necessary, we'll swamp the front part of the field with the water from the vats."

"But—But we need that for—"

"We won't have any use for it if the indigo is burned. Hurry now. But keep the youngest children in their houses. I don't want anyone hurt."

Laykee appeared as Joseph dashed back out the door. Her shift was rumpled and her hair tangled; her eyes were narrow with concern.

"The indigo's on fire, Laykee. Come with me. We'll do what we can."

She ran across the lawn with Laykee beside her. Sure enough, at the far end of the field the night was seared with leaping flames.

Her heart pounding, Eden slogged along a row of indigo shrubs, the graceful plants in full flower creating a shadowy canyon for her to follow. Laykee walked behind her.

As they neared the end of the tunnel, they smelled the burning plants and felt the heat increasing. Crackling closed out other night sounds, and the glow drew them like moths into the hellish scene.

No sooner had Eden broken from the path and surveyed the blaze than Joseph and eight shirtless workers arrived, each carrying two buckets. She immediately saw the hope-lessness of the situation. Only nine men and a few women against a roaring fire covering over two acres and spreading rapidly. But they must try.

"Make a line!" she shouted. She and Laykee each took a bucket and headed for the river. If the fire had started on the opposite side of the field, there would have been no chance at all.

Her shoulders ached from the previous day's work, but she ignored the discomfort and carried bucket after bucket, trading off with Laykee, working in unison, never pausing as she threw every ounce of strength she possessed into getting water to the field.

After half an hour she was climbing the embankment when she slipped in the damp earth and fell to her hands and knees, dropping her bucket and losing its contents. Briefly, she was light-headed, but she was able to turn and sit quietly, holding her head in her hands.

"You all right, Miss Eden?" came Joseph's soft voice.

Without looking up, she said hoarsely, "Yes, thank you, Joseph, but we're losing. How did it happen? Was it lightning?"

"No'm." He hesitated. "No'm, 'twasn't God who done this. It was man."

Surprised, she looked at him squatting beside her. "Man? You mean—someone started the fire on purpose?"

"We found burnt torches over there in the corner. Foot-prints, too, in the mud. Boots, looks like. But probably jus' one man."

She was shocked, appalled at the thought anyone would do such a thing. And why? She had no enemies. Charles had been respected and loved. No one had anything to gain. The terrible thought that crept into her mind was beyond belief. Yesterday she had rejected Derek's proposal. He knew she was starting her harvest today—and he would lose Palmer Oaks if she successfully sold her crop. Admittedly, she was on the brink of collapse and wasn't thinking clearly, but who else would have done it?

Derek. The very idea drugged her senses. Sitting there, she bit into her lips and tried to think. How well did she really know the lord from the mountain fortress of central Europe? He had fought vicious battles before to hold onto his land. His careful plot to gain Palmer Oaks by marriage had failed. He knew nothing about the second lien with Bull Hawkins, but believed her failure would deliver to him the title to her plantation. It must have been a blow to his pride to live as a pauper these past months, looking across the river daily at a lovely home he had expected would be his. And then to make matters worse, she had lashed out at him and then ridden away, leaving him to stew over the demise of his devious plan. Could this be his answer to her rejection of him?

"I'm goin' back to work, if youse all right, ma'am."

"Oh yes, please do," she muttered. Again she put her head in her hands. This was the final blow. She decided she didn't care about the indigo, Palmer Oaks, or taking one more breath, for that matter. She would never be happy anyway without the man she loved at her side. She was sorry for everything now, especially for herself. She gazed beyond her fingers across her filthy skirts to her mud-caked slippers. She was only vaguely aware of a pale glow beyond the burning field, the first blue tint of a new day—one that held only devastation and disappointment.

Tears seeped through her lashes and between her fingers. She might as well have a good cry and get it over with. Then she would go back to the large vats and order them dumped over into the fields, though she doubted that would do more than save a handful of the plants, at best.

"There—over there—come here, Kurt! Get the line going from that shallow bend."

Who was shouting? Not Joseph. She twisted around to see dozens of men silhouetted against the fire and the brightening dawn. Then more, coming swiftly, coming to help, coming from Waldenburg.

She jumped up and hurried toward them. One man shouted orders. Karl Hansen. And there was Kurt Mueller and even Hans Messenbaugh. Derek? Was he here, too? She didn't see him.

She ran across the field to Karl. "Thank you," she gasped breathlessly. "Thank you. But it may be too late."

"I've got plenty of men. We'll stop it all right. Though you've lost nearly half already, I'm afraid."

"Where is Mr. Walden?"

"I saw him earlier tonight on the bridge, but not lately. Oh, there he is now."

She whirled to see Derek approaching from the east on horseback. His expression was stern and unreadable. Was it possible he had started the fire? Her heart rebelled at the thought, but her mind refused to let it go.

As if in a vision, she saw him as the warrior he had been. His horse reared near the flames; he rode expertly, controlled the animal, lifted in his stirrups to shout orders at his men. He rode like a horseman of the apocalypse, his hair tossed like fired bronze in the eerie light, his skin dark gold along his cheekbones and throat, his chest revealed where his shirt lay open. His jaw worked and his eyes roved across the chaotic scene, falling at last on her.

With both hands containing the frightened stallion, he rode in her direction. Kurt hurried away to rejoin the others.

Eden held her ground, refusing to be defeated by either the fire or the baron.

Arriving beside her, he pierced her with a haunted look.

"I'm indebted to your men, sir," she said in a voice that held no sign of weakness. "Did you bring them to my aid?" Even her own ears detected bitterness in her tone.

"I can't take credit for sounding the alarm. Our lookout saw flames. I responded with the others."

She noticed now that both Derek's hands were bandaged,

apparently with pieces ripped from the bottom of his shirt. "Have you been injured?" She wanted to ask if he had burned his hands when he torched her indigo—but she dared not.

"Singed them. I'll recover." His voice was as acidic as her own.

"This was arson," she announced, her tone openly accusing.

"So I heard." He nudged the horse near and leaned toward her.

She saw fierceness in his look, indigo fire in his eyes. "Do you believe *I* did this, *fraulein?* Is that what you're suggesting?"

The passion in his gaze caused her to hesitate. She had no proof. She didn't want to believe it.

"After all that has passed between us, Eden, I see we're complete strangers.

There was desolation in his face, but his chin was set, his tone harsh and laced with anger.

"I didn't accuse you of anything," she said lamely.

"But it was in your mind—that I would destroy your crop to gain your property."

"It was a fleeting thought. I prayed it wasn't true."

"Verdammen." He cursed deep in his throat. "And you expect me to deny it?"

"I think an innocent person would—"

"Enough." He rose in the saddle and stared at her from behind a mask made of steel. "Good-bye, Mistress Palmer." His words rang with finality as he spun his mount and headed back to where his people worked now in orderly precision.

He didn't start the fire. At that instant Eden knew it with absolute certainty. Whatever else she thought of Derek Walden, she knew he would not have stooped to such stupid cruelty, such cowardly meanness, such an act of petty revenge—not even to own Palmer Oaks. "Derek!" she cried starting after him. "Please—come back." Either he didn't hear her or chose not to. Stumbling in the furrows, she saw him ride toward the bridge and caught the sound of his horse's hooves pounding across the wooden planks he had built to join his land to the river road. He was gone for good. She was sure of it. Gone. A far greater loss than her indigo—or even Palmer Oaks. Even if she apologized, she could never undo the damage she had done, not only tonight, but yesterday as well. She had shredded his pride and accused him of a criminal act. What could she expect? She had destroyed whatever chance she could have had at life's happiness.

Karl Hansen came to stand beside her. "We found this, Mistress Palmer. Near where the fire started."

She looked at the golden object he held in his palm. An earring—a large hoop, common with pirates, just like—just like the one Bull Hawkins had worn when she saw him in Barbados. Hawkins. Why, of course, he would be arriving in Charles Town to claim the balance of what she owed him, due in a few days. But why would he burn her crop? She took the earring and turned it over in her hand. She remembered what he'd said about owning land and becoming a gentleman. He didn't want her payment—he wanted Palmer Oaks, and he was rascal enough to pull such a dreadful stunt to get it.

Heaving a sigh, Eden closed her fingers over the earring. Why not Hawkins? she thought as fatigue and resignation overcame her. Everyone else wanted her land. Hawkins was just one of many. After a pause, she looked at Karl. "Thank you, all of you, for your help. I'll find some way to repay you."

"We were glad to help, mistress. It's under control now. I'm only sorry we couldn't get here sooner. It was the bridge, you see."

"The bridge?" she asked listlessly.

"Whoever fired the field tried to burn the bridge. Derek

saw that first. We were hanging back, but he ran right onto it and pulled burning timbers away. It would have gone up like a torch. We rode over as soon as we could."

Her throat constricted. Fire. The one thing he feared. Perhaps the only thing he feared. Her next question was barely audible. "Is that how he burned his hands?"

"Yes, but he says not badly. Don't worry, he's a tough fellow. But you can see why we all admire him." He smiled at her as if they shared the same feelings. Apparently he knew that she and Derek were more than just friends.

Desolate, Eden nodded and walked away. Yes, she and Derek had been more than friends, but she had ruined everything with her absurd suspicions and cruel words. He had opened his heart to her, offered her his hand, and she had put her pride and her fierce determination to own Palmer Oaks above everything. After all, he had come from a land where to be a man was to be powerful, decisive, and protective of womankind. He didn't understand her independent nature. She should have understood *him*—then led him gently into a new way of thinking. Now he would never love her, and she couldn't blame him. Katya waited with open arms—lovely arms that would enfold him, comfort him, and remind him of their common heritage.

A short time later she was hardly aware when Laykee came to tell her the fire was out. Half the field was gone, but half saved, and the water vats remained intact.

"We'll rest today," Eden said thickly. "Tomorrow we'll harvest what's left, then see what price we can get at market."

When she got back to her room, she allowed Laykee to strip away the filthy rags that were all that remained of her clothing. Mechanically, she bathed and crawled into bed. Her hair smelled of smoke and her fingernails were black with mud. Today she would sleep, tomorrow, somehow, begin again. She didn't even hate Bull Hawkins. He was a pirate, after all, and she had elected to deal with him. What could a body expect? Her last thought was of Derek's face bending near when she accused him of burning the crop. It would be her personal hell to remember that look every day for the rest of her life.

Two days later the harvest was complete and the barrels packed, waiting to be shipped.

Eden strolled to the end of her dock. Beside her padded Queen Elizabeth, freed now of the burden of feeding her puppies, who could forage on their own. Not a breath of air moved through the trees or stirred the last fading roses in the garden. Eden knew autumn would soon flow almost imperceptibly into the mild season of winter.

She sat on the wooden bench beside the walkway. Queenie stretched out beside her and rested her chin on her mistress's slipper. It was good to relax after the feverish pace of the past two days. She had pushed herself to the breaking point overseeing the production of the indigo. Everything had gone smoothly: the paddle wheels had worked to perfection, turning day and night until the limewater was carefully added to end the process of fermentation. The dye stuff had settled, then been cut and packed. Bull Hawkins's instructions had worked out beautifully.

Shading her eyes, she gazed across the water, a sluggish, silver ribbon, almost blinding in the late afternoon brilliance. Across it stretched the lands of the Swiss—and Derek was there somewhere, her enemy now, she supposed.

Sighing deeply, she reached to pet Queenie's head. "It's a terrible mess, Queenie," she murmured. "We may have to leave here, old girl." She continued talking to the dog, finding some solace in her silent companion. "I'll have to decide what to do with the money. With only half enough, I'll have to choose between paying the Crown or Bull Hawkins. If I pay Hawkins, the Crown will take the land and give it to the Swiss. If I pay King George, Bull will step in and execute his second lien. Either way I lose. I could ask

Landon for the money, but he would insist we marry—and that will never happen, if I have to become a begger on the streets of Charles Town." She sighed again. Queenie thumbed her tail on the wooden planks.

"Derek," she said softly, "not only did you prove yourself innocent of arson, but you proved you truly cared for me. If all you had wanted was Palmer Oaks, you could have let the whole field burn." She shook her head sadly. "Oh, Queenie, what can I do? He must surely hate me now. And I wouldn't blame him."

Lost in thought, she didn't hear the footsteps until they were close upon her. Startled, she looked up to see Derek walking toward her.

For one second her heart leaped with hope. But then she saw the cool look in his eyes, sensed his well-controlled hostility. Pride stopped the warm greeting that had almost betrayed her joy at seeing him. Mustering her dignity, she rose to face him. Queenie jumped up, wagging her tail in a friendly hello.

"Hello, Derek. I'm glad to see you." She thought his look softened for a fleeting second.

"Good afternoon, Eden," he said stiffly. "From appearances, you'll soon ship the indigo to market." His tone was as polite and distant as his expression.

"Tomorrow the barges arrive at daybreak."

"A successful crop, then," he observed.

"Yes. Well, half a crop, at least." She glanced at his hands. One remained bandaged. She was painfully aware this was the first time since they had met that he hadn't reached for her hand or drawn her into an embrace. The loss of his love hurt so deeply she wondered how she could stand it. Keeping up a brave front, she said, "I'm glad you came by. I wanted to thank you, and ask about your hands. I only learned after you'd ridden away how you had saved the bridge and the balance of my indigo."

"I helped, but the men did the majority of the work."

"I tried to catch up with you that night, but you were out of hearing. Had you not come by today, I was going to visit Waldenburg. I owe a great deal to your people." Eden stepped toward him, feeling the familiar throb inside her as she saw him standing, bathed in sunlight, neatly groomed and incredibly attractive.

"Did you expect me—or my settlers—to stand by and let your crop be destroyed?" His words fell like chips from a block of ice.

She folded her hands before her. "I was wrong, Derek. I apologize."

"It took a near disaster to prove my innocence. I'm not sure I can count on that luck throughout a lifetime."

She looked down at her hands as tears threatened. She deserved that. She knew it. But oh how deeply his words cut into her heart. "What can I say? I jumped to conclusions. I have some excuses, but none of them are adequate. I can only beg your forgiveness."

When she looked up at him, his face was hard as flint.

"I forgave you, Eden, for your first anger when you learned of my claim to your land. I should have told you right away of that conflict. I failed to fully understand your deep desire to bring in the crop and pay off your mortgage. I assumed you would be content to accept my name and my protection—and my love, of course—as most women traditionally do from their husbands. I see now that you're not like other women. I respect your spirit and your intelligence, though I might honestly prefer a bit less independence in the woman I call my own."

She considered his words. Was he offering her another chance? He was here, after all. He had come to see her. "Derek, I can't undo the past—my foolish fears and stupid assumptions. But I would like to begin again. Do you think—that is possible?"

He gazed at her for such a long time, she thought he must hear her heart pounding its frantic rhythm. Finally he said,

"You dealt me a severe blow. I came here today to speak to Laykee about the herbs for Anna. Otherwise, I wouldn't have bothered you."

Her hopes plummeted. "Anna," she murmured. "Yes, whatever happens between us—we must help Anna, if we can." Through the mist in her eyes, she saw again a sign of softening in his face. Turning to look blindly at the river, she said, "Come again someday, Baron. You'll always be welcome here."

Throughout the long silence that followed, she felt his nearness, his power, and—she prayed—the weakening of his firm stand against her. She wanted him more than life, but she would not be reduced to futile pleading.

After an eternity he said huskily. "I'll stop by tomorrow. Maybe I can be of help."

She heard him walking away. But she only looked skyward and said a prayer of thanks. Maybe there was hope, after all.

With the return of hope came a surge of ideas. Before Eden retired for the night, she had a plan of action.

The next day, Derek returned to Palmer Oaks just as the sun lifted above the smoky hills. He had spent plenty of time mulling over the problem with Eden. She had accused him of arson and immeasurable greed. She obviously thought him as low a varmint as Landon, offering marriage to gain control of her plantation. But she had little worldly experience, and he had made the mistake of hiding the truth from her in the beginning. It was easy to see how she might assume all men were alike in their desire to control as much property as possible, to attain wealth at any cost, and to turn their women into pampered possessions. With time, he could have reassured her of his deep respect for her and of how her property was more of a problem than an asset as far as their relationship was concerned. He had lain awake wondering how long it would take for him to match and surpass her financial worth. Not to feel superior, but to be worthy of a woman such as she.

But the night of the fire had nearly been his undoing. He had seen the accusation in her eyes. Pain, anger, and disillusionment had followed in quick succession. She had hurt him beyond measure when she accused him of starting the fire. But yesterday he had seen misery and remorse etched in every line of her face. That look would have brought tears to a stone-hearted villain. And hopefully, he didn't yet fall into that category.

The eastern sky was alight with pink and gold as he mounted the steps of the back veranda, the aroma of bacon and coffee wafting on the cool morning air reminding him of the breakfast he'd missed. Perhaps he'd come too early, he thought, hesitating before the door.

It swung open suddenly and Laykee appeared carrying a tray of steaming loaves of fresh-baked bread.

"Good morning, Mr. Walden," she said, showing no surprise to see him there as she walked onto the porch.

"Good morning, Laykee. Is Mistress Palmer about? I could return later."

"Oh, she's been up for hours. Baked the bread for the hands. Today is a big day, you know."

"Indeed I do. That's why I've come. I thought I could help in some way."

"Miss Eden's in the kitchen. Go in, if you like."

He smiled warmly at the dark-eyed maiden, and strode through the open door into the back hall. Half the night he'd tossed and turned, choosing, then discarding speeches of reconciliation. This very house stood between him and the woman he loved. How could he convince her he loved her without appearing to covet her property? Sooner or later she would have to trust him, trust his words and the sincere emotions behind them.

He walked to the kitchen door and halted. Eden stood at the table, her sleeves rolled above her elbows as she washed bread tins in a large bucket of soapy water.

He stood there watching, silently memorizing the sight of the woman he loved dearly, a rare beauty, innocent and enchanting, as she worked in the fresh sunshine streaming through the kitchen window. Whatever happened in the future, he would cherish this moment, lock it away in his heart forever.

He cleared his throat and doffed his hat.

Startled, Eden looked up at him.

"I met Laykee on the porch and she invited me in," he explained.

"I'm glad to see you," Eden replied with a hint of a smile.

"I thought I could help. I've a strong back, though perhaps a dull mind." He hoped his attempt at humor might help mend the fences between them. "If not, I won't interfere."

Her lips curved upward. "I have my schedule well in mind."

"Of course. But isn't there something I can do?"

She wiped her hands on her apron. "I might think of something."

Her aloof manner was unsettling. He had been harsh with her yesterday. Maybe she deserved it, maybe not. But today was a new day, and she had suggested a new beginning. He was willing to try. He took a step toward her. "Eden, we must talk."

"Yes. I do have something to tell you."

He moved near, close enough to see the flecks of gold in her eyes. He also saw confidence there, and determination. The woman he knew and loved. Yes, the barrier between them was beginning to crumble. "What is it?" he asked.

"I have accused you of concealing the truth. I am just as guilty of that as you. You see, I've let you believe you would secure the title to Palmer Oaks if I must default."

"Yes. That's my understanding from the documents in Charles Town. But you won't have to default now. There should be enough profit from the indigo to pay off the king."

"The truth is you are *third* in line for the property— behind the holder of a second lien."

"What?"

"I took out a loan to buy the indigo plants. I would have paid off the king and the second lien with the proceeds from the entire crop. Now—I must choose."

Dammit, why hadn't he considered she had other options? And he could guess who held the second mortgage. Despite his dismay, he smiled across at her. "I must say it is ironic, isn't it? No doubt your cousin Landon made you the loan. And now you must choose—between your blood kin or a foreigner whom you can't find it in your heart to trust. The joke is on me, it appears." He actually managed to laugh.

She smiled slyly, like a clever fox toying with its victim.

He wasn't amused. "Choose between us, Mistress Palmer. You and Palmer Oaks are prizes any man would fight for. But I won't fight Landon Palmer for your hand. I want the choice to be yours. I'm sure you can see there's a difference between Landon and me. If you can figure it out, it might help you make your decision."

She tilted her chin, refusing to let his speech destroy her confident air. She walked around the table and grasped his arm.

God, how he would like to kiss those lovely lips into submission. "What now?" he snapped.

"You can help—since you've offered."

He *had* offered—he would have to do what she asked. "I'll oblige," he said gruffly. Damn, she was so stubborn. How could anyone so exquisite, so soft and loving, have an invisible suit of armor to equal any knight?

"When the barges are unloaded in Charles Town, I'm to meet the buyers and arrive at a price. They don't like to negotiate with women, or so I've been told."

He lifted an eyebrow. "I rather pity the man who must bargain with you, *fraulein*. He's certain to underestimate your powers of persuasion—your will of iron."

"I intend to be fair," she said. "But I know the value of the dye. It's just that a man by my side would lend substance to my argument."

"Why not ask Landon to act in your behalf, considering his interest in your profit?"

She eyed him for a long moment. "Well, I could, but you have offered to help me and he has not. Besides, I intend to see Landon at tea later today."

Derek almost flinched under the whip of her words. If she was meeting Landon, she must have already made her choice. She would let the property go to Palmer—and Palmer would certainly insist on marriage. Pain cut through his insides like a heated lance. Sometime since yesterday she must have changed her mind about giving their love another chance.

Smoothing her hair, she said, "And *you,* as well, Derek. I'd like you to come to the Oyster House at four o'clock, if that's convenient. I've reserved a private room; there will be four of us at the meeting."

He took a deep breath. What game was this? "If you like. Four guests, you say? You, me, Landon—a cozy group for tea. Who is your fourth guest?"

"You'll see when you arrive."

He shook his head. "By all that's holy, Eden, you are a most amazing woman. Of course, I'll help you if I can—both at the docks and at your tea. You keep me jumping through hoops so I can see what will happen next."

She smiled now, a smile of true pleasure. "A woman's privilege," she said. "But it does take skill to make it happen."

He smiled back at her. "Skill—and brains—and a heart like a rock."

"We'll see, Baron. We'll see."

Eden dressed with great care in the boudoir of her town house. She felt a bit like she was dressing for her execution. Her gown was of kincob, a rich brocade in shades of azure swirled with threads of indigo-blue, a fitting color considering her activities of today. The square-cut neckline was trimmed with a tiny white ruffle which was repeated along the insert of the stomacher. Full pinked ruffles finished the elbow-length sleeves and fell gracefully to the bell-shaped skirt draped over a swaying hoop.

She turned before her long mirror and studied the back, cut in the popular style of the Watteau sack, draping in box pleats over the skirt. Peaking beneath the ankle-length skirt were her high-heeled shoes made from matching brocade.

Gazing at the wondrous creation, she remembered how happy Charles had been last year when the dress arrived from London. Never had she owned such a gown, nor had her poor dead mother. "For your first ball," Charles had said. "And perhaps for your engagement party. I've placed a second order for two bolts of white satin. You can design the wedding dress of your dreams."

His extravagance at such a time was so foolish, Eden had burst into tears, but had insisted they were tears of joy. Not only did she know they were destitute, but the idea of marriage had never entered her mind.

But today she was glad to have the dress, if for no other reason than to give her confidence to face the ordeal that lay ahead. Laykee had helped her wash and arrange her hair, securing it with a pert lace cap at the back of her crown.

As usual she wore gloves, not to be stylish, but to hide her damaged hands and blunt nails. She would never have the hands of a lady, she thought, stepping away from the mirror and collecting her purse and a velvet pouch from the table. She worked like a field hand, bargained like an Indian merchant, and plotted like a master spy—but for once she looked like a well-bred lady of means. She would have three powerful men dancing in attendance. And her entire future would be decided in the span of a few minutes.

At precisely 3:45 she arrived in a rented carriage at the Oyster House and asked the coachman to wait. She wouldn't be staying for tea, she explained, and would go directly to the courthouse after her meeting. Her three guests could stay if they liked, but the chances of that were none to impossible.

She entered the small, luxurious private dining room and came face-to-face with Landon. Her plans had included his arriving first. She saw at once he was distressed by the sight of the elegant table set for four guests.

He swept into a bow, then kissed her hand. "My dearest Eden, you look magnificent. Why, I've never seen you so . . . so utterly exquisite. You've been hiding your beauty under simple attire for as long as I've known you. And what have you been up to, chérie? I've missed you these past weeks."

She was not surprised he had no knowledge of the harvest season in progress. His disdain for farming or any serious labor had always been obvious.

Moving to the head of the table, she gave him a benign smile. "You could have found me at Palmer Oaks if you'd been really interested," she observed sweetly.

"I have planned to call for days," he simpered while

pulling out her tufted armchair. "In fact, I'll do so tomorrow. Unless you plan to be in town. In that case, we'll attend the concert tomorrow evening. Would you like that, my dear?"

"I may be resting tomorrow, Landon. I've been extremely busy lately bringing in the indigo crop." With a loud thunk she placed the velvet pouch on the table before her. "I sold it today for a very good price."

He pulled up the chair at her right and looked at the pouch. His eyebrows arched as he fingered it. "You mean . . . the proceeds are here? Why, they should be in the bank, or in my private safe." He gave her a condescending smile. "Poor dear, you do need a man to guide and protect you. I hope that pleasure and honor will soon be mine. You did promise to set the date, did you not—after you harvested the indigo?"

Eden was at a loss for words. How could Landon have forgotten their last meeting, brushing aside her rejection of him and his scandalous behavior with Fanny Picket as if it never happened?

"Now, who else is coming for tea today? I'd hoped we could be alone," he said with a critical tone.

Before she could answer, the door opened and Derek Walden strode in. He wore the same forest-green suit he'd worn at the celebration in Waldenburg, and his powerful presence filled the small room, making Landon's elegance seem false and foppish.

Landon rose from his chair, wearing a look of cool disdain.

"Good afternoon," Derek said, directing his greeting primarily toward Eden.

"Hello, Derek," she responded. "Please have a seat."

With barely a glance at Landon, he pulled up the chair at her left.

A waiter appeared and offered goblets of brandy or wine.

Eden chose a light claret while the men selected the dark rich brandy.

Taking a sip, she found herself enjoying her little game. She had worried and fretted for so long over this moment, lived it, rehearsed it so many times, that now that it had arrived, it seemed like a play moving smoothly toward its climax. She wasn't certain, of course, of the ending, but the plan was in motion and could not be halted.

When the door opened next, in walked none other than Bull Hawkins, resplendent in a scarlet velvet suit, no doubt the pride of some long-dead Spanish grandee. His red cocked hat held a swooping white feather; his black silk hose clung to bulging calves, and he wore high-heeled slippers with rhinestone buckles. Why, he even had a sword buckled to his side, and every finger displayed a sizable ring. His beard was full, but recently trimmed, and golden loops dangled from his ears.

Eden stifled a laugh as she observed the stunned looks on the faces of Landon and Derek.

Landon half rose from his chair, then sank back as if too shocked to stand.

Derek merely stared in speechless surprise. When recognition flared in his eyes, he quickly recovered from his astonishment. "Hell fire, it's Bull Hawkins," he exclaimed. "And dressed for a fandango." He looked at Eden, his expression a mixture of chagrin and amusement. "Mistress Palmer has assembled a rather motley group for her tea party."

Bull looked as surprised and annoyed as the other two men. He flashed a hard look at Eden. "I thought we had business, Mistress Palmer. *Private* business."

"We do, Mr. Hawkins—if you'll take a seat."

Hawkins marched to the end of the table opposite Eden and sank into the cushioned chair.

Landon paled and pushed as far back in his seat as possible. "Eden, who is this outrageous fellow?" he sputtered.

"Mind your tongue, sir," growled Bull. "I may not be a gentleman yet, but I expect to be in about five minutes."

"Landon, this is Bull Hawkins," she announced. "Mr. Hawkins sold me my indigo plants. To his credit, they did indeed flourish in South Carolina soil."

"Until the fire," Bull hissed. "I heard all about your misfortune."

Derek stiffened. "You knew about the fire?"

Eden said calmly, "Mr. Hawkins not only knew about the fire—he started it."

Bull rose partly from his chair. "That's a lie."

"It's the truth and you know it," she said sharply.

"You ain't got no proof."

"Only this." She laid a gold hoop on the table—an exact match of the two he was wearing. "This was found where the fire started, along with torches."

"You can't prove that's mine," he said. "I've been at sea this past month anyway."

"Your *ship* has been at sea. But you came ashore a week ago, then promptly left. I have the word of a dock steward."

"That doesn't prove I burned your crop."

Derek stood and clutched Bull's collar. "I've heard enough."

Bull scowled and reached for his sword.

"Did you do it?" Derek demanded. "I've never known Mistress Palmer to lie. I'll have your hide, you damned pirate—"

"Sit down, Derek," Eden ordered. "It doesn't matter now anyway."

Reluctantly, Derek released Bull and sat back in his chair.

Bull straightened his collar while keeping an angry eye on Derek.

"What's this all about, Eden?" Landon asked. "I thought you sold the indigo."

"I did."

"What?" Bull bellowed, giving away his guilt once and for all.

"Don't worry, Mr. Hawkins. You're right. I don't have enough proof to send you to jail, though I'd like to more than I can say." She looked at Derek. He was gazing at her as if she were a stranger. She would like to have reassured him that all was going as she'd planned, but that would have ruined everything. Instead she addressed Hawkins. "We have a business arrangement, sir. Have you brought the lien to my property?"

"What lien?" gasped Landon.

"I gave Bull a lien on Palmer Oaks in exchange for the indigo."

"Bull Hawkins?" Derek snapped. "But I thought—"

"I didn't say *who*, did I?" she said crisply to Derek.

Derek leaned back in his chair and took a long swallow from his goblet.

"Now," Eden said, "I want that lien, Mr. Hawkins. Here is the money I owe you." She pushed the pouch across the linen.

He squinted at it like it was pure venom. "Umph. Well,

dammit, I didn't want the money. I thought yer crop burned, a pity of course, but I—"

"Wanted Palmer Oaks." She completed his sentence.

"Har. Well—"

"You are not alone in that desire, Mr. Hawkins. Now give me the lien."

From the corner of her eye she saw Derek throw her a narrow look. Fortunately, he kept himself under control and drowned his ire with another swig of brandy.

Bull handed her a wrinkled piece of paper. She glanced at it, then tore it in half. "Take your gold, Mr. Hawkins. You'll find it the correct amount."

He stood, grabbed the pouch off the table and stuffed it under his coat.

"You see," she continued, "only part of the crop burned. Our friend, the baron, saved the rest. Wasn't that fortunate?" Her voice dripped honey.

"So be it," he grumbled. "But I'll be a gentleman one day, somewhere or other. You'll see." He stomped out of the room and slammed the door.

"When elephants walk on water," Derek mumbled.

"That was ghastly, Eden," Landon said, first rising, then falling into his seat in a display of indignant horror. "That beast, that criminal—you in debt to him. You could have come to me for money. After all, I'm your fiancé."

Derek put his goblet down heavily, spilling a portion of the contents on the white tablecloth. He said something under his breath in guttural German, but it was lost on the two present.

"That is a matter we'll soon discuss, Landon. But first I must explain that Bull Hawkins held a *second* lien on the property, not a first."

"I don't know what you're saying."

"I'm saying that there has been a *first* lien on Palmer Oaks since my stepfather acquired the grant seventeen years ago.

He has paid on that debt every year—until now. The final payment is due—November first."

"Oh—well, I suppose you'll pay it and own the place."

"Not quite. You see, I gave all the money I had to Bull Hawkins just now. I can't pay it."

"What? But you'll lose it, then. The Crown will foreclose."

Derek coughed, but Eden ignored him. "That's right. Unless . . ." She reached in her purse and removed a paper. "This is a document signing Palmer Oaks over to *you*. Only one payment remains. If we choose, we could sign it—if you want to, Landon."

His eyes grew wide. Color rushed into his face. Why, she would swear he was drooling at the idea. She thought she heard Derek curse, but she kept her attention on Landon.

"Why, naturally I want Palmer Oaks. I've always wanted a plantation upriver—a profitable plantation like the Poinsetts'. You're saying it could be mine for one small payment to the Crown?"

Derek interjected, "Unless you'd prefer to pay her a *fair* price for the property."

"Oh, I don't need to do that, do I?" Landon hastened. "I mean, she's my betrothed, after all, and I expected to have the place for nothing."

Derek leaned forward and clenched his fist.

Before he could speak, Eden motioned for him to remain silent. To Landon she said, "There's one more requirement, cousin, if I sign over the property."

He was inspecting the paper she handed him. "What's that, my dear?"

"I have *another* document for you to sign. It's a written release of our betrothal—officially breaking our engagement."

"Hm," Derek muttered, leaning back in his chair.

Landon gaped at her. "What? You don't want to marry me?"

"No. I thought I'd made that abundantly clear. In fact, I will not marry you, no matter what you decide about Palmer Oaks. I would just like proof of your agreement."

He appeared shocked, but not exactly devastated. "You mean you'd break our engagement—and still sign over your property?"

"That's my offer. I think it's a good one. You don't love me, dear cousin. Why don't you be honest with both of us. Your taste runs to another type, after all."

He studied her, apparently uncertain whether she could actually be serious. Finally he shrugged his shoulders. "Well, if you don't love me, I suppose I can't say I truly love you. Although naturally you have my undying affection. We are cousins, after all. Where do I sign?"

She handed over the second document and a stylus. "There." When he finished, she looked at the paper, enormously relieved. "Now that we're no longer engaged, Landon, you can sign the first document giving you the right to buy the plantation."

"Eden—don't," Derek said in a low tone.

"Stay out of this, Walden," Landon snarled. "It's none of your business."

She gave Derek an appreciative smile. "Thank you, but I'm not quite done yet." She addressed Landon. "Before you sign that agreement, there's one thing I should mention. The indigo crop I sold this morning will be the last ever produced at Palmer Oaks."

He blinked at her without comprehension.

"I'm sorry to say a plague of locusts destroyed Mr. Walden's indigo just across the river. The creatures are sure to make indigo a risky investment for the future. But if you work very hard, you can restore the rice fields and irrigation canals. You'll have to hire labor or buy slaves—many slaves to make it pay. And the house needs immediate attention—a new roof, paint, several major repairs. But I'm sure it can be livable in a month or two. You'll have to live there, of course, or all will go to rack and ruin. It isn't easy being a farmer, Landon. Look what happened to your uncle Charles."

She waited, watching his face change from confident pleasure to misgivings to an ugly scowl. She felt her own tension like a taut bowstring. Her heart raced furiously beneath her ribs.

"So, Eden—you tricked me," he said at last.

"Tricked? Why no, I'm just being honest. Ask Mr. Walden. If you like, he'll show you his ruined crop."

"But without the indigo, there's no real profit."

"No *easy* profit, Landon. The land returns a profit when it's properly worked—and loved. I was foolish to try for quick wealth. Now, as you can see, I've lost everything. So—there is the agreement. You may sign it now."

He straightened his spine and glared at her. "No, I don't believe I'll take over the plantation, after all. I have no intention of working like a slave and burying myself at some backwater plantation surrounded by a lot of foreigners."

Concealing her relief, she raised her hands in feigned amazement. "My my, cousin, I am *so* surprised."

"I'm sure you are, but that's the truth," he said flatly. "I don't want the place after all. Let the king have it. Maybe he'll send a few more Huns over to take charge of it."

Maybe he will," she said, not daring to look at Derek.

He got up from the table. "I'm going to the theater. Oh . . ." As if he had an afterthought, he turned to look at her. "What will you do, my dear—now that you're a free woman?"

"How nice of you to ask. Possibly I'll return to Wentworth in England. To my mother's family."

"Good idea. And since I am now also free—"

"Good-bye, Landon," she said sharply.

"Well, good luck, Eden dear. Let me know when you've made your plans." He left the room, closing the door behind him.

She sank into her chair. Without looking at Derek, she carefully tore the unsigned agreement into several pieces and laid them aside, then folded the document releasing her from her betrothal and put it into her handbag. She took a long drink from her glass. Everything had gone perfectly, but the most important revelation lay ahead. She was acutely aware of Derek's silent scrutiny from his place beside her. At last she raised her eyes to meet his, and found his expression one of abject admiration tinged with amusement.

"My darling Eden, you are an amazing woman. I can see I underestimated you by a thousand leagues."

"I appreciate the compliment, but I don't agree. You're looking at a ruined, homeless, and penniless orphan. I have bought my freedom at a very high price."

"I salute you, nonetheless, Miss Palmer. Your wit and courage are something to behold."

She held her breath, hoping he would say more. She knew as well as he that Palmer Oaks would now revert to him through his grant from King George.

The words she had prayed for were not spoken.

He stood and offered her his hand. "I'll go now. I want to get back to Waldenburg before dark."

Her throat tight, she took his arm and walked with him from the room.

When they reached her carriage, he opened the door. His manner was relaxed and pleasant. "Where are you going now?" he inquired.

"To the courthouse—to sign the deed over to the Crown."

"Then, *auf wiedersehen,* Eden. I'm sure you've done the right thing today." He closed the door as she sank back into the padded seat.

As the carriage moved along the cobbles, she knew she had gambled and lost. Baron von Walden would have Palmer Oaks, without the necessity of marrying its former owner. Her relationship with him was over; she had the truth at last. The problem was, it was tearing out her heart.

She arrived at the courthouse in minutes.

"Please sir, I'd like the deed and the mortgage to Palmer Oaks on the Ashley River." Eden had to hide her grief for only a little while longer.

The elderly official left the desk and disappeared for a time. When he returned he carried two documents. "Here you are, Mistress Palmer. Good bit of interest today in these musty files."

"Yes, well, the mortgage is due soon." It took several seconds for her tired brain to register his remark. "Interest? Someone other than me?"

"Yes, ma'am. A gentleman was here earlier. Had a legitimate claim on the property, he said."

Derek. So he'd already been here. Even before her meeting. The thought of his greed was appalling. He must have known she'd never marry Landon, not after she had loved him so completely. He'd already made arrangements to take possession of the property. She could have cried, but was too disgusted for tears. She decided she might learn to dislike Derek more quickly than she'd anticipated.

"Well, I must sign the papers, too. You have the deed and the mortgage from the Crown?"

"Yes, ma'am. You do need to sign the deed. But the mortgage isn't required. Only your acknowledgment."

"Oh. Well, let me have it."

The fellow opened the yellowed paper. "This is the mortgage. Since its been paid, you just need to—"

"Paid!" She grabbed it and took a close look. Indeed, the word PAID was marked in large blue letters across the face of it. She saw her stepfather's original signature and a place for her to sign at the bottom. There was no other name on the document.

"But it *can't* be paid," she gasped. "It's not due until November first."

"As I said, the gentleman came earlier today and paid it off in full."

Her head was spinning. "What gentleman?"

"A stranger in town, Miss Palmer. A tall man with sort of an accent."

Her hands were shaking when she picked up the deed. Of course, it was Derek. But he had no money—and he didn't need to pay. The land was his free from the English government. She looked at the official document of title. Her breath stopped. It wasn't signed to Derek at all. It was signed to *her*—to Eden Palmer, the title, free and clear.

"Are you all right, Mistress Palmer? You look a bit pale."

"When did you say the gentleman came by?"

"Early afternoon, 'bout two o'clock I'd say."

She could barely speak. "Where do I sign the deed?"

"There."

She picked up the pen, then stopped and looked at the old man. "When he paid, did you ask him to sign the deed, since—since he was paying off the mortgage?"

"I did. I even told him he had to prove his right to own the property. He showed me his land grant and everything looked in order. But then he said he didn't want Palmer Oaks. Said the place was a pain in the—well, a problem for him. Sounded odd to me, but he insisted. Still don't know why anyone would pay for something they think is such a nuisance."

"I believe I do." She signed her name on the title and handed it over. "Thank you, sir." She started to hurry away.

"Wait, Miss Palmer. You'll want a copy—"

"Later. I'll get it later," she called over her shoulder.

She ordered her carriage driver to race toward the stable. She had to find Derek, to ask him, to learn his reason—if only he had made such a gesture because he loved her.

At the stable she leaped from the coach and ran into the barn, only to be told Mr. Walden had ridden away minutes ago.

Back into the coach. A fast clip along the river road, with the light fading, her head poked out the window as she searched for a lone rider.

In a few minutes she saw him as he jogged slowly along the familiar path. "Stop!" she cried to the coachman. "There he is!"

The driver reined up and assisted her from the carriage.

"You can go back to Charles Town," she told him. "I expect to ride on with my friend."

Derek had halted and dismounted at her first cry. As the coach wheeled and started back to town, he led his horse toward her, stopping when they were within arm's length, his face relaxed, but revealing nothing of his feelings.

She looked at him, waiting, hoping. He merely stood there in the shadowy twilight, looking at her with his absorbing, enigmatic blue gaze.

She finally asked, "Why, Derek? Why did you do it? You didn't have to."

"I know how you love the place. I was afraid you'd marry Palmer to keep it."

"I don't love Landon."

"I know that, too. That's why I wanted you to have your home, without obligation to anyone."

"You don't think I'm now obligated to you?"

"No."

"But you paid for it—for the mortgage! You could have signed the deed, owned it yourself."

"The payment was very little compared to the ones your stepfather made over the years. The land should go to the daughter he loved. And . . ."

"And what?" *Say it, Derek,* her mind screamed. *Say the words I want to hear.*

"We're friends, after all. Good friends, I would hope." He gave her a half smile. "Besides, I didn't want Landon Palmer for a neighbor."

Friends? *Friends?* "You could have had Bull Hawkins."

He chuckled. "Hell, that one took me by surprise."

"Derek, forgive me for asking, but you said you had no money. Naturally, I intend to pay you back, but it may be a while. I hope this doesn't cause you financial hardship." Her words sounded calm, businesslike. Her heart was turning somersaults inside her.

"Not at all. I just got rid of something I didn't need anymore. Not here in America."

"Oh? What did—" A stunning thought entered her mind. She reached for his right hand. His baronial ring was gone. "Not—Not your ring," she whispered.

"I told you I'm not a baron anymore. What use is a—"

She threw herself into his arms, pulled his face to hers and kissed him, held him, let her tears moisten her cheeks and his. "You love me," she cried when their lips parted. "You *do* love me."

"*Liebchen,* sweetheart," he murmured, holding her off the ground, hugging her to him. "Eden, my God, of course I love you."

She kept her arms tightly around him. "Derek, I've been a fool. Forgive me."

"Shh, little one. I've been more foolish than you." He chuckled and she felt it deep in her heart. "Two fools are we. What a happy life we will have together." He kissed her again, fiercely, possessively, lingering as if time had no meaning and the road they were on led only to their private paradise.

At last she looked up and said, "Take me home, Mr. Walden. And don't ever let me go."

He picked her up and perched her on his saddle, then swung up behind her. With his arms tightly around her, he put the horse into an easy canter.

She thought she would burst with happiness. Her heart was soaring, her mind in a whirl. Then she felt something small and round being pressed into her hand.

"I didn't sell *your* ring, *fraulein*. It's yours this time—for good."

Clutching the ring, her joy was overwhelming. She turned so she could gaze up at him. "Derek," she murmured, "we could stop on our way. There's a place—a place where we might see an egret fly."

"True. I know the place. But it might be cool this time of year."

"I don't think so. No, I doubt it very much."

"Hello! Are you there?" came a masculine voice.

Eden jumped up and pulled off her gardening gloves. Derek was here; the pruning could wait. Tipping back her skimmer, she raised an arm in greeting as she saw him walking his stallion at the far end of the field. "Hello," she called. "I'm coming." She was pleased to see Anna mounted in front of him, her legs dangling from the animal's broad shoulder, the tips of her tiny boots protruding from the frilly eyelet ruffles of her skirts.

She saw Derek bend his head to speak to the child. Then Anna waved vigorously toward the sound of Eden's voice.

"Good morning, Anna," Eden called, deeply touched, as always, by the little girl's happy manner. For two weeks now, every other day, Derek had been bringing Anna to Palmer

Oaks, at first to have tea and play with the puppies, and eventually to begin short sessions in the gazebo with Laykee. The Cherokee girl was wonderful with Anna, inspiring her confidence from the first. In her quiet, caring way, she had won the child's trust, become her friend, and now the two shared many secrets. Only two days ago Derek had reported with great satisfaction that Anna had spoken of her days in Neuchâtel for the first time since the massacre in Switzerland. Laykee was very encouraged and announced that today she would do the healing ceremony and use the herbal mixture on Anna's eyes. She had said not to expect an immediate miracle—but Eden had spent many recent hours in prayer on Anna's behalf.

Eden held up her skirts and made her way between the faded rosebushes toward Derek and Anna. "I'm coming," she called. "Meet me behind the house. The puppies are there."

Ignoring the mud clinging to her boots, she hurried to the back porch, where Derek had dismounted and lifted Anna to the ground. As Eden always did now, she greeted him with a warm embrace.

"What a ferret you are, Mistress Palmer," he said with a cocky smile that set her heart pounding. He brushed dirt from her cheek, then leaned to give her a quick kiss on the spot.

"You've chosen a farmer to love, my lord," she said.

Anna had located the puppy box, which Eden always placed in exactly the same location. "Oh," she squealed as her plump arms disappeared into the chaos inside the box. "They're getting so big, Miss Eden. May I have one today? May I? Please, please?" she wheedled.

Eden laughed, giving Derek a nod of approval. "They're nearly grown," she said.

"Please, Dirk, may I?" Anna begged. "I've got one picked out. This one." She held up a pudgy, squirming creature then hugged it under her chin. "He's a girl—I think. I'll call her Robin."

Derek's eyes were laden with love for the child. He lifted his eyebrows and smiled at her. "Robin? Sounds a bit more, ah—birdlike than doglike, don't you think, *liebling?*"

"Maybe. But she feels like that bird sounds—that bird you called a turkey. But I don't want to name her Turkey. Robin is better. Robins can sing, too. Dogs can't sing, but I can sing to Robin. Isn't that a good idea, Dirk? I'll make up a song. Miss Eden can help. She sings so pretty, don't you think so, Dirk?"

Eden felt her cheeks rouge as she recalled her earlier encounter with Derek in the hold of his ship. "Not as pretty as you, Anna," she said, feeling Derek's amused eyes on her. "And I think Robin is a lovely name for your puppy. She's the first puppy that looks just like her mother, Queen Elizabeth. Brown spots and all."

"Oh, I'm glad," said Anna, petting the pup with gentle strokes.

Laykee came out of the house and went straight to Anna. "Good morning, Tau-yie." This was the Cherokee name chosen by Anna as her very own.

Carefully, Anna replaced the pup. "Hello, Laykee. Today is our special day—the story you promised." She covered her rosebud lips with one hand cupped inside the other. "Oh, oh, it's a secret. I didn't mean—"

Laykee put an arm around her and stroked her curls. "It's all right, little one. Only those who love you are present. Maybe we'll share some of our secrets with them someday."

"Yes, I'd like that," Anna said, reaching out to hug Laykee. "Let's go to our lodge. When we're done, I'll play with the puppies. Maybe today I can take Robin home."

Holding hands, Laykee and Anna walked toward the gazebo in the shade of a stand of young pines not far from the river. Before they entered their "lodge," Laykee threw an encouraging smile over her shoulder toward Derek and Eden.

Eden waved in response. *Please God, let it work,* she prayed silently. *Use Laykee's magic and my prayers, and Derek's, to help this innocent child to see again. There is so much beauty in Your world. Take away the terrible sights from her mind and let her see all Your wonders.*

Derek slipped his arm around her waist and stared for a time toward the gazebo. He echoed her thoughts when he said in a voice husky with emotion, "I pray this works. I would give anything, everything, for that darling child."

"I know," she murmured. "It's in God's hand. Our God and Laykee's Cherokee God. Who knows, maybe they are one and the same."

Lost in thought, they strolled to the veranda and sat on the steps.

"Would you like some fresh peach tea?" she asked after a moment. "I'm thirsty after puttering in the garden all morning."

"Good idea," he agreed. "Summer's heat has lingered late this year."

In minutes she was back with two tall glasses of the tea sweetened with peach juice. She was outwardly calm, but nervous inside over Anna's treatment today. Taking a breath, she tried to put it from her mind for the time being. She watched Derek tip back his head and drink deeply. She loved him beyond belief. At Christmas, just over a month from now, they would be married in the new church at Waldenburg.

He set aside his glass and pulled her into his arms. She controlled the beginning of passion and relaxed against him, enjoying his warmth, the steady throb of his heart, the tenderness in his embrace. His lips were close to her ear when he said, "I'll love you until my dying breath, Eden, and even after that, God willing."

She held him close, this hero of hers. Her love had no boundaries, no questions, no demands. It was all-encompassing and complete. She knew she could give without limit—and her gift would always be safe in this wonderful man's keeping.

She eased away when she saw Laykee and Anna approaching. "Derek, they're back. Do you suppose—"

Quickly, he helped her to her feet. "We shouldn't get our hopes up, Eden. It may take time—weeks, months, who knows?"

With baited breath Eden watched the two walking through the garden. Anna skipped along holding Laykee's hand. Eden looked at Derek.

He was staring at Anna, his brow knitted in concern.

At the same instant their hearts plummeted to their toes. Nothing had changed.

Eden watched in dismay as Laykee led the child back to the puppy box. Anna knelt beside it and fumbled in search of her puppy.

"Oh—it didn't work," Eden whispered.

Derek's hand clasped her shoulder. "Remember what I said," he murmured. "We can't expect too much right away." His bleak tone gave away his true feelings.

She forced herself to hide her disappointment and followed him to the box.

"Well, Anna, how was your visit today?" he said with forced merriment. He looked questioningly at Laykee.

Anna raised her face toward him, her dimples deep beside her happiest grin. "Oh it was wonderful, Dirk. Laykee told me about the magic of the Cherokees, and then she—and then—" Her smile waned, then completely disappeared. "We talked about some secret things, some bad things. She put something that smelled funny on my eyelids."

"That's all right, pet. You and Laykee may keep your secrets. There will be plenty of time for you to share more

255

with her." He knelt beside her, ignoring the dirt sure to stain the knees of his breeches. He stroked the child's hair and fumbled with a ribbon at the neckline of her dress.

At the sight of his pain, Eden felt her own heart ache, her own disappointment multiplied a hundred times over. Maybe it just took time, she reminded herself.

"We should go now," Derek said, unable to keep hoarseness from his voice.

"But come again soon," Eden suggested. "Laykee can have another private visit with Anna any time."

"Oh yes, I'd like that," Anna said, her smile returning.

"I would like that, too," Laykee said softly. "Who knows the ways of magic?" She gave Derek a meaningful look.

"Can I take Robin today, Miss Eden?" Anna chimed. "Is she ready to go home with me?"

Eden looked at Derek, who had stepped to the hitching rail. He gave her a sad smile of approval.

"I think today would be perfect," she said past the lump in her throat. "She's been eating scraps for several weeks— but she'll cry for her mother for a while, I expect."

"I'll let her sleep in my bed," Anna said, picking up the wriggling puppy.

"I'm sure you'll have to ask permission for that, dear. Usually dogs have their own bed to sleep in."

Derek led his horse close. Turning to Eden, he drew her into a parting embrace.

She could almost feel his anguish. "Don't worry," she whispered. Give it time. And pray."

"Pray? You've given me new life, Eden, but if this doesn't work, my soul may be in danger. I've prayed so often before to no avail—and now this failure."

She hugged his waist and pressed her cheek against the front of his shirt. "Be patient," she said softly. "She's such a happy child. Surely she can be healed."

He looked at her with great tenderness. "Thank you for

caring, my love. I'll see you again as soon as possible. Tomorrow we harvest Kurt's garden. There's much to do."

"Soon, Derek, soon." Reluctantly, she released his hand.

He placed Anna in front of the saddle. She cradled the puppy in both arms.

"Good-bye," Eden called, attempting a grin. "Anna, take good care of Robin."

"Miss Eden . . ."

"Yes? Is something wrong?"

Anna turned toward her. "What color are robins?"

"Well, rather brown—with a red breast, very pretty—"

"My Robin doesn't have a red breast."

"No, but—" The child's strange comment fixed her attention.

Anna continued. "She has a nice brown patch around her eye. See? But she doesn't have any red at all." She pointed to the puppy. "I like the brown circle around her eye here." With one finger she circled the pup's markings, following the line exactly.

Eden felt the breath leave her. She moved near and took a close look at the puppy. It did indeed have a wide brown circle surrounding its right eye. She stared at Anna, seeing her blue eyes, her mouth bowed with concern.

The child merely blinked and gazed back at her, obviously seeing her, and not in the least surprised, as if nothing was different from a second ago.

"Anna?" Derek leaned over to look into her face. "Anna, did you say the pup has a round patch—a brown spot around its eye?"

"Yes. But I do want to call her Robin. Do you think it matters that she doesn't have any red on her stomach?"

Derek straightened abruptly and gazed skyward. Eden knew he was hiding the tears of joy he couldn't hold back.

She looked at Laykee, who was smiling now. The Cherokee woman placed one finger over her lips and shook her head.

It was a precious moment, fragile and miraculous. Eden understood she was not to question it, but let Anna say or do whatever felt right to her.

She gnawed her lip to hide her emotions. Their prayers were answered. Anna could see, and appeared to have no memory of her blindness. It was as if she had lit a candle in a familiar room, one she had known well but that had temporarily been lost in darkness.

Looking now at Derek, Eden received from him a secret look of elation. "As I was saying," she said casually, "God does answer prayers from time to time."

Anna's attention was completely on the pup. "Now don't cry, Robin. I'll take good care of you," she purred near the puppy's floppy ear.

Derek cleared his throat. "If Robin is settled comfortably, we'll be on our way."

"She's fine," said Anna. "We can go now."

"Good-bye Eden—and thank you, Laykee." Plainly overcome, he reined the horse around and loped toward the gate.

Eden watched his departure, swept with happiness and love. What a miracle they had shared. And how very much she adored him. Had such a man ever existed? She doubted it. She was surely the most fortunate woman on earth. "Come back soon, my love," she whispered to the departing figure. "I'll miss you until I'm in your arms again."

❦ Epilogue ❧

Palmer Oaks Plantation—August 1734

"What the hell are those, Eden?"

"What do they look like, sweetheart?"

"Worms."

"Very good, Derek. They *are* worms."

Derek shrugged out of his military jacket and pulled up a chair beside Eden, who was holding a brown wooden box.

Shaking his head, he stared at the crawling caterpillars. "I suppose you expect those creatures to make us rich someday," he said with an indulgent smile.

"Maybe," she answered pertly.

"You'd better explain, darling. I don't fancy depending on worms for our future."

"You have your vineyards—I have my worms. Between the two, we can hope to raise enough funds to educate the children at a proper English university."

"Lord, Eden, Anna's only eight, and Charles just three months old." He turned to gaze into the cradle at Eden's elbow.

"I thought we were going to call him *Derek*," Eden said.

"Anna calls him *Dirk*. When he's old enough, we'll let him choose what he wants to be called—like the Cherokees. Now—back to the worms."

"They're silkworms. All we need is enough white mulberry trees, and we can sell silk to everyone here in the colonies. Think how much cheaper it will be than importing it from abroad. Why, we'd be rich in no time."

He laughed and reached to brush an errant wisp of hair from her temple. "You'll never change, my love. I'm surprised the East India Company hasn't made you their director."

"I'm only interested in farming, Derek. And raising babies." She leaned near the crib, beautifully decorated in handmade lace. "Isn't he an angel?" she cooed, and rocked the cradle gently. "And the ladies from Waldenburg outdid themselves to make all this exquisite lace."

"I told you my Swiss people would learn to love you, didn't I? It just takes time to win over some folks' hearts."

Setting aside the box of silkworms, Eden took a long look at her husband. "Derek, how did it go today—the maneuvers at Waldenburg?"

He reached into the cradle and pulled the satin cover up to his son's tiny chin. "Fine. Except you know how I feel about this business of raising a militia."

"Yes, but the king requires it of every community. Besides, there isn't any war in sight. Marching just gives the men something to do on Saturday afternoons."

"I don't like it. I've had enough of war to last a lifetime. And when men are required to wear uniforms and practice marching and shooting instead of playing with their children, it bodes ill for the future."

"But the American colonies have no enemies, Derek. I'm sure we'll never have any reason to go to war."

"Not in our lifetime, perhaps—but maybe in Charles's, or our grandchildren's."

"Dirk—I want to call our baby Dirk." Anna skipped onto the porch, her blond curls bouncing with each step.

Eden put her arm out to enfold her. She knew without doubt that she and Derek had spoiled her terribly since they adopted her. "Don't you think two Dirks in one household is too many, dear? Think of the confusion when our baby gets older."

"No. You call Papa 'Derek.' I call him 'Papa Dirk.' Our baby will know the difference when we speak his name. Please, Mama. Please, may we call him Dirk?"

Derek ruffled her hair. He could never deny the child anything she asked for. "We'll see. Run inside now and get some cookies from Laykee. She has a surprise for you."

"A surprise? Really? What?"

"It's not a *what*. It's a *who*. Go along now. I want to speak to your mother."

"Hurray! Bryan's here!" She scampered off toward the kitchen.

"Anna is certainly taken with Laykee's nephew," Eden observed.

"She's fascinated with his Indian ways. Natural enough, I think. She's never forgotten her own Cherokee name is Tau-yie. And someday she'll understand how Laykee helped her regain her sight."

"It's amazing how she never realized she was blind. Like it never happened."

"Thank God she was cured."

"Yes, thank God. Now, what did you want to talk to me about that is so private."

He gave her a crooked grin. "You know I'm not prone to gossip, but I did hear astounding news at the village today."

"Tell me," she said excitedly. "I do love gossip, you know.

"Do you recall Virginia Hardy?"

"My goodness—I'll never forget that scandalous creature. I figured she had been hung by now. She and her dreadful brother."

"Quite the contrary. The latest word from England is that she escaped the noose and married an English lord who hasn't the slightest idea of her checkered past."

After her first astonishment, Eden laughed. "Fancy that. The wicked fox. Honestly, Derek, she was going to kill you. It's unfair that she's prospered. Who told you about her?"

"Katya."

"Umph. Might have known. So it could be a bald-faced lie."

"Now, Eden, you should forgive Katya. She was only a young girl three years ago, full of youthful infatuation."

"I'll try, but she's never too friendly—to me, anyway. And she did cause us a great deal of trouble."

"Nevertheless, Max keeps her busy—especially in bed. She's with child again, I'm afraid."

"But she just had the twins last Christmas. My, she is certainly helping to populate Waldenburg in a hurry."

He scooted his chair next to hers, slipped his arm around her back and pulled her against him. His look was heated, suggestive. "My darling Eden—maybe we should continue to do our part as well. You may remember, I'm responsible for the success of Waldenburg—its survival in the American wilderness—"

His words were lost in her kiss of welcome as her arms encircled his neck. The baby, the silkworms, and Katya were all temporarily forgotten, along with the humid breeze drifting across the Ashley.

❦ Author's Note ❧

In creating my heroine for *Indigo Fire,* I borrowed freely from the true story of Eliza Lucas, a remarkable teenage girl who lived in South Carolina at her father's plantation and who is credited with introducing indigo as a cash crop into the colonies. While her father served in a government post in the West Indies, the girl hired a French expert to help her produce indigo as fine as that raised in France. It became a major export by the 1770s, and Swiss and French planters doubled their investment every three or four years.

Several elements worked to eliminate indigo as a source of prosperity in South Carolina: the American War of Independence, the introduction of chemical dyes, and ravages by grasshoppers and other pests. In the years following the revolution, King Cotton predominated, requiring millions of acres and multitudes of black slaves toiling to produce it.

While researching my own Janssen family tree, I came across the story of the first German and Swiss settlers in the Carolinas and Georgia. One man in particular, Baron Christopher de Graffenreid from Berne, brought 1500 settlers from Switzerland and purchased ten thousand acres of land. In 1710, 650 Palatines arrived at the Neuse River and established the town of New Berne in North Carolina, and from the Alps in upper Austria the Salzbergers came to Georgia to escape religious persecution. In 1731, John Peter Purry of Neuchâtel in Switzerland visited Carolina. Soon after, the English Crown, which was eager to establish

263

industrious Protestant communities in America, agreed to give him land and 400 pounds sterling for every hundred effective men he could transport from Switzerland to Carolina.

My imagination was fired by these hardy and industrious pioneers who left their mountain homeland in central Europe to find religious freedom and economic opportunity in the gentle climate and verdant lowlands of the American south.

Add to this mixture of divergent cultures the large influx of French Huguenots and the well-established and remarkably civilized Cherokees occupying the southern Alleghenies, and the scene is set for the dramatic events that would eventually lead to the War of Independence, the Civil War, and, for the unfortunate Cherokees, the devastating ejection from their homeland in 1838 and the forced march that would become known as the Trail of Tears.